Totally Bound Publishing books by ML Uberti

On the Island
Island Distraction

I0681390

On the Island

ISLAND DISTRACTION

ML UBERTI

Island Distraction
ISBN # 978-1-83943-851-6
©Copyright ML Uberti 2018
Cover Art by Posh Gosh ©Copyright April 2018
Interior text design by Claire Siemaszkiewicz
Totally Bound Publishing

Published in 2020 by Totally Bound Publishing, United Kingdom.

ISLAND
DISTRACTION

Dedication

To my wonderful, inspiring friends.
They love, they listen, they support, and they
laugh at every one of my jokes.

Chapter One

Elle and I stared at the gleaming white monstrosity of a house while the Uber we were crammed into maneuvered the circular drive, our mouths hanging open in shock and envy.

"This is the *vacation* house?" Elle whispered, just in case raising our voices wasn't allowed when we were several feet away from a huge Georgian mansion, bigger than any house we had ever seen in our lives, on the ocean of the east Atlantic coast.

"Ava told us he's rich." I scanned the tall Greek columns and sweeping wraparound porch.

"This isn't rich, Marley. This is like P. Diddy, gold faucets, sneezing into cashmere Kleenex rich," Elle said, still whispering, still staring.

"Whatever. The Reed Whitakers still put their pants on one leg at a time, just like us, right?"

"No, I'm sure they pay someone to dress them in their tailored Armani slacks every morning. Two people—one for each leg."

"Then they're supporting the local economy! So, they can't be that bad." I dragged my honey-blonde hair up off my neck into a low knot, then let it go, deciding against it. I had spent the better part of the morning blow-drying and taming my mid-back-length hair and a ponytail would make it all bumpy and I'd have to start all over again. Playing with my hair had become a nervous habit for me in third grade—I couldn't seem to let it go. And my nerves were about as frazzled as they could be right then.

Elle and I were both anxious about traveling from Columbia, South Carolina, to the Yankee-wealth-stronghold of the north, Martha's Vineyard. But our college roommate, and one fourth of the 'tribe' we had spent four years sowing our wild oats with, was getting married five years after we'd graduated—to Reed Larrick Whitaker the Second. Ava had been smitten by him from the get-go. He was just the kind of man she'd always wanted—one who would let her avoid working for a living, spoiling her and insisting she stay home to raise their future tow-headed babies while shopping on weekends for couture with his paycheck.

I wouldn't call it love at first sight. Reed had tried in the beginning to keep things casual, but Ava had wasted no time locking him down with incredible blow jobs and ultimatums, and now we were three days away from her dream wedding at his family's colossal summer house.

"Good news is that we can steal the silver to pay the rent." Elle flung her door open and stepped out.

That didn't seem like a bad idea. We were already two weeks late and our landlord was a creep of epic proportions who'd told Elle to her face that she could work off the rent if she happened to be *an ass virgin, willing to let him come in her without a condom'*. Word for word, that was verbatim what Mr. Vindap had said when she'd told him we might be a few days late last month. Now we were late again and I swear Elle had started walking backward up the stairs in case he came up behind her, poor thing.

I shoved out of my side of the small sedan and took the bag the Uber driver propelled at me, holding his hand out for a tip.

"Uh, one sec." I bugged my eyes at Elle over the roof of the tin can he had picked us up from the ferry in, and nodded toward Ivan, our driver.

She gave a loud sigh and dug out a five-dollar bill from her bag. Ivan scampered over to retrieve it, speeding away before we could even call out a "thank you."

"Fuck," Elle said, as we stood in front of the steps of the expansive house, craning our necks to consider all three stories of heavy leaded windows and jutting balconies above us.

"Yeah," I agreed, whispering again.

The door to the house flew open and I heard Ava rather than saw her.

"You're here! Oh, my lord almighty, you're here!" she called out, loud enough that no doubt everyone on this side of the Atlantic could hear her. I guess we didn't need to use our inside voices.

"Hey." Elle held up a hand and waved.

The porch stretched wide and the steps were formidable, so it took Ava a while to reach us. But when she did, she threw her arms around both of us in typical Ava fashion, and hugged us so hard she almost cut off our airflow. She wore a size four but took her yoga seriously.

"I missed you so much! You both look wonderful! I'm so glad you're here!" she gushed.

"Missed you, too, Ava." I said and that was true — we did miss her, though I doubted we looked *wonderful* after several hours of crowded and humid travel. But we weren't glad to be there.

Elle and I both liked Reed fine — he made Ava happy and seemed like a decent dude, if not a tad snobby and self-centered, but Ava could be, too, so I suppose they were well-suited to each other. Not to mention they both had cause to be snobby. They hailed from upper class backgrounds and had landed lucrative jobs right out of school, thanks to their families' connections. But Elle and I came from and had nothing — a couple of girls from a Podunk town in the middle of South Carolina — who now lived less than an hour from where we'd grown up and had jobs that barely paid us enough to afford the rent on a dilapidated two-bedroom walk-up in the red light district. Elle taught preschool and I worked at a non-profit food pantry that paid me so little they told me to supplement my income with free loaves of bread and jars of peanut butter. And I did. I had to.

Ava and our other roommate at Clemson, Sloane Riley, weren't like Elle and me. Ava was refined and cultured, spending her childhood vacations in Austria and attracting the kind of man whose parents had a beach house the size of an office park. Sloane came from old money, *really* old money. Her dad is a United States senator, her grandfather was the Secretary of Education two administrations ago and her great-great-grandfather had been a vice president. Both Ava and Sloane were stylish and sophisticated, drawing from padded bank accounts with more money in them right then than Elle and I would see in our lifetimes — *combined*.

Of course, we hadn't cared when we'd befriended the two girls who were above our station in life when we'd been eighteen years old and embarking on our higher education, spreading our wings and getting our bearings — and eating the same over-cooked chicken fingers and charred French fries the dining hall offered. But standing up in one of their weddings while spending almost a week with Ava's upper crust parents and Reed's affluent family seemed daunting, to say the least. We'd downloaded three etiquette apps on our trip up here and still didn't know what fork to use for dessert.

It's gonna be a rough five days.

Nevertheless, we were here for Ava. We had packed our seven-hundred-dollar bridesmaids dresses for Ava. We had thrown a bridal shower alongside her sister, cousin and Sloane for Ava. We would deal with whatever stuck-up pretty boy she forced us to stand up with, for Ava. And Elle and I were going to freak out to each other in whispers and corners the whole time we were here.

A long black town car steered into the drive behind us, and Ava at last relinquished us from her Herculean hold.

"That must be Sloane and Slater!" Ava almost shoved us out of the way to greet her new guests. "Sloane!" she shouted as the driver heaved the passenger door open and Sloane stepped out.

"The gang's all here!" Sloane declared, throwing her arms around Ava and tossing Elle and me a wide smile. Yeah, someone had stocked vodka in that limo. I'd bet my life on it.

Sloane is not what I would describe as chipper. She came across as cool, in more ways than one. She was aloof and uninterested, and I know if she hadn't been forced into the dorms freshman year she would never have deigned to look at us twice. But somehow, all three of us had won her over and for four years we'd all been inseparable. Then we'd graduated and gone in different directions but maintained close ties through email, texts and social media. And now we were all here. To usher the first of us into wedded bliss.

Sloane gave us all hugs and I could smell some kind of liquor. Jack Daniel's, if my two years of bartending recalled correctly.

"Little nip of JD on the ride over, Slo?" I teased.

"It's Slater's favorite. Slater, you remember the girls, right?" Sloane turned and waved her hand toward her brother.

I doubt Slater would remember us, but we *all* remembered him. Slater Riley had presence. He stood well over six feet tall, sculpted of pure muscle and oozing sex appeal. I didn't know if he was smart, or fun or well-read — I only knew that he looked fucking phenomenal every time I saw him. He also mirrored his toffee-nosed sister — polite and uninterested. Elle and I once spent a four-day vacation in Cabo with the male Riley and wasted most of our time drooling over him and imagining him naked. He'd ignored us completely.

Slater gave Elle and me a courteous and remote nod, then kissed Ava on the cheek. Seemed he and Reed Whitaker being friends meant Ava could be afforded a touch of affection. *That lucky bitch.*

"Hey, Ava," he murmured and I got goosebumps. I could only imagine Ava creaming her pants right now. She might be getting married, but she wasn't dead. And during those four days in Cabo, Ava had shared our fascination with the guy none of us could ever have.

"Hi," Ava breathed, stumbling against him and crowding him, without even realizing it.

A gust of wind came over the top of the house, washing over us with the strong scent of the ocean. I inhaled the smell—I had missed that. It had been months since Elle and I had taken a day-trip to the South Carolina coast to lie on the beach and read mystery novels. The fresh air, the sound of the waves crashing, a gorgeous man in our midst—I had the distinct feeling this weekend would be epic. As in, life-altering and different from the sullen buildings and oppressive heat Elle and I had left a few states behind us.

Slater glanced once more, impervious, at my roommate and me then returned to the car.

"Wow," Elle exhaled when he disappeared from sight.

"He spent the entire ride over here texting with some guy about a hipster bike shop he's buying and yammering about some shitty bluegrass band he wants to see when we get back to New York. He's become *so* Brooklyn. Every girl he's dated this year smells like patchouli vag oil and doesn't shave her pits," Sloane sneered.

"Okay, gross visual. Thanks." I held up a hand to get Sloane to stop.

A woman in a trim gray dress and starched white apron came down the steps and offered to take our bags. Elle and I refused and held onto our own luggage. Sloane passed over her three bags without a second thought.

"Well, I still haven't finished deciding who's standing up with who yet. I'm thinking of putting Slo with Slater—" Ava drew us back into wedding mode and Sloane shook her head hard. "Or with Elle. You're both tall," Ava finished.

"I—uh, I might not— I don't know." Elle let out a nervous twitter then cleared her throat. "I'm not good with guys like that."

"Guys like what?" Sloane raised an eyebrow.

"Guys who—" Elle puffed up her cheeks and curled her biceps to mime her meaning.

"Have tribal tattoos?" Ava questioned.

"Are afflicted with asthma?" Sloane asked.

"Compete in weightlifting competitions?" I frowned.

"Are rich and hot," Elle filled in.

"I didn't get that at all," Sloane said, crossing her arms.

"Me neither. You could've done like a dollar sign or maybe made a duck face or something," I said.

"Oh! Or taken off your pants!" Ava suggested.

All our eyes swung to her.

"You said he told you he was well-endowed," Ava said to Sloane with a blink.

"Yeah, but Elle isn't. What's she going to show us? Her bush?" Sloane gestured to Elle.

"I wax now. We got this kit from the drug store and it's like the best investment we ever made." Elle glanced at me.

"Hands down, greatest forty dollars we ever spent. Oh, and we got a foot bath. We do our own pedicures. We are living the dream, ladies. Envy us," I fake-bragged.

We all chortled and I remembered why I loved these girls. We were self-deprecating and silly and had a connection born from coming of age in one another's space. It could never be replicated and it would never go away. Even though this weekend would be a stark reminder of the life I would never have, and I would have to withstand everyone we met looking down their noses at me, I could hang with my girls again. The fearsome foursome, my BFFs until the end of time, my ride or dies. *It's going to be great.*

"Come on. I'll show you to your rooms. We're all staying here and the guys are staying at Reed's aunt and uncle's house a few addresses down. His mom seemed scandalized by the suggestion that the wedding party all stay in the same place. She claims the boys and the girls can't be trusted together." Ava took over one of Elle's bags.

"I don't trust me around any boys, either. It's been eight fucking months since I've been laid. And I didn't bring my vibrator. So, I'm on a manhunt that anyone not getting married is welcome to join in." Sloane skidded her gaze to Elle and me. "Unless one of you two has suddenly found yourselves a man."

"Marley finally fucked her boss," Elle blurted out and we all stopped in the giant foyer because the words bounced and echoed off the walls.

"Thanks, Elle. Appreciate you waiting about three minutes after we got here to publicize that to the entire household," I muttered.

"Sorry. I didn't know the acoustics would be so good in here." Elle dropped her voice to a whisper.

"You fucked your boss?" Sloane asked, staring at me.

"He's not technically my boss," I muttered when Ava peered at me over her shoulder on the way to the stairs. "I mean, he's the CEO, but I have like a boss under him."

"So, you're under both your bosses? Like a little ménage-à-trois action?" Ava grinned.

I flattened my lips into a thin line. "We aren't and we haven't. We slept together *once*. It's not serious. I don't even know what we are. He won't define it and I won't ask. So we've been just – hanging out."

"Hanging out? Babe, those ovaries won't last forever. You should really get your head in the marriage game." Sloane poked me in the ribs. I knew she must be kidding—she stayed as far away from marriage as someone ever could.

But her words hit a nerve. I didn't know what Ben and I were, either because Ben harbored an untold fear of getting fired for dating me or because Ben was—*Ben*. No doubt he represented a good catch. MBA from Duke, worked hard and dedicated his life to making a difference in the world.

But every date prior to the last, where we'd consummated our pseudo-relationship, had ended with a chaste kiss and some minor groping. He'd had to imbibe several beers before taking things further with me and even then, as soon as it was over, he'd left within thirty minutes of me faking my orgasm and him getting off. Not only did I end up sexually frustrated, I had no idea how he really felt about me.

At work the following day, he'd acted like nothing had happened. The date had been two weeks ago and he hadn't mentioned it or asked me out again. And, worse than that, I had no idea how *I* felt about that. He seemed like the kind of guy I *should* end up with. I knew that.

But it seemed that what I *should* do and what I *was* doing were becoming more and more at odds with each other the older I got.

"Don't worry about my ovaries, Sloane. They're firmly in place and I have no intention of pollenating them with little white-tailed semen any time soon," I told her when we all hit the stairs, where two guys came into view, descending.

Both of them stared at me. One grinned wildly—at my ovary-semen comment, no doubt—and the other had his phone up to his ear. I took both of them in with a glance, but I darted my eyes back to the guy with the phone. *Wowzer. What a looker.* I didn't think I had ever seen someone so handsome in real life. And he was just that — *handsome.* Not cute or hot or pretty. No, he had a classically good-looking face that could span generations of attractiveness.

As his eyes met mine, they flashed then narrowed. His body, too, stilled for just a moment, but he pushed himself forward even faster than before, his brow furrowed in concentration as he continued his phone call. He mumbled a few words about absorption rates and comparable market analysis that made no sense to me.

Even *that* was attractive. The guy appeared one-hundred-percent together, hyper-focused on whatever had his attention, ambition pouring out of him. Even though our eyes had met and I'd thought I'd seen — *something* — he seemed all business.

"You have to file the J-51 paperwork ahead of working on the involuntary alienation clause."

His words sounded like gibberish, but the sexiest gibberish I had ever heard. He also sounded annoyed. Well, I knew I would be annoyed as hell if I had traveled to an island paradise and had to deal with involuntary alienation clauses — if I had any clue at all what those were.

Then I remembered my embarrassing statement from moments before and blushed. By this time, both guys were nearly out of the front door on their way to wherever. They glanced behind at us one last time. The one on his phone still barked out jargon, his posture stiff and irritated. The other guy shot us a grin and a nod. "Welcome to the island, ladies," he said and they both walked out, the handsome one keeping his eyes on mine until the very last moment.

"Well, that was embarrassing," Elle noted, as we all stood and watched the two guys disappear.

"Yeah, especially since that's the guy you're probably standing up with, Marley," Ava added.

Yeah. Awesome first impression. If I don't feel like a hick out of water already, that certainly did it.

And it only got worse. Our rooms were sumptuous and gigantic, connected to en-suite bathrooms stocked up with fluffy, snow-white towels, claw-foot tubs and the adjoining sleeping areas had oversize beds with piles of pillows and blankets, each at a thousand thread count or higher. I was so awed by everything, I think I managed a "g'all darn" and "gee whiz" while I took in the opulence. I was Carolina through and through and no amount of time up north could alter that.

After Elle and I had prattled on about our rooms, Ava suggested we change for dinner. I dressed in a different T-shirt and shorts. I had brought several outfits, not sure what to wear, but everything looked wrinkled and felt plain. *I* felt plain.

I didn't usually feel that way. I was tall and stayed fit thanks to the most inexpensive exercise in the universe — running — and I had been blessed with flaxen hair that grew quickly, naturally shiny and thick. I had interesting green-brown eyes, with a small cluster of freckles across the bridge of my nose. However, no matter what I pawed through on my quest for this evening's attire, nothing felt *good enough.* So, I just threw on the items closest to me.

Sloane popped her head into my room, took one glance at me and made me come with her to find something more appropriate, agreeing with my derogatory inner monologue.

"I have dresses here, Slo," I argued, though I didn't think any of them would do the trick, especially after she revealed half the items she'd brought with her, which had to be nearly fifty couture outfits.

"Are they from Walmart?" she asked with a knowing glance.

"Target," I murmured.

"Yeah, put this on." She tossed a garment at me—a pale gold Halston halter dress, with a price tag still on it. Four hundred and ninety-five dollars, nearly the same amount I owed in rent. *I should sell this thing on eBay when I'm done.*

The dress fitted like it had been made for me, even though I was a size eight and Sloane barely a six. It had an intricate back design that bared my shoulders and dipped down to just above my ass. I looked stunning.

"This is gorgeous." I twisted to give myself a once-over in the large standing mirror.

"Yeah, well, unfortunately I have four inches and two shoe sizes on you, so I hope you have something to put on those pretty little feet to match it up." Sloane waved a hand at my t-strap sandals, which were indeed from Walmart.

"Um, I brought a pair of nude pumps," I said, slipping off one shoe.

"Jesus, did you think you were going to a hoedown?" Sloane pushed herself off the bed.

"I can't afford much right now. I blew all my savings on the dress and shoes for the wedding *and* the gift *and* the airfare to get here, not to mention the ferry and the food I'm going to have to eat, as well as all the alcohol I'm going to have to chug down in order to forget that I spent all this money to get here."

Sloane stopped. "Why didn't you ask me to help?"

"I'm not going to ask you to pay for my bridesmaid dress," I argued.

"I would have."

"And I appreciate that, but I do have some pride," I muttered, toeing off my other shoe.

"Just not enough to stop you from banging your boss," Sloane said, a wicked smile growing across her perfect lips.

"Just once! I have no idea what the guy is looking for. Or what I'm looking for. I have no real dating prospects. I think we're both just wasting time," I said.

Sloane threw the door open. "Wasting time? Come on, Marley. I've never known you to do something careless like just *waste* time with a guy." She walked down the hall toward my room.

Sloane was right. I hadn't. This kind of behavior didn't befit me at all, but Ben had entered my life as an enigma. One minute, he'd gazed at me, telling me that we would be perfect for each other, and the next, he ignored my text messages and acted like we'd never even met. I'd been on a teeter-totter with him for months and I'd moved no closer to and no further from figuring out what we were.

"It's...casual," I offered, tagging along behind her.

She snorted. "You? Casual? This is Marley Jackson, right? You don't do casual."

Match point, Sloane Riley.

"Get the pumps. I'm going to find us something to drink," she ordered, going for the stairs.

I did what she told me, then went to grab Elle from her room on the other side of the steps.

I knocked and she instantaneously flung the door open, in just her underwear. "I forgot my toothbrush!" she cried out, near tears.

"Okay, well, I'm sure we can find you one," I said when she gripped my arm and yanked me inside the room, banging the door shut behind us.

"And tampons. And anything but my flip-flops and Keds!" Her voice grew more frantic.

"Did you get your period?"

"No! But what if I do?"

"They have stores here, Elle. I think we'll be okay."

"Yeah, the tampons probably cost thirty bucks a box. And the toothbrushes are probably fifty bucks. And I have no shoes for this!" she shouted, her voice growing louder and more agitated.

"Elle. Slow down. You and Ava are the same size. I'm sure she can—"

"Slater kissed me!" she burst out then slammed her hands to her mouth.

"Slater kissed you? When? Just now?" I asked, glancing around the room as if he would magically appear.

She nodded. "Yes. He came in here, said this is where he had stayed whenever he would come to hang out with Reed when they were younger, and cornered me. Over there. By the armoire." She pointed a shaking finger toward the antique oak closet near the window.

"Okay, then he just slipped you the tongue?" I stared at her.

"Yes!"

"Well, that's um—unexpectedly—awesome?"

"I don't know! I mean, he's Sloane's brother!" she scream-whispered.

"Yeah, and you're both adults, and he's hot and you're hot and—"

"And he's Sloane's brother!" She'd started yelling now, in a house full of people.

"Keep your voice down. We don't want the world to know, do we?" I asked. Maybe we did. I mean, if I'd made out with Slater Riley, *I'd* want the world to know. Like, big-time. I'd hire a sky-writer.

"I think he's drunk." She chewed on her bottom lip.

"Well, maybe he had some drinks but it's not even four o'clock in the afternoon. I doubt the guy's blasted."

"His eyes were glassy. And he smelled like bourbon. And weed." She covered her face with her hands. "I'm such an idiot."

"How are you an idiot? If a hot guy comes in my room on this trip and lays one on me, I'm kissing him back. For sure," I said.

"But what about Ben York?"

"Ben York is in Columbia, we are barely dating and he basically fist-bumped at the end of every date we had."

"Except when you nailed him two weeks ago," she reminded me.

"Yes, except then. But I'm not tied to Ben, Elle." I said this to both of us, knowing I had to get my shit together in the relationship department. And soon. Sloane had been right about my dwindling ovaries, even if just in jest. Not to mention, I wasn't quite comfortable riding a slow downhill slope to spinsterhood. I wanted to be with someone, in ways that meant something. I wanted what Ava and Reed had. I just wasn't anywhere *close*.

The bedroom door swung open and I think we both half-expected Slater, but Ava strolled in.

"Hey, ladies, you all ready?" she asked, twirling in a lace skater dress with gorgeous, jeweled peep-toe heels.

"You look amazing," I said, smiling at her.

"*I* look amazing? Jesus, Marley. You can't wear that!" she scoffed. "No one will notice *me*!"

I glanced down at my dress. "It's Sloane's. And that's total bullshit, you know it is."

"No it's not," Elle said, then shrugged an apology to Ava.

"That dress is perfect for you. And you have J-Lo curves and everything." Ava harrumphed.

"So do you!" I countered, but Ava just shook her head.

"I have no boobs. You have boobs! And an ass! I have a pancake ass!" Ava spun around and threw her dress up to show us her ass squeezed into a barely-there white thong.

Sloane threw the door open, a bottle of champagne in one hand and four glasses in the other. "Whoa, do I have awesome timing or what?"

Ava glared at her. "Don't give Marley any more outfits. No one has a chance around her unless she's wearing her Sears Specials." Ava snatched a glass and the bottle from Sloane.

"They're from Target," I added, but I just got a nasty glare. From all of them.

"Heard you and my brother made out." Sloane collapsed on the bed and addressed Elle.

She burned bright red. "I well, I um —"

"Whatever. Go with it. Just use protection please. And double it. Just in case. I love my brother but I don't think he's ready to be Daddy Slater. You have been warned." Sloane held up an empty glass to Ava.

"I'm not, either!" Elle protested in response.

"Even more reason then." Sloane winked at her.

Ava popped the top off the bottle and poured us each a glass as we gathered around the end of the bed.

"To Holmes Hall, suite 306." I raised my glass.

"To Lightsey Bridge 1, room 402," Sloane said.

"To the Orchard, room 101," Ava replied, her glass lifted.

"To Rosewood, room 221," Elle finished, and we all clinked glasses, shared smiles on our faces.

"To making out with cute boys — fiancés included," Sloane added once we took a sip. *Now, that I can toast to.*

We polished off the bottle of champagne in no time flat, Ava got Elle a pair of shoes that didn't have laces and we caught each other up on whatever we hadn't shared through Facebook or group iMessage.

Elle had wrapped up the school year and planned to spend her summer tutoring. She still worked almost five full days a week and spent her weekends at the library teaching a group of high school kids who needed help with math.

Sloane had booked a trip to Thailand, but in pure Sloane style, she wouldn't be backpacking and tromping through dirt-floor temples. No, she'd reserved a two-bedroom villa in Phuket on the banks of the Andaman Sea.

Ava and Reed were house-hunting and disagreeing on where they wanted to end up. Ava wanted to head to the suburbs of New Jersey but Reed was dead set on Connecticut. With a housing budget of *a mere* eight hundred thousand dollars, they couldn't seem to find what they wanted.

Then the girls wanted to grill me about all things Ben, so I side-stepped that and asked Ava wedding questions instead — how many people were coming, what the menu consisted of — all the details I didn't really care about but would rather discuss than my confusing love life.

Once we were all caught up with one another, we traipsed down the stairs and out of the house to the beach, on our way to the first of many parties to celebrate everyone's arrival on the island. Tonight's festivities included the Welcome to the Island Party, then tomorrow night Reed's parents' friends were hosting the Jack and Jill party — a gambling soiree, with the proceeds donated to Reed and Ava's favorite charity, the Essex County Humane Society. Friday night's agenda involved the rehearsal and dinner, followed by the wedding on Saturday. Sunday we would all be heading home, nursing our hangovers and pretending Ava had just lost her virginity on her way to hightailing it to Antigua for her honeymoon. The truth is Ava had lost her virginity the first night we got to Clemson, at a dorm party with some guy named Cooter. We had never let her live this down and never would.

On the beach behind the house, plank flooring had been laid under a huge white tent, with tables full of seafood and finger sides, and soft music playing in the background. A few dozen people milled around and Ava took over the monumental task of introducing us to all of them. We already knew her parents, Sloane's parents and Reed's parents, who we had met at Ava's shower in Virginia last month. But there were many other friends and family to meet, all with names like Buster and Muffy, drinking old-fashioneds and white wine spritzers. We did our best to be cordial, but after about twenty minutes straight, Sloane insisted we take a champagne break and we downed another bottle between the four of us.

"Where's Reed?" I glanced around. The party consisted of just old couples and women — not one guy under the age of thirty-five was in attendance.

"The guys are doing some kind of cigar and bourbon thing." Ava rolled her eyes. "Reed's best man Brooks is still pissed he couldn't throw a rager stag night since we're having a Jack and Jill instead, so they're all up at

Reed's aunt's house, planning to watch some fake-titted bitch take off her top while they smoke Cubans."

"Really?" I stared at her. I knew Ava well—and she is not the kind of girl who would be okay with her fiancé ogling some naked chick three days prior to them saying "I do".

"Well, I may have found the info for the stripper in Brooks' phone and called and canceled her, then ordered a different dancer from the Big and Beautiful Transgender website." Ava gave a casual shrug.

All three of us burst out laughing.

"You did?" Elle asked, a wide smile on her face.

"Whatever. They deserve it. They wanted to get lap dances like an hour before we had to greet all our wedding guests! That's just tacky." Ava shuddered.

"Agreed." Sloane finished her glass. "And who knows? Maybe Big and Beautiful will get lucky with Holden."

Sloane and Ava shared a giggle and Elle and I peered raised-eyebrowed at each other.

"Holden Pierce," Ava filled in. "The guy on the stairs with Mitch Oliver when we came in, with his phone attached to his ear."

"I see him all the time in New York and he barely acknowledges me. The man is dealing with some serious issues *and* he's a rampant workaholic. Our families have been friends for years and still, every time I see him, he's on his phone, checking emails or reading some kind of investment magazine. I mean, it's not like I expect him to Snapchat me and get us matching best friend necklaces, but, for crying out loud, he lacks even the most basic interaction skills," Sloane complained.

"What does he do?" I asked, trying to sound casual, like I didn't give a shit what one of the best-looking guys I had ever seen in my life did for a living.

Honestly, I hadn't been able to go more than three minutes since he had sailed past me without thinking about those chocolate eyes and that very attractive face.

"Whatever it is seems to occupy his brain twenty-four-seven," Ava observed. "I met him last night and he talked on his phone the entire time! He barely even said a word to any of us!"

"Well, he sounds like a fun companion to be paired up with this weekend," I deadpanned.

Ava shifted her eyes to the side — a dead giveaway. "Uh, Ave —" I started.

"I'm sorry!" she sputtered. "Someone had to stand up with him!" She threw out a dramatic arm. "Elle would just cry any time he said something rude."

"Thanks." Elle frowned.

"I mean that in the nicest possible way." Ava patted her arm. "And I'm sure he'll be on his best behavior," she added for my benefit.

Sloane shot me an unconvincing tight-lipped smile. "Oh, yeah. I mean, it's like a wedding and his parents are here and…"

Yeah. Great. There went any hope I had of getting to know the *GQ* stunner. *Pity.* Maybe someone else would have helped clear up the confusion I had about Ben and our dying-on-the-vine courtship.

Ava's sister Nanette walked into the party and we all exchanged hellos, and soon after her cousin Cece, the last of the five bridesmaids, appeared dressed to the nines and we exchanged hellos again. Cece forced Ava to sit down and tell us all who she coupled up with whom, stating out loud her determination to catch the bouquet. She also insisted whoever the garter was tossed to must be single and searching.

"Well, okay," Ava started, doing her best to make Cece happy. "Brooks is best man, so he's standing up with Nanette." The other Burcar sister, Ava's junior by three years, looked like Ava's polar opposite. My former roommate had white-blonde hair and liked to wear pastel, whereas Nanette's hair had been dyed jet black, same color as all her clothes, and she painted on emo eye makeup for all occasions. She also preferred girls to boys, a fact that Ava's conservative family took surprisingly well.

"Lucky bitch," Cece muttered under her breath and Nanette scoffed.

"Yeah, I'd be luckier to stand up with Marley. Could that be arranged?" Nanette licked her lips and dragged her gaze up and down my figure.

"See? That dress does wonders," Sloane noted with a nod at me.

"Oh, it's not the dress. I've had Marley in my spank bank for a while now. That dress isn't doing it for me. But hopefully we can go to the beach tomorrow and I can see whatever bikini you packed for the weekend." Nanette wiggled her eyebrows at me.

"Well, I didn't pack a bikini. And I'm flattered. But you know that's not my gig, Nan," I told her once again.

"A girl can always hope." Nanette shrugged, taking a sip of champagne. She'd been flirting with me since freshman year—we'd met when the fifteen-year-old Nanette had visited her big sister at college—and she hadn't stopped, no matter how many times I had told her I didn't play for her team.

"Back on task here, Ave." Cece tapped an impatient finger on the table.

"Oh, yeah. Cece, you're standing up with Mitch," Ava went on.

"Be sure to schedule your penicillin shot today," Nanette offered. "From what I've heard, the guy is an unmitigated manwhore with at least three kinds of VD."

"Charming," Elle mumbled and I snickered in response.

"Elle is with Slater," Ava continued.

"Which will be interesting, considering you got here an hour ago and you two have already made out," Sloane noted.

Cece thrashed her head toward Elle. "*You* made out with *Slater Riley*?"

"We didn't really make out. I mean, it lasted like two minutes," Elle corrected.

"Was there tongue?" Ava asked.

Elle hesitated then nodded.

"Then you made out," Ava judged.

"Like I said, just double bag his junk—you don't want to end up with a weekend hangover *and* Slater Jr in your oven," Sloane advised. "And me?" She prodded Ava.

"You're with Ethan Forrester," Ava continued.

"Yeah, I know him. He's one of Slater's bros. And he's a total *duh*. But he looks good in a tux, so I'll take it." Sloane shrugged.

"And, Marley, you're with Holden," Ava finished.

Cece stomped her foot under the table. "Not fair!" she whined.

I glanced from Sloane to Ava. "I thought the dude couldn't be bothered to pay attention to anything but his cell phone."

"He's super-rich. And fucking gorgeous. So who cares if he's an asshole?" Cece said.

"Well, I care. I'm the one stuck with him. Can't you move us around?" I asked and Cece nodded, jumping on the bandwagon.

"Cece is like five foot nothing and Holden is over six feet. It'll be weird for pictures." Ava scrunched her nose.

"And aren't the programs already printed up?" Elle added.

"*And* if you're stuck with Holden, maybe you'll come over to the dark side by the time Monday rolls around." Nanette waggled her eyebrows at me.

* * * *

After we'd squared away each of our assigned partners for the weekend, the six of us sat at a small, round table covered in a navy-striped damask with pillars of floating candles in sailboat-shaped holders. I noticed a subtle nautical theme with all the décor — from the message-in-a-bottle place cards to the rocks glasses etched with frosted anchors flanked by Ava's and Reed's initials. Even the silverware set at each place had been engraved with the happy couple's initials besides the phrase *my anchor and my sail.*

The entire space was softly lit and romantic while a small string quartet played light versions of classic rock songs and once again I found myself envious of the kind of life I would never lead. Strange the way fate dumped a gal into one life, then crossed her path with someone who made her see all she'd even thought to have.

I forced myself not to dwell on the things outside my control, at least for now, and listened while Nanette talked about her work with her Ph.D. in philosophy at SUNY. She attempted to explain her thesis to me, but I got lost after the fourth word in her eighteen-word title. Cece prattled on about all the available men who would be attending the celebration this weekend, her sole focus seeming to be becoming Mrs. Cece Something-Or-Other right after Ava and Reed exchanged vows. After an hour or so, and another shared bottle of champagne, a group of young men came wandering over, smelling like cigar smoke.

"Hey, babe." Reed bent and laid a sloppy kiss on Ava.

When I'd first met Reed, I had been visiting Ava and Sloane in New York. They had both gone there right after college and hadn't settled more than a month before Ava had met Reed at some Yale alumni mixer she'd gone to with her cousin. Well, begged Cece to take her to so she could meet some Ivy League eligible bachelors. Just a few short years ago, Ava used to be a lot like Cece was now.

She'd told us all Reed looked like a Chris Hemsworth clone—turned out she meant *Liam Hemsworth* which is nothing to sneeze at but, come on—he's *not* Chris. Still, she'd described Reed as tall and good-looking, with a full head of dirty-blond hair and a mischievous smile affixed round-the-clock to his face. She'd also informed us that he had a reputation as the ultimate party boy, and while it had taken some time to convince him they should be more than just fuck-buddies, Ava had managed to train him to become her faithful puppy dog, trotting after her and fulfilling her every whim.

"Hey, hon, how was the stag party?" she asked wide-eyed.

"Mammoth," one of the guys joked and I had to hide a smile under my hand. That must have been the stripper's stage name.

"I want to introduce everyone around." Ava stood and took Reed's hand. He gazed at her, adoration in his eyes. "I'll do the girls and you do the guys."

One of the pretty boys chuckled and another one looked at him and guffawed. *Oh, great. Welcome to an entire weekend of penis and vagina jokes with this crew.*

"This is my sissy, Nanette—I think most of you have met her—and my cousin, Cece," Ava started, pointing to each of them. "You probably know Slater's sister, Sloane, too, and these are my two friends from Clemson—Elle and Marley."

"Marley? Like the dog?" One of the guys snorted a laugh.

"Yes, like the dog. That's *soooo* original. Never heard it before," I said, putting on a fake, wide smile.

"Really?" The guy gawked at me. He seemed like the kind of guy who often came across as 'not in on the joke.' He had bright blue eyes surrounded by white-blond eyelashes and his hair matched the eyelashes. With his high, prominent cheekbones he could probably model—he definitely had the mental incapacity for it.

"She's fucking with you, Ethan," Holden, my groomsman said, his eyes on the phone in his hand. I wanted so badly for him to glance up, so I could get another peek at those soulful, dark whiskey-tinted eyes.

"Oh. Really?" Ethan asked, surprised.

Yeah, Sloane had been dead-on with this one—he was a *duh.*

"Well, that's Ethan, the dumbfuck," Reed pointed to the guy with the terrible jokes. "Slater, Brooks, Mitch and Holden." Reed nodded toward each guy, who gave a wave when Reed said his name.

Brooks stood beside Ethan as his mirror opposite—with a head of dark, longish hair, and prominent brunet eyebrows over eyes an interesting shade of gray. He didn't stand as tall as the rest of them, but his body was thin and muscular like a soccer player's. He had diamond studs that flashed in each ear and bright Japanese-style tattoos on both forearms.

Mitch Oliver stood off to the side, the prettiest of the group, blue-eyed and blond-haired. With that deep tan and relaxed attitude, he looked as though he had just climbed onto the shore with a surfboard tucked under his arm. He came across as calm and cool, his arm resting on the back of a chair, and leaning to the side. I would guess this guy had never had a real problem in his life, and it showed.

Holden, still had his attention on his phone, giving no indication that he intended to get off it.

"Hi, Holden." Cece wiggled her fingers at him. He looked up, giving her a tight smile in response, then went straight back to staring at his phone.

"Well, we have to get to dinner. We have place cards for each of you, so everyone can sit by their respective partner for the weekend." Ava gestured toward the table with the small glass bottles on it.

"Where's dinner?" Elle asked, standing and taking me with her. I swayed a little bit, all the champagne running to my head.

"Over at Reed's aunt's house." Ava pointed. "Maybe introduce yourselves to each other on the way?" She gave Elle a huge, obvious wink and gestured to Slater. Elle burned bright red but Ava just grabbed Reed and headed across the beach where the party was starting to file out.

Each couple paired off and I waited for Holden to move, finish with his phone and maybe acknowledge me. And I waited. And *waited*.

"Uh, Holden?" I questioned after almost five minutes of being straight-up ignored.

He let out a loud, annoyed breath and glanced up at me, his eyes flashing just as they had during the brief moment of heat we'd shared on the steps earlier. The annoyance fell from his face and his eyes went dark.

"We're supposed to head over, and uh, get to know each other," I said, tucking hair behind my ear and taking a tentative step toward him. *Goddamn*, the guy was fucking gorgeous. He had messy brown hair, styled effortlessly, a sharp jaw and a clean-cut, preppy style. He stood at least a couple of inches taller than me, and I topped out at around five nine in the three-inch heels. His shoulders were broad and his waist narrow, and I saw a hint of sophisticated ink winding under his button-down with its sleeves rolled to his mid forearm. He had a flashy watch on one wrist and expensive loafers on his feet.

"Yeah?" he asked, giving me an appraising once-over then returning his gaze to mine.

"Yeah," I said, not sure what to do then.

He stared at me for another minute, a voice coming through the speaker on his phone. He simply powered it off and kept his eyes on me, dropping the device into his pocket. "You're Marley?"

"Uh, yes," I replied, chewing my bottom lip. I couldn't tell if he seemed happy about that or not.

"You're Marley," he repeated, "the girl I'm standing up with?"

I nodded. I don't know why he found this such a tough concept to grasp.

The phone in his pocket rang and he kept his eyes on mine before drawing it out and answering. "I need a minute," he said and I had no idea if he had been talking to me or whoever called on the phone. His eyes were directly on mine still—he hadn't even blinked. He just kept staring at me.

I shifted and glanced around. The tent we were in had cleared out, except for a few of the staff who were busy boxing up the remainder of the table cards, champagne bottles and glasses to haul toward the other location.

"Let me help," I said, stepping over to the one of the waitresses who juggled several items at once. I needed to take a breather there. I felt as though a string was tied around my ribs, drawing me toward Holden Pierce, and I couldn't explain why. That was, of course, until he answered the stupid phone.

"Oh, no, I got it," the waitress replied, her eyes going wide. She obviously didn't want a guest mingling with the help, but this girl couldn't know that under any other circumstances, I would *be* the help.

"It's no big deal. We're going to the same place." I divested her of a few bottles and a handful of glass flutes.

"Are you sure?" she asked, glancing at the two guys who were packing up the rest of the bar with her and watching me.

"Of course. In fact..." I walked over to Holden and shoved several items at him.

He bobbled his phone, then jostled it into his pocket and wound an arm around the glass I'd almost let shatter at his feet.

His head whipped up. "What are you doing?"

"We're helping. Carry this." I handed him several more flutes by the stems.

"Sorry, I— *Fuck*. I'm in the middle of a deal in the city and I can't seem to get it closed."

"You're a busy man. I get it," I said with a slight shrug.

His mouth gave a slow curve upward. "Fuck the phone," he said and my insides fluttered. Goddamn, he had a nice smile. It reached all the way to those Hershey-colored eyes.

I walked back to the three wait staff and grabbed a few more bottles and flutes.

"We got this. Y'all can get everything else. We'll see you over there," I said to their stunned faces.

One of the guys flicked his gaze between Holden and me. "Uh, you sure?"

"Of course," I told him with a smile, which he returned by leaning toward me a bit and giving me a wolfish grin.

"You ready, iPhone boy?" I called over to Holden.

He glared at the waiter with the flirty smile then eyed me for a long second. "Yeah, I guess I deserved that," he murmured, falling into step behind me.

His phone rang again, but this time, he ignored it and continued to follow me, so I slowed down until we were side by side. His phone kept right on ringing and he huffed out another breath and hiked up the bottle under his arm. "You're Ava's friend from Clemson?" he asked, his voice low and deep. Even though I guessed him to be around about my age, he seemed older, holding himself as if he were beyond his years, his voice one of the sexiest sounds I had ever heard.

"Yep. We were roommates. All four years," I replied.

"Never seen you before. You must not hang with this crowd," he said and I slowed my feet at the implication in his statement. He took a few steps forward and stopped, glancing back at me. My eyes were hard and narrowed on his. "Anyone who grew up with these people wouldn't bother helping a waitress." He shrugged.

"Well, that's a clever deduction, Sherlock, but you don't call someone *poor* to their face," I said, my voice thin.

He tightened his jaw. "I didn't call you poor."

"Yeah, well, I am poor and it's pretty clear what you were inferring. So, let's do each other a favor and not talk about our own net worth for the rest of the weekend, shall we?" I plastered on a fake smile and started walking again.

"That is not what I meant at all, Marley. I don't give a shit about your net worth. And not having grown up with these people is not an insult, trust me."

"Didn't *you* grow up with these people?" I shot back.

"Yeah, and that's the reason why I'm saying it like a compliment. You're not like them. They wouldn't have done this. *I* wouldn't have done this." He nodded down at the items in his arms.

"A little hard work never hurt anyone, you know."

"I'm not afraid of hard work." He sounded offended.

I eyed him, skepticism in my gaze. A blind person could see this guy had been born with a silver spoon his mouth. He seemed like the kind of man who had never come across a problem money couldn't buy him his way out of.

"Not like the rest of these people here," he added in an angry mumble.

"Including our friends?" I stared at him.

"These people are not my friends." The words "these people" coming out of his mouth sounded sour.

"Why not?" I asked, my steps slowing. For some reason, I didn't want to reach our destination and share him with a room full of people yet.

"Because they're a bunch of spoiled pricks who haven't done shit in their life but whatever Mommy and Daddy told them to. They don't care about building their own standing or creating wealth for themselves. They're happy just to spend their trust funds and hold out their hands for more."

"But not you?"

"Fuck, no. Anything I have in my bank account I made on my fucking own. And I'm not going to piss it away on a half a million dollar wedding to show it off."

Sloane had hit the nail on the head—Holden had issues locked up tight behind those dark eyes and any inkling that he didn't earn what he had, he took offense to. *Workaholic through and through.*

I found the bar that had been set up on the expansive stone patio at the back of the house that hosted the next party and dropped off my bottles and glasses.

"I have to finish this call." Holden came up beside me, drawing a few watchful stares from the people milling around outside. They all looked at him with familiarity, but he just grazed over their glances with a casual nod and brought his eyes back to mine.

"Have at it."

"Will you wait?" he asked, taking a step toward me.

"Am I y'all's keeper?" I asked.

"*Y'all?*"

"Are you going to make fun of my accent now?" I asked. "Because that's pretty obvious. So is the fact that I'm poor. Oh, I'm sorry, I mean not 'like everyone here'." I made air quotes with my fingers. "I also still sleep with a nightlight on and never learned to swim. You can add that to the list of my flaws." I went to walk past him.

Damn, I had a chip on my shoulder. I hadn't even realized. All my years of hanging out with Sloane and Ava had made me think I had grown beyond this kind of class warfare. But I guessed not. *One guy with money says one thing and I take it the wrong way, throw it in his face and try to stomp off in a huff.* I hadn't been fair — to either of us.

"Marley, wait please," he called.

I stopped dead and spun around, almost knocking into him and toppling us both over. He held out his hands to steady me, keeping us upright. As soon as he touched me, my body flushed with heat and shifted near to him, without me even wanting to. He smelled like a sweet cigar and a woodsy, faint cologne and when I caught the scent of it, I moved even closer.

His eyes flared when he examined me, the brief flash of warmth I'd seen earlier returning. "Just a quick call. Two minutes. I want us to walk in together," he murmured.

I swallowed down the rising lust I felt and the emotions that crept up with his statement. I didn't know why he wanted us to go in together, but I didn't want to look a gift horse in the mouth.

"I can wait," I told him and he gave me a stellar smile. He moved his eyes down my frame and back up to my face in a slow sweep, wetting his bottom lip with his tongue. He regarded me as if he wanted to devour me and I slid even closer, sort of wanting to let him. The heat in his gaze increased a thousand-fold and we were both moving toward one another as if connected by a taut, tightening string.

"You have exactly two minutes. Starting now," I breathed.

Humor sparked in his eyes. "Understood." He stepped back from me, releasing the combustible air that had started to build between us, and took out his phone.

I let out a shaky breath and walked over to the bar where I had set down the bottles.

"I think you could use this." The waitress handed me a champagne flute from the tray she'd started arranging.

"You have no idea," I muttered and took the glass, giving her a grateful smile in return.

She glanced at my companion on the phone. "He's a fucking babe," she muttered then her eyes grew wide. "Oh, shit— I mean, shoot! I'm sorry." She burned bright red with embarrassment.

"Don't worry about it. I was thinking the exact same thing. You just said it earlier than I could."

"Some guy at the last party we catered told my boss I said the s-word and I almost got fired. And still I didn't learn my lesson," she mumbled.

"Well, your secret is safe with me. And what a shitty reason to get fired, no pun intended."

"Yeah, well. It wouldn't be the first time. A girl got canned last week for wearing navy shoes instead of black."

I stared at her. "Are you serious?"

She nodded, still filling up champagne flutes on the tray. "Totally. Nate got reamed just this morning because he didn't have the liquor labels facing out on the back bar. He has to forfeit all his tips tonight for it." She nodded toward Nate, the one with the flirty smile.

"That is the most ridiculous thing I've ever heard."

"Yeah, well, that's the island for you." She shrugged.

I didn't quite know what she meant, having never been here before, but I had a feeling she meant this place seemed just like I'd thought it would be— pretentious and snobby. I would never make it here long-term—good thing I had a flight back first thing Sunday morning.

Holden came walking over to me, finishing up his call then shoving his phone into his pocket. He gave a narrowed-eyed stare at Nate, who had his eyes on me, and held out his hand. "Thirty seconds to spare."

I fitted my hand into his and my skin tingled. "I'm proud of you, iPhone boy. You're improving."

He let out a low laugh, holding open the door from the patio into the house for me. I mumbled a "thank you" and tried to slow my breathing. The guy had *something*. No doubt about it. Not just his style, his deep, mellow voice or the expensive attire. He had a charisma, impossible to ignore. Men like him were dangerous and, if there was one thing I had become adept at doing, it was avoiding danger.

I had made an art form of being careful when it came to life decisions. Sure, I would throw back a few too many or drive over the speed limit on occasion. The riskiest thing I had done of late had been to date my boss, *technically* not even my boss. We weren't breaking any rules—our organization didn't write a fraternization clause into our employee handbook and neither of us was attached to anyone else. We were two consenting adults, even if it had fallen apart before it'd even started.

My parents had always taken risks and it had cost them countless jobs and thousands of dollars. My biological dad had ridden a motorcycle fast and hard and it had killed him in the end. My mom sank every dollar she had into whatever get-rich-quick scheme presented itself—and always lost it all. My stepdad gambled any money we had on horses and spent the rest on cheap bourbon. I'd never had security, never been able to predict the next day or week, never been able to breathe without difficulty, even as a small child. Neither of my parents had ever had a kind word for me or my brother and, anytime we'd gotten into trouble, rare though those occasions had been, my stepdad had been sure to let us know what losers we were turning into, what failures we were going to be, what disappointments we had always been. My mother had become the kind of woman hesitant to intervene. She subscribed to the 'tough love' mentality even if the tough was severe and the love was miniscule – because my stepdad did. They were clichés I refused to become, and that meant that I had to always be cautious, color between the lines, walk the straight and narrow. And in my twenty-five years, I had *always* done that.

I wouldn't allow myself to make decisions that could send disruptive ripples into my life for years, upsetting all the hard work and solace I'd struggled to build. I didn't want to live out my years in a loud, angry household like the one I had grown up in. I wanted to live smartly, peacefully.

I did not intend to show up at Martha's Vineyard for a weekend and throw it all away. No matter how sexy Holden Pierce smiled. Or how good he smelled. Or the fact that after five minutes of banter, my panties had grown damp and my head swam with lust.

I didn't know how to swim, which meant I had to keep my feet planted on the ground. For good.

The rest of the wedding party had been seated at a long table at the front of the huge room. It mimicked a wedding reception and I wondered how many times this weekend were we were going to have Ava's 'wedding'. I guessed a lot – Ava no doubt had been looking forward to five days straight of adoration and attention. She had been positioned front and center of the enormous, opulent room, large vases of flowers framing her and Reed's places. Each table looked ornate, with lofty, tapered candles burning, and a soft harp was being plucked melodically in the center of the room. The room oppressed, relieved a little by the life-size cut-outs of Reed and Ava in key places around the perimeter.

I skated into my assigned seat and Sloane leaned over her partner, Ethan, and nodded toward the giant photos. "I already have Reed overload and we just got here."

I snickered and went to withdraw my seat, only to have Holden appear at my side, holding out my chair for me, then tucking it into the table after I'd settled in.

I didn't say thank you that time, and I avoided Sloane's piercing stare and instead downed half of the champagne sitting in front of me.

"Think that's for the toast, babe. You need a drink?" Sloane asked.

"It's been like two minutes since my last one. I'm dying here," I said, sucking back the rest of the glass.

Sloane passed over her rocks glass filled with liquor. "I can get another."

Ethan slung an arm around the back of Sloane's chair. "I can get you something, Slo. Whatcha want?"

"Just bring two of whatever she's having." Sloane gestured to me and Ethan twisted toward me.

"What can I get you?" he asked, shifting his eyes to my cleavage in a way I could have predicted.

"Oh, um, something easy. Wine, champagne. Whatever." I waved my hand.

"I'll get it." Holden stood when Ethan did.

"I can get it, man." Ethan nodded to him.

"You get your date's and I'll get mine," Holden said, his voice level and even.

I spun my head around toward him and our eyes met. The intensity still lived there, burning its way into me, and I couldn't help but return it. *Fuck, he's sexy.* He drew me into him without trying, even while trying to put me off. He provoked a strange sensation—a push

43

and pull I had never experienced. We weren't 'dates,' but in that moment, I wanted to be.

Ethan peered down at Sloane. "Are you my date?"

"Depends on how nice you are to me." Sloane batted her eyelashes.

Holden put his hand on the back of my chair and leaned down toward me, creating that charged space between us again. "Just a glass of wine? Anything else?" he asked, his voice low and his eyes on my mouth.

My stomach descended into my toes. I felt a fever in every cell in my body, my blood pumping in my ears. "Um, that's all. Thank you." He tore his gaze from mine then straightened, moving around the table and toward the bar at the back of the room. *Whoa, that was hot.* I almost started fanning myself.

Ethan hustled after Holden to the bar and Sloane shifted over into Ethan's empty seat. "What took you guys so long to get here?" she asked, tipping her head toward Holden's retreating form.

"He had to take like a dozen phone calls," I explained, taking a sip of Sloane's glass and passing it back to her. I didn't feel prepared to confess my growing attraction to the man she had outlined as a head case and a workhorse. That would just be asking for a lecture.

"And why is he calling you his date?" She continued to prod.

"Who knows? Maybe he thinks it'll get him laid. Which it won't." *Yeah, not gonna confess I want that, too.*

"You sure about that? All the rumors I've heard about Holden Pierce are that he's a man hell-bent on satisfaction — and packing a monster between his legs."

"How many rumors have you heard?" I asked, trying to sound casual. I doubted I did, evidenced by the fact that I almost panted and my face flushed with heat.

"A lot." She lobbed back her drink. "But you know, all these guys fuck around. What else are they going to do with their time? Work?"

"Holden claims he works. You basically called him a textbook overachiever," I countered, trying not to ogle Holden as he leaned on the bar, his long frame relaxed while Ethan whispered something and made an obscene hand gesture, which Holden responded to with a half-smirk.

"Yeah, he is. I know he does investing and boring real estate, and I heard he works at his dad's law firm, too. No idea what he does there. Last I knew, he had dropped out of Yale Law so I know he's not an attorney."

"But he's not um, you know, like with anyone?" *Totally obvious.* I didn't sound cool at all. But God love Sloane — if she noticed it, she ignored it.

"Don't think he has a girlfriend, but half the girls I grew up with have slept with at least one of the guys in this wedding party. Just kind of the way of life with this crew," Sloane explained.

"That seems sort of incestuous, doesn't it? How everyone knows each other and all the parents are friends with the kids just pairing off with one another?"

"Very," Sloane remarked. "Which is why I would never date, fuck or mingle with one of these guys. Though I will admit, going on looks alone, Holden and Mitch make a girl think twice."

I peered around her and down the table to where Mitch sat without a care in the world, sipping a beer and listening to Cece talk nonstop and make wild gestures.

"He's pretty. Like California-boy pretty. Almost too pretty."

"Psssh," Sloane scoffed. "There's no such thing as too pretty." She shifted back into her seat when Ethan and Holden returned.

"Yeah, there is. Especially when it comes to the guys you like. What about the one guy who was really a girl? Way too fucking pretty," I reminded her.

"Yeah, well, *she* had a beard! I mean, how would I know?" Sloane tittered when Ethan handed her a glass.

"We all told you her name was Stacy!"

"That can be a boy's name, too!"

"Here's your drink." Holden set the glass down hard in front of me. It spilled a little over the top and I picked it up and licked the side.

Holden's eyes followed the motion of my tongue. "I don't want to miss any," I muttered then jumped when Holden danced his fingertips across my arm. He gave me a dangerous smile that went straight between my legs.

"It's your job to keep me entertained," he informed me.

I crossed my legs and twirled my frame toward his. "It is? Since when?"

"Since now," he said, watching my legs when I rearranged them. He dragged his hand through his thick, dark hair and moved his eyes back up to my face. "And up until Sunday morning."

"Oh, really?"

"I'll make it worth your while." He took a long sip from his rocks glass. I watched the liquid move down the column of his strong throat. The man seemed as though he consumed pure adrenaline and converted it to energy and attraction. Every part of his carved, muscular body was on full alert and focused on me.

"I'm not interested in your millions, rich guy."

"*Billions*, sweetheart. I have billions." He said it matter-of-factly, with no bravado in his voice at all.

"Not interested in those, either."

"What do you want?" he asked, his eyes hooded.

"Pleasant conversation."

He watched me for a moment. "That's it?"

"Sure." I shrugged.

"Okay, then. Fire away." He sat back with his glass still in his hand.

I leaned forward, my head propped up by my elbow. "Okay." I thought for a minute. "How much money do you donate to charity?"

"Whatever gives me the biggest tax break," he answered, without missing a beat.

"Okay, what charities do you give to?"

He shrugged. "No idea. My accountant handles all that."

"You have an accountant?"

"Yeah. I have a lot of people who work for me."

"How many?" I asked.

He thought for a moment. "Ten. Full-time. I also have a PA at my building and one at my investment firm. And one at the office."

"The office? Investment firm? Your building? Are these three separate places?" I asked.

"Yes, three separate places. Staff at each one. What do you do?"

"I work at a food pantry," I replied. He set his hand on my thigh as we spoke and fire rushed through my leg. It felt heavy and warm and the longer we talked, the closer we shifted to one another and the more fervor grew in his gaze.

"A food pantry. Like a grocery store?"

"No. Richland Hope. It's a food bank. We give food to needy families and seniors."

"For free?"

"Yes, for free. If they need it." I leaned closer to him, the bond between us increasing.

"What do you do there?"

"I manage the mobile food pantry." He stared at me, so I went on, "We have five food trucks that go out into the community and deliver to schools, homes, at festivals, things like that. I coordinate the locations and disbursements and work on the truck. I hire all our interns, too."

"By yourself?"

"Yes, by myself. There's twenty-five of us who work across four locations. We all do like three jobs. Just like you."

He rewarded my teasing with a dazzling smile. "What did you go to college for?" he continued.

Sloane giggled behind me and knew she had been eavesdropping. "Plant and wildlife science," I replied.

Holden stared at me. "What?"

Sloane laughed harder.

"Plant and wildlife science," I repeated.

"What the hell is that?"

Sloane cackled and I whirled around to shoot her a glare, then shifted back to Holden. "It's the study of agricultural technology and biological systems."

"Tell him about the Agronomy Club!" Sloane called down to us and I leaned closer to Holden.

"Don't ask me about that," I told him.

"Tell him about being on the soil judging team!" Sloane continued with pealing laughter.

"Really don't ask me about that," I said, picking up my drink.

Holden's mouth grew into a wide grin. "You were on a soil judging team?"

I sighed and shot Sloane another dirty look. "Clemson hosted the regional soil competition in 2014. I was one of the judges."

"The *head* judge!" Sloan corrected, her voice designed to carry.

"I know, it's ridiculous. Just don't call me Dirt Girl. Because *they* did for an entire year." I jerked my thumb toward my former roommates scattered down the table from me.

"I like a dirty girl," Ethan said, leaning in from behind.

I spun toward him and Holden flexed his hand on my thigh, digging his fingertips into my skin. When I rotated back at him, he shook his head slightly. "Eyes on me, sweetheart," he commanded, his voice low and quiet.

I should have yanked his hand off me, tossed it at him and let him know I didn't like it when a man told me what to do. Because I didn't. But I'll admit, that "sweetheart," that dark, intense gaze and that handsome, perfect mouth made me acquiesce, made me more and more drawn to him, and from what I could tell, him to me as well.

I kept my eyes on him as I continued, "Incidentally, my team won that year."

"I have no doubt." What the hell was it with this man? He was irresistible, even with my worries and innate desire to protect myself from the unknown.

Holden Pierce represented a *big* unknown. We'd shared less than an hour together and yet, somehow, I had become captivated by him, in a way I had never been by any man previously. Boyfriends from college, dates I'd had with guys since I moved to Columbia—

none of them held a candle to the fire building between this near stranger and me. I knew he'd never be the kind of man who fitted into my world, nor I in his, so I should have been more wary of him than anyone else. But I couldn't help myself.

Reed's father stood to make a speech and my attention veered away. But Holden's hand didn't. He kept it on my thigh, inched it up a little higher and stayed it put through Mr. Whitaker's speech, then the prayer from the chaplain, then the toast from Ava's aunt with all kinds of exposition about the linking of the Burcars and the Whitakers, akin to the melding of two precious metals. Her metaphor, not mine.

On occasion, Holden would stroke my skin, but he decided that his hand over my dress didn't suffice and slipped his fingers on my knee then under my borrowed dress. It didn't feel obscene — it felt comforting. I was a fish out of water, experiencing this torrid connection to a man I didn't know, and his touch somehow kept me grounded. He rubbed his thumb across my skin and gave me a gentle squeeze from time to time. His fingers started to feel like a brand and I knew when they went away, I would miss them.

Once the speeches were done, the staff came around and delivered plated dinners.

"Hey." The waitress from earlier scurried up behind Holden and me to deliver our dinners. "Thanks again for the help." She dropped a small bottle of Don Julio tequila onto the floor between our seats. "Already chilled," she murmured and disappeared.

Holden flicked a glance to the bottle then back at me. "That's interesting."

"Sometimes it pays to be nice to people." I reached down, uncorked the bottle and poured a healthy amount into my empty ice glass. "But I'm kind of a disaster when I drink tequila," I confessed.

He cocked an eyebrow when I filled up the glass he was holding.

"Don't let me near a karaoke machine. Unless you want to hear every Bon Jovi song ever recorded, sung horribly off key," I whispered.

He paused then threw his head back, laughing so hard he drew stares from the people around us.

I handed the bottle across Ethan's lap to Sloane.

"What's so funny over there?" Sloane asked, nodding toward Holden, who hadn't stopped chuckling. And who still had his hand on me.

"Bon Jovi." I shrugged and took a sip of my drink. *Damn, that's strong.* I needed lemon and salt for this.

Sloane shifted her gaze to Holden. "She sang *Livin' On A Prayer* five times in one night during a trip to the Keys last summer. I've *never* been kicked out of a bar for singing too much hair metal. But I was that night."

"He's a wordsmith, that Jon Bon Jovi. The songs are classics," I protested.

Holden kept his eyes on mine, twinkling with amusement. Another sharp, oppressive heat blossomed between us and I couldn't tear my gaze away from him.

"Holden, dear." A woman with a pretty, though Botoxed face, stepped up to the table and set her hand on his arm.

With purposeful slowness, Holden shifted his attention to her, his body locking tight and rigid. His hand left my leg with reluctance and his whole presence morphed into something heavier, dragging the whole atmosphere around us downward.

"Yes, Mother?" he asked, his voice like ice.

"You need to come sit with your father and me. Tish Martindale is at our table — it's been ages since you've seen one another. She would like to say hello." Holden's mom flicked her eyes to me then literally turned her nose up.

"I'm seated with the wedding party. I'm *in* the wedding," Holden replied in an obvious and irritated tone.

"Just for a moment, dear. Come along now." She walked off, assuming he would follow her.

And he did. But he hesitated, taking a deep breath, throwing back the remainder of his drink, then brought his eyes to me. "Going to get this over with," he said, as though I shared some secret. I didn't know what he meant or why he meant it, but I nodded.

"Okay. I'll be here," I said, giving him a wry smile.

That made his lips curl upward. "And that means I'll be back soon."

"Should I hold onto your phone so I know I'll see you again?" I teased, but his face went serious.

He leaned over me, resting one hand on the back of my chair and one on the table, leaving mere inches between us. "I can promise you'll be seeing a lot of me this weekend, Marley."

I shivered. "Okay." My reply was breathy and wanton. I couldn't help myself. It just came out of me.

He shot me another sexy-as-fuck grin and sauntered over to the table where his mother waited for him, tapping her nails on the table and regarding her watch in a cartoonish fashion.

He sat on the edge of a chair at the table near a gorgeous redhead, who flung her arms around his neck and practically shimmied her way into his lap.

"Tish Martindale," Sloane said beside me, jerking my attention away from the auburn-haired bombshell and my 'date'. "She's a total slutbag. And she's been trying to get her hooks into Holden since they were in fucking diapers."

"She's gorgeous." I took a drink of tequila and let it burn down my throat.

And she was, in a way I would never be. Oh, I could be pretty enough. I'd been prom queen of my high school, homecoming queen at Clemson my senior year, approached by modeling scouts once or twice. But I didn't have that effortless beauty that came from having a good life. I didn't have hair that cost hundreds of dollars to be lowlighted and highlighted, sleek and straight. I didn't have a blinding white smile from dentist-office bleached teeth. I didn't wear clothes that were tailor-made for my frame, or shoes with red soles.

I grew up a poor girl who had gotten lucky with generous genetics and a nice figure. But I would never be the kind of woman who could catch and keep a man with billions – even if I wanted to. Which until today, I hadn't. But within an hour, the man on the phone had become something else – a fantasy, maybe, a desire licking at the edges of my skin and niggling its way into my brain. He had felt it, too. I knew he had. It had radiated from his fingers clenched on my leg and the depth behind his stare. I wasn't fooling myself. I knew he returned whatever growing attraction there was between us.

But as Tish dangled herself over his arm and pressed her surgically enhanced chest into his shoulder, I knew I would never get the chance to be with a man like him. Destiny didn't work that way.

"She's a skeeze. Bet she has crabs. I hope they don't crawl off her twat and onto our plates," Sloane said.

"Yeah, probably true," Ethan agreed and shifted in his seat, cradling his junk.

Sloane stared at him, aghast. "Damn, Ethan, *really*? You hit it with Tish Martindale?"

"It was at college! I hit everything in college!" Ethan tried to defend himself.

"Yeah, but everyone knows she's a double bagger," Sloane said. "One bag for your dick and one for her face the morning after you wake up and the beer goggles wear off."

I sipped my drink. "Bullshit. She's stunning." I glanced again at the subject at hand and found Holden's gaze on me—or, more accurately, on the space between Ethan and me, which had shrunk as I moved closer to Sloane. I swung backward without a second thought.

"Nah. She's all made up. She's got bad skin." Ethan took a drink.

"And a terrible personality," Sloane added.

But that didn't mean that Holden came back. I'd finished my dinner and dessert by the time I realized he hadn't kept his promise to me. I doubted he planned to return—but hadn't been given a plate at his new table.

I stood and slunk around the side of the small risers we were seated on, picked up his plate and refilled his drink, weaving my way through tables and setting it all down in front of him. "Food's getting cold. And I'm sure you're hungry," I said and he blinked up at me, his face blank. The warmth vanished and I told myself I just wanted to make sure he had something to eat, but the truth was I was hoping to see that heat in his gaze again—I didn't.

"Oh, Miss, thank you. Can I get another gin and tonic? Two limes?" a woman at the table requested.

"And another Glenfiddich here, babe," an older man ordered, shaking his glass at me.

"Oh, I don't work here," I said, taking a step backward.

They all stared at me as if I'd told them I came from planet Neptune.

"You look like you do," Tish muttered under her breath with an unattractive snort.

See? Even in Sloane's five hundred dollar dress, they could tell I wasn't the kind of girl who would be mistaken for a wealthy princess.

Holden stood with a snap, grabbing his plate and glass and backing me up when he came forward. "See you all in a bit," he said, nodding toward our table.

I turned and walked back, and he slipped into the seat beside me, dropping the plate down with a loud clank and drinking all his tequila down in one long sip. "Don't do that," he growled at me.

I stared at him. "Do what?"

"Deliver my fucking food to me."

"It was just sitting here. I didn't think you were coming back."

"I told you I'd be back."

"Well, you hadn't been," I replied.

He faced me and yeah, the fire flared back in his eyes — but, under the surface, anger bubbled, too. "You're not working, Marley. Don't bring my food to me, don't carry champagne bottles for the staff — don't do anything but enjoy your fucking weekend."

"I am!" I said, searching his eyes for something, some hint of what had him so charged up. Twenty minutes with his parents and the hot redhead and he had lost any of the relaxed nature and attraction that had been building between us.

He poured another glass of tequila and drank it all down. "Fuck," he muttered to himself.

He bunched his shoulders, giving away just how far he had gone from composed to agitated. His whole body was clenched tight as a bow-string, seemingly ready to strike.

"Want to get out of here?" I ventured, my voice soft.

He stared at me a long moment. "More than anything."

I tipped my head toward the doors and he nodded, standing and helping me out of my chair. He clasped his hand in mine and I glanced behind me at Sloane, who watched Holden lead me through the room at a swift pace. I pointed to my bag on the table.

Sloane nodded as Holden cleared the doors to the patio. There were a few smokers hanging around with drinks, cigarettes or cigars in hand, and he crossed the patio and went down a small dune toward the beach.

"Wait," I begged, tugging on his hand and forcing him to pause.

He stopped and I used his forearm to balance while I tugged my shoes off.

"I have to wear these all weekend. I don't want to get them full of sand," I said by way of explanation.

Holden watched my mouth as I spoke, then spun around and kept walking. He kept us together, hand in hand, until we reached the shoreline and only then did he halt just short of the tide.

We stood there in silence a moment, side by side.

"You going in?" I teased, elbowing him in the side. He yanked on my hand with a hard jerk so I fell into him and he wound an arm around my waist.

"I fucking hate the Vineyard," he said, pressing his fingers into my side.

"Is this a vineyard? I thought it was Montauk," I asked confused, glancing around.

"Montauk is where you took the ferry from. This is Martha's Vineyard. Montauk's south and Nantucket" — he pointed out across the waves — "is over there."

"Oh. Huh. I thought this was all one big blob of Massachusetts." I squinted across the ocean and shielded my eyes from the setting sun.

He squeezed me tighter. "No. But it's all shit."

I glanced around us. "Doesn't strike me as shit. In fact, I don't even think they let the animals shit here. They probably staple the seagulls' asses closed."

He chortled and shook his head. "Where the fuck did you come from?"

"Greenwood, South Carolina. Well, technically Angler's Haven, but Greenwood is the census city."

"Census city?"

"Yeah, like there's so many tiny crappy towns across Carolina that they have to have designated census cities, so everyone can be accounted for. My parents' house is in Angler's Haven, but Greenville is the census city."

"So a suburb."

"Greenville isn't big enough for suburbs."

"And you went to Clemson," he said, repeating one of the few facts he knew about me.

"Yes, where I was the head judge for the 2014 soil competition." I blew on my knuckles and rubbed them on my shoulder.

He had at least a half of foot on me with my heels off and a good fifty pounds more of muscles. Which were substantial now that I could feel them pressed against my body.

"Where did you go to school?"

His smile fell and he twisted his gaze back out at the water. "I don't want to talk about myself."

"Okay." I stepped out of his grasp and moved to the side. "Let's go swimming."

Yeah, I had thrown caution out of the window even though I had *just* told myself to be, but something about this guy brought it out in me. Maybe seeing him with a woman who was more his speed, maybe the tortured way he'd sounded when he said he didn't want to talk about himself? Or maybe I had grown sick and tired of always doing the right thing when the bad thing had the potential to feel *really* fucking good.

"What?" he asked, his voice taut when I tossed my shoes to the side and took the filigree comb out of my hair.

"Swimming," I repeated, reaching for the hem of my dress.

"I thought you said you couldn't swim."

"I can't. But I'm not going in that deep. You're wearing underwear, right?"

"Yeah," he ground out then peered behind him and back at me. "Fuck it." He went for the buttons on his shirt.

"I haven't been in the ocean in a year. I miss it. I haven't been anywhere in a year except my apartment, my job and Angler's Haven. That's pretty pathetic," I confessed, removing the five-hundred-dollar dress with care and setting it gently on a patch of tall grass that separated the beach from the houses behind it.

I circled around to see Holden staring at me.

"Yeah, tattoo. I was young and stupid." I ran my fingers over the large lily I'd had inked above my hip bone. "Don't judge me."

"I'm not," he said, dropping his shirt to the sand. His body was sinewy and toned, with a hint of a six-pack and a light dusting of hair across his pecs, making a trail down into his shorts. He had an elaborate black-work tattoo going up one arm and across his shoulder blades. "And I got this six months ago. Not young and stupid." He shucked his pants.

"I don't know. You're going swimming in your underwear with a near stranger and there's a house full of people a hundred feet away. That's pretty stupid," I observed, backing up toward the water.

"Well, then, I'm not young. I'm almost thirty," he called to me.

"Wow. I never would've guessed you were such an old geezer. Do you dye your chest hair?" I asked, my feet hitting the water.

He grinned, starting toward me. "No. How old are you?"

"Twenty-six," I replied. "On Sunday, actually."

He stopped moving a moment. "Your birthday is Sunday?"

"Yes. But don't tell any of the girls. I hate birthdays," I begged, inching into the water.

"Why?" He closed the gap between us.

I shrugged. "It's a boring reason. Now, hurry up before someone catches us." I turned, dipping down under the surface and coming up a moment later.

"I can't believe you did that."

"Did what?" I asked, wiping water out of my eyes.

"Went under."

"You're not going under? It feels amazing. It's a little chilly but not bad. And it's only, like, three feet deep here. I'm not going to drown."

"You fucked up your hair and makeup."

"Yeah, I guess I did." I squeezed the water out of the ends of my dark hair and wiped the dripping mascara from under my eyes.

Holden wound an arm around my back, drawing me against him again. I could feel his cock between us, half-hard and almost visible under his gray boxer briefs. God, I didn't know how much I would love that sensation, the pressure of his want on my skin. But I was enamored with it.

"I've never met a girl like you." He pushed my hair off my face.

"Well, that's not surprising. I doubt a lot of poor folk cross y'all's path," I said, laying my accent on thick.

"That's not what I meant." He stroked the side of my face.

"Soil judges?"

He gave a slow smile. "Yeah, first soil judge I met."

"I won homecoming queen my senior year at Clemson, too. But that's not as cool as President of the Agronomy club."

"You were president of the dirt club?"

"It's agronomy. Not the dirt club. And yes, I was," I replied, my voice dropping when he shifted closer to me in the water.

"And now you manage a food pantry." He moved even nearer. Not only could I feel his dick getting harder but his legs, chest, arms were all pressed against me. He dug his fingers deeper into my hair, stroking my cheek with his thumb. The heat from his eyes blazed like a fucking inferno now, threatening to consume me.

The man knew seduction and he worked it like a master on me. I had met him just short of two hours ago and responded to him as if we had spent a lifetime learning the ins and outs of each other's bodies and minds. I wanted to blame the sun, the scenery, being out of my element and desperate to leave my drab life behind, if only for a few days. But it was more than that. *He* was more than that. Underneath the overriding tension and obvious desire lived a man with incredible depth, not just another simple rich boy, like the others I had met in my travels with Sloane and Ava. Complexity and depth abounded in him, I could feel it.

"Yes," I replied, my mouth just inches from his.

"And you like Bon Jovi."

"Yes."

"And your birthday is Sunday," he whispered, closing the small gap between us.

"Yes," I breathed.

"Happy early birthday, Marley," he murmured and, just as his lips almost hit mine, someone shouted his name.

"Hey! We're going to the bar. Come on, lovebirds! Let's go!" Ethan yelled, his hands cupped around his mouth.

"We'll pass," Holden called back, still holding me close to him.

"You can't pass, bro. We're all going. Reed's idea," Ethan hollered.

"You could meet us there," Sloane called, hitting Ethan on the shoulder and saying something in a quiet voice to him.

"No, we're coming!" I moved out of Holden's grip. His eyes were on mine. "We should go," I said, looking away.

Did I want to stay? *Yes.* Did I want him to kiss me? *Yes. Am I pissed we were interrupted? Yes!*

The interruption had come at the perfect time—I needed to keep coloring inside those lines, get my head on straight for a second. I couldn't get burned by Holden's fire. I didn't come here for a fling with someone out of my league. I came for Ava, her wedding and a much-needed vacation that had sucked away all my savings. I had Ben back home. I had my job back home. I had a life that, had it not been for a random dormitory lottery when I'd been eighteen and starting college, would have never crossed paths with a man like Holden Pierce. And I should probably keep it that way, mundane as life had become. Because I knew in that moment that if I stayed, if I let Holden Pierce kiss me in the Atlantic Ocean in our underwear, I was reckless. I'd crossed a line into carelessness. And I wouldn't be able to walk back over that line once it happened.

I waded out of the water and back to our clothes, tugging my borrowed dress back on. Holden trudged up beside me and didn't say a word.

"I need to go change," I told him, picking up my heels.

"Then go." His voice sounded tight, his eyes distant.

"Okay. Um, you want to wait for me?" I asked, against my better judgment. I shouldn't prolong this, whatever *it* was. But I couldn't help myself.

He dug his ringing phone out of his pocket and took a long moment to answer me, his eyes averted. "I'll meet you there."

I stared at the muscles in his back, bunched up near his shoulders and flexing as he spun away, already gone in body and mind. Back and forth, up and down, calm and torrid. He couldn't seem to settle. And my desperation to find out why grew.

"That looked cozy," Ethan murmured, clapping Holden on the back. I ambled toward them through the sand and grass.

Holden ignored him, back to his phone, back to his work.

"I warned you. Guy's got a one-track mind," Sloane said once they were both out of earshot.

"Yeah, you did. And now I look like a drowned raccoon." I swallowed down rising tears.

I'd thought there was a connection. I'd thought there was something building between us, even if I didn't want it to. But he'd gone cold before we got all the way to hot. A warm, natural fire hadn't built between us — more like kerosene thrown on a grease flare. A burst of flame that devoured skin and bones in an instant. Yeah, mundane worked better for me. It didn't end in heartbreak. And I'd already had enough of that to last a lifetime.

"Let's get you into that Walmart dress and drink more tequila." Sloane threw an arm around my shoulders.

"It's from Target." I didn't smile back.

* * * *

I threw off Sloane's five-hundred-dollar dress back at my room, reapplied a thin layer of makeup and blow-dried my hair enough so that I was presentable, fluffing half of it back in a large barrette. I'd had enough of pretending to fit in — my sale-rack dress from Target seemed good enough now. I slipped on my twenty-dollar T-strap sandals, giving up on the good life, heading downstairs to meet Sloane and Elle in the foyer.

"Slater's waiting for us with the car," Sloane said when I reached them.

"Did you make out with your usher dude?" Elle asked, her voice shrill and carrying through the expansive hall.

"Um, no. Almost, but no," I said, tucking my clutch under my arm.

"Why not? Where's your dress? Is your hair wet?" Elle fired at me.

"Holden had to take a call. It's upstairs. And sort of," I answered her questions one by one, then walked around her to the door, wanting to get more alcohol in me fast. Champagne and tequila weren't doing it for me. I needed something stronger like moonshine or absinthe.

"Wait, he took *another* call?" Elle scurried after me, persistent.

"Yep. Dude's got to make them Benjamins," I said, trying for a lighter tone, forcing myself not to get caught up in disappointment with a man I barely knew. I had already been disappointed in most of the men I *did* know.

Elle snorted at my joke, then stopped dead once we cleared the steps. Slater waited by a town car, smoking a cigarette. "You girls ready?" he asked, glancing at the three of us, but settling his eyes on Elle.

I swore I felt her blush beside me. "Yes," she murmured and he opened the door for her, giving her a wink. She blushed redder.

Elle glided across the seat and I sat next to her, poking her in the side and skating my gaze to Slater. She chewed her lip and shrugged. I wiggled my eyebrows and she snickered.

Good for her. I didn't know what was going on with them, but when Slater climbed into the front seat, he twisted his head around and gave Elle another sexy grin. Damn, that man had a nice smile.

"If you guys are going to make googly eyes at each other the whole time, I'm gonna barf." Sloane lit a joint and held it out for me.

I wrinkled my nose and shook my head. "I'll just end up falling asleep."

Sloane offered it to Elle. She hesitated then, when Slater lit his own, she took it from Sloane's hand and inhaled.

"I haven't smoked weed since the Keys trip," Elle admitted then exhaled.

"God, that was so fun. We should go again." Sloane took the joint back.

"We blew our wad on this trip. Maybe next year," Elle said.

Sloane shrugged. "I'll pay for it."

"No," Elle and I both said at the same time.

"You're so lame. I mean, if I want to do it, just let me. I need as many good deeds as possible to cancel out the bad ones."

"I don't think that's how it works, Slo," I said.

"Okay, how about this. I miss you guys." Sloane threw an arm around my shoulders. Yeah, cool Sloane was gone, to be replaced by lovey Sloane, helped along by lots of alcohol and marijuana.

"Come see us in Columbia," Elle suggested, taking the joint back.

"You guys are boring at home. You're always working. And you smell like little kids."

I laughed. "Oh, *so* sorry we live in the real world."

"Yeah, the real world sucks," Sloane muttered.

"No shit," I agreed.

"Do little kids smell?" Elle asked, a blank look on her face.

Sloane and I exchanged a glance and laughed.

* * * *

The place in town we went to was called Admiral's. The downstairs included a restaurant, with a bar and loud music upstairs. Most everyone had already arrived, including a half-drunk Ava.

"You're here! I can't believe you're here!" she cried, running up to us and hugging us all tight to her. We lost Slater in the fray and Elle watched him walking off, shoulders drooping in dejection. I'd seen that look before. Elle had a tendency to fall fast and hard in love with any man who paid attention to her. I didn't understand it. She was beautiful, with soft, auburn hair and cornflower-blue eyes, but her confidence sucked and she always seemed stunned when any man wanted her — then did her level best to get and keep that man, even when he was a complete loser.

I had a bad feeling I would be picking up the pieces when she fell apart on Monday during our trip home.

"You can't believe we're here at this bar?" Sloane asked, glancing around.

"No, I mean, here here!" Ava squealed. "You're my best friends. Ever. Ever ever *ever*. Let's dance!" she shouted and dragged Elle to the dance floor.

"I need a drink first." Sloane wrenched my arm and dragged me over to the bar. We stood and waited to order. "What happened at the beach with Holden?"

"Nothing," I said, trying to get the bartender's attention.

"It didn't seem like nothing. What about your boss?" Sloane asked.

"I don't want to talk about him."

"Okay, let's talk about Holden Pierce."

"I don't want to talk about that either. I don't want to talk about *any* of this." I sighed.

"It's not like you to go jump in the ocean with a strange dude. In your underwear. I mean, you had one one-night stand in college and the dude ended up tracking you down to go out on a date. So, it didn't even really count," Sloane commented, ignoring my request.

"I know this."

"So, now you're having casual sex with the CEO of your company *and* making out with strangers in the ocean?"

"I'm not having sex with Ben."

She raised a knowing eyebrow at me.

"Okay, I had sex with Ben. *Once*," I clarified. "And after —"

"After?"

"After. Well, nothing." I shrugged.

"He ghosted you?" She was incredulous.

"Sort of. I mean, we work together, so it's not like he can fade into the great unknown. But our last uh *date* happened two weeks ago and since then, well, he's been—unavailable," I admitted. Sloane could always get to me reveal anything. I didn't know why. She didn't come across as the easiest person to talk to. She was full of opinions and liked to give advice then get pissed when we didn't take it. But Sloane and I had shared a lot during our friendship and no one knew me better, not even Elle.

"So, it's over?"

I shrugged. "I guess so. I mean, do I really need a notarized letter delivered by certified mail to tell me the dude ain't into it? If he was, he would come back for seconds." I gestured to myself.

"Well, it's his loss."

"You always say that."

She pinned me with a serious stare. "Because it's true, Marley. Any guy you've had around has been scarce worth the effort. And I'm sure this one is no different. The right guy will lock your shit down fast. He'll know you're the best girl he could get. By far."

"That weed made you sentimental," I told her and she laughed. "Sometimes," I started, pausing to collect my thoughts, "sometimes, I think that maybe I'm too careful and it's not doing me any good. I mean, I knew Ben for a year prior to going out, then we slowly started dating and even after me, you know, being careful — the guy still took off on me. I'm not naïve — I know the guy probably got what he wanted then bailed."

"Maybe he didn't," Sloane interrupted but I shook her off.

"No, he bailed. I've seen him ten times since we went out and he hasn't said a fucking word." I sighed. "This is a good lesson, though, right? Maybe I need to be a little more — spontaneous. Seems being careful isn't doing shit for me." I forced a laugh.

"You're spontaneous," Sloane retorted.

"No, I'm silly when I'm drunk and do stupid shit. I'm not spontaneous. I'm not a daredevil. I don't ever do anything long-term casually, without, like, eons of forethought. And maybe I need to start doing that." Maybe I would and maybe I'd end up the charred remains of myself when someone doused me with gasoline and walked away. Like Holden had.

The bartender plunked down two margaritas. "Those guys got them for you," he said, and nodded toward where Ethan and Mitch were standing at the other end of the bar.

Sloane picked one up and tipped it toward them in thanks. I gave them a little wave and grabbed my glass.

"You want to throw caution to the wind, I support that. I think you should. But isn't that what you did by sleeping with your boss?"

Sloane was almost too perceptive, too blunt. It made fooling myself incredibly difficult around her. "Yeah, I guess it is." I let out a long breath.

"You know I think the world of you, Marley. Always have. You got me through the hardest shit in my life."

Sloane had not had an easy first year at college. She had been forced into a situation at a frat party by a guy she knew from one of her classes, and hadn't wanted to tell anyone. When she had, she'd only told *me*. Sworn me to secrecy. I'd agreed but only if she saw a counselor. Only if she talked to me about it. Only if she agreed to think about pressing charges.

She hadn't wanted to, but I'd *made* her. I'd been gentle but firm. We'd talked to the police and her counseling had helped, especially when her grades had taken a tumble and she'd almost gotten kicked out due to absence and poor test scores. She'd joined a support group, had managed to put the pieces back together and she still went to meetings to this day. She'd ended up with a degree in social work to help girls like her and she worked part-time at a rape crisis center in New York City. It was almost the only thing in her life she took seriously and I was glad she did. *She's changing lives. I know she is.*

"I think the world of you, too," I said, my nose tingling with tears.

"And I want to see you with a guy who deserves you. Not some dude you work with who's flung your fling, or a rich kid with hang-ups and a surgically attached iPhone," Sloane declared.

"You think Ben's flung it?" I asked, feeling vulnerable all of a sudden. He wasn't the one, but admitting I had been tossed aside hurt, no matter what.

"Yeah, babe. It's flung. It's flung like cow dung." She squeezed my arm.

"Gross." I made a face and sipped my drink. "That's a terrible rhyme. Don't ever say it again."

She giggled as Mitch and Ethan walked up to us. She looked at Ethan. "Come on, date." She handed me her glass and grabbed his hand. "Let's dance like fancy pants."

"That's better than cow dung!" I called after her and she twirled away laughing.

I gave Mitch a smile. "Hi." First ovaries and semen, now cow dung. *This guy must think I'm one classy gal.*

"Marley, right?"

I nodded, sipping my drink. "Mitch. Cece's groomsman," I said.

"Yeah." He had a pleasant, open smile. "I think I lost her."

"No, she's standing over by the bar staring daggers at me." I nodded behind him.

He rotated his head and peeked over at her, then back at me. "Yeah, she's persistent. Nice girl, just not my type."

"What's your type?"

"Girls who don't ask me what's in my bank account five minutes into a conversation."

I stared at him. "She didn't."

He tipped his beer back and swallowed. "Yeah, she did."

"Wow. That's, like, super tacky," I said.

"Agreed."

"And obnoxious."

"That, too."

"And fucking rude."

"Yep."

"Did you tell her seventy bucks so she'd leave you alone?"

He snorted. "No. Didn't think of that. I guess I should've."

"Well, if she asks again, just be all, I don't believe in bank accounts. I've got a hundred bucks shoved in a *Playboy* under my mattress."

He gave a loud laugh. "Good idea."

"This is a very strange world to me," I admitted, glancing around.

"What is?" He shifted closer to me.

"All this — money, the wealth, the glitter. It feels weird."

"Yeah, well it feels weird to me, too, and I've grown up with it."

"Does it?" I asked.

He nodded, taking a swig of beer. "Yeah. I think if it ever feels normal, I'm fucked."

"Probably," I agreed.

"So, what do you do?" he asked then glanced over the top of my shoulder.

I sensed Holden as soon as he walked up behind me. He smelled like salt water and a hint of that cologne I'd gotten a whiff of earlier.

"Hey, Mitch." Holden nodded at him, stopping beside me.

"Hey, man. Where you been?" Mitch asked.

"Had to change," Holden said. I felt his eyes on me, but I refused to look at him. "Your date is waiting for you at the bar." He tipped his glass toward the bar behind Mitch.

"Yeah, I know. That's why I'm over here." Mitch shot me a wink.

I grinned in return and Holden tensed beside me.

"You got a minute to talk?" Holden said in my ear.

"I'm going to dance, actually," I answered, setting my and Sloane's drinks down on the table next to me.

"Two minutes," Holden replied, not taking no for an answer.

"I don't want to talk," I protested as Holden held out a hand toward me. But, without knowing why, I slipped my hand into his, and he towed me away from a curious-eyed Mitch and toward the back of the bar.

I sighed in spite of myself. "Do you always get what you want?" I asked at his back. He led us around and through clusters of people drinking and talking.

"Yes," he replied. He took us through the doors and onto a long balcony that wound around the side of the building. Once we were in a dark corner, clear of almost everyone else, he caged me in so my back was against the wall and he was on the other side of me.

In a heartbeat, that warmth emanated between us again, starting at my core and rushing through me, swarming my chest and up my neck, onto my face. I had to be blushing, even if he couldn't see me in the darkness. Flushed, because he looked so goddamn handsome, because he intimidated me, because he was sexy and mysterious and all the things a woman always told herself she didn't want, but she always did.

He tossed back the rest of his drink and twisted his body, setting the empty glass on a table and turning back to me, moving in even closer.

I shifted farther into the wall so I was flush with it. Holden made a noise like a growl and pressed himself against me. "Stop trying to get away from me," he bit out.

"I'm not!" I protested.

"We were right here, just like this, in the ocean and you practically ran away."

"No, I didn't. We should've gone back to the dinner. We're here for Reed and Ava."

"I don't give a fuck about Reed and Ava."

"Well, that's just ridiculous. You're in the wedding, tough guy. So, you can claim not to give a fuck, but here you are, all weekend, giving fucks while they tie the knot." I scowled at him.

"Reed's my brother's friend. I'm a stand-in because he's not here. But I don't want to talk about any of that shit. I just want to get through this goddamn weekend and I want to do that with you."

"Well, okay. I mean, I'm standing up with you and we're like paired off so I'll be right with you," I said, giving him a blank stare. Wasn't that kind of obvious? Things were moving in a direction at a rapid pace that I had wanted a couple of hours ago, but now I hesitated.

I had *just* told myself I didn't want to get burned and I had *just* told Sloane I wanted to throw caution to the wind. I needed to drag myself back to earth so I didn't lose myself up in the stratosphere of bad decisions.

"Not like that, sweetheart," he said then closed the gap between us and captured my mouth with his.

That did it. I was definitely on terra firma now. And *loving it.*

Holden didn't kiss me with hesitation or softness. He didn't ease me into him with nuzzles or sighs. No, he took my mouth with force, shoving his tongue between my teeth before I could even react. But it wasn't unpleasant. Quite the opposite.

I had grown accustomed to guys who were careful, like I was. That was not Holden Pierce's gig. Oh, no. We were in a public place, a few feet away from bystanders and he'd pressed me against a brick building as though he wanted to consume me.

That spark I had been searching for for the past few months with Ben? The nonexistent one that I'd kept crossing my fingers and toes, praying it would appear as if by pure magic with every guy I had ever been with? It flared up like a fireball in the sky. Right there. Right then. With *this* man.

I spun my tongue around his, drawing away a few inches then moving into him again, nipping at his top lip, sucking in the air he was expelling, clutching his shirt in my fists for fear that if I didn't hold on, I would fall over. But he took care of that. He groaned into my mouth and hauled me hard against him with his strong arms. He dug his erection into my stomach and I went on my tiptoes, slanting my head and deepening the kiss even more.

He gripped my ass in one hand and slipped the other between us, dipping his fingers between my thighs and up the skirt of my dress.

"Wait, wait," I panted, standing back. Yeah, I was right back to where we were before Sloane's stern talking to. I wanted this. I wanted to be reckless. I could feel the excitement of it pulsing under my skin and between my legs.

"What?" he breathed.

"I'm down for, you know, hanging out and making out and uh, other stuff, but not here," I admitted to both of us, ducking my head behind his shoulder and nodding toward the people who were a stone's throw away — though none of them were paying any attention to us.

"Let's leave, then." He clutched my hand and headed toward the door.

"No, wait, Holden," I said, stalling our movements, though it wasn't easy. He was a man on a mission. I had to jerk on his arm to get him to stop. "You may not give a shit about anyone, but I'm here for Ava. She's one of my best friends. I'm not taking off fifteen minutes after I got here because you want to bury your dick in me."

He seized the back of my head and dragged my mouth almost to his. "Don't talk about my dick inside you unless you're ready for that to happen," he warned, his voice hoarse, his lips a breath away from mine.

"Okay, noted." I swallowed hard. "Give me an hour. I'll have a drink, I'll dance. You can dance with me."

"I don't dance."

"Okay, well, I'll do that. You order some jalapeno poppers and a soda and chill out for a little while."

He gazed at me a moment then shook his head, amused. "Fine. I'll *chill out*. You go on and dance. But I'm giving you just an hour. One hour." He held up his watch for emphasis.

"Okay, Father Time. Got it. Sixty minutes. Thirty two-minute breaks." I went up on my toes and kissed him fast and closed-mouthed. "Keep your pants on until then."

I compelled myself to walk away and back into the club. My friends weren't hard to find, in the center of the dance floor, whooping and hollering and holding their drinks over their heads while they spilled all over the place.

"Marley Mae! You're here!" Ava threw her arm around me and sloshed half her drink down my back. I let her get away with using my middle name and the vodka soda on my clothes because this was her weekend.

"Hey, Future Mrs. Whitaker!"

She sighed. "Mrs. Whitaker. I can't wait!" she said, dancing back toward Elle.

Sloane grabbed my arm. "Where'd you go?"

"Out for some air," I said, starting to move to the beat.

"I got my eye on you. I'm not going to let you go too far down this New Marley Spontaneous Adventure Road. I won't let you get hurt," she said.

"And that's why I love you." I threw my arms around her neck and kissed her.

We danced like mad, made requests for Michael Jackson and *Call Me Maybe*, our college anthem. And after a while, some of the other guys, including Reed, Slater, Ethan and Mitch, made their way to the dance floor, pairing off with everyone. Cece gawped at Mitch, hope in her eyes, but he looped an arm around my waist and tugged me against him.

"I've been holding your drink for an hour," he said, his body close to mine and his voice in my ear.

I snickered. "You have not."

"No, but I did drink most of it."

"Well, you paid for it."

"Ethan paid. This is all on his tab." He moved to the beat and wound an arm around my waist. "So order whatever you want."

"I don't think I need anything else. All the champagne from earlier is rushing to my head," I confessed in his ear.

"Perfect," he replied with a wide, boozy smile.

We danced for a while and made small talk over the music, which proved challenging — the music screamed and the bar flashed with blinking strobe lights that made me feel like I would seizure. My head already felt dizzy from all the drinks and all this thumping and blinking wasn't sobering me up at all.

Mitch told me he worked on Wall Street for a brokerage firm and that he lived in Brooklyn, "with the rest of the hipsters."

I shifted my gaze downward at his Dockers and deck shoes. "Not a hipster. Not at all."

"Yeah, well, I live with Brooks, and he's half-hipster. So that counts."

"Where is Brooks?" I asked, glancing around, finding him at the bar — standing next to Holden, whose eyes were dead set on me.

"Talking to Holden about boring-ass money shit." Mitch wound another arm around me and hauled me closer to him. "You smell good," he noted, running his nose over the shell of my ear.

"It's sea water," I croaked, tearing my eyes from a still watchful Holden. I could tell from there he was not happy. He wore a dark expression in his eyes and gripped the glass in his hand so tightly I thought it was going to shatter.

Mitch's chest rumbled against mine. "No, it's something else. Vanilla. Sugar. Something." He took a deep breath and nuzzled against my neck.

I swallowed hard, making a move backward, but it was unnecessary. An arm drew me away from him ahead of even getting a chance, and whirled me in a half-circle into Holden's frame.

"It's been an hour," Holden said, winding a strong, possessive arm just about all the way around my side.

"It has not."

"Close enough."

"No. Not close enough. I have three thousand and six hundred seconds and I'm not leaving this dance floor," I said, tossing my arms around his neck. "So you'll have to stay here with me until my time is up."

"I don't dance," he repeated, dropping his mouth to my ear.

"It's all just sweat and bodies in here. Dancing is basically like fucking with your clothes on," I protested.

"So then you've been fucking Mitch for twenty minutes," he shot back.

"Because you've been glued to the bar with Brooks."

God, we sounded like an old married couple. I didn't want to end up like this, let alone *start* like this. I twisted his wrist so I could read his watch. "Fifteen more minutes. Then I'm all yours."

He narrowed his eyes at me then stepped back off the dance floor. But he didn't go far. I moved through the throng of people and found Elle and Slater well-nigh humping next to the bathrooms, Ava and Reed making out near the DJ booth and Sloane sandwiched between Ethan and Mitch.

"Hey!" Sloane called as I chose her to join, positioning me in front of her, which put Mitch at my back. He slid his arm around my waist and jerked me back against him, gyrating his hips behind me.

"I didn't think Holden was the jealous type," he said as we danced.

"I don't think he is. He's impatient and I said I would ride back to the house with him," I lied.

"Well, that's a bummer. I was really hoping you would ride *me* back at the house."

I turned to face him for a second. "That's presumptuous. You barely know me."

"You barely know him." Mitch threw his head backward toward where Holden stood, watching.

"That's true," I said. "But he called dibs."

Mitch laughed, the sound long and loud. "Did he?"

I shrugged and flipped back to my friend. "You having fun?" I asked Sloane.

She nodded, a loose smile on her face. "Totally!" she called. She flitted her eyes over my shoulder, then brought them back to mine, glaring at me. "Look before you leap, babe." She twirled around and faced Ethan as a hand circled my wrist and dragged me away from Mitch and Sloane.

Holden heaved me against his hard body for a second time and started to shuffle to the music. Mitch moved into my place against Sloane and I peered up at Holden. "You don't dance."

"It's just fucking with clothes on. And that I can do."

I slithered my hands over his shoulders and drove one of my hands into his hair as we moved. "You're not bad at this."

He didn't respond, just kept a close hold on me, shooting a scowl at any guy who came within striking distance. And when fifteen minutes were up and we had gotten sweaty while barely moving, glued to one another, turning me on so much I thought I was going to burst, he spun on his heel and walked out, trailing me behind him.

Sloane wiggled her fingers at me and I grabbed my clutch off the table when we passed by it. Holden had me down the stairs, outside and into a town car before I could even think.

"That was kind of rude. I didn't even say goodbye to Ava or—" I didn't finish, because Holden slammed the car door and pounced on me.

Just like before, his mouth was on mine, his tongue in my mouth, our teeth and lips clashing as he pawed at me, crawling up my body and pressing me down into the seat and car door.

This was the point where I would as a rule make things stop, take a breath and cool my jets. I would have an internal conversation, weigh the pros and cons and determine if moving forward seemed prudent at this juncture.

But prudence was not on my mind—oh, no. For the first time in my life, I let my body rule my mind. His heavy weight pressed against me and I lived in that sensation, letting it wash over me and make all my decisions.

I had told myself that I could do this. I had been cautious with Ben and it had gotten me nowhere. Maybe not being cautious with Holden wouldn't get me anywhere, either. But it would save me a hell of a lot of time worrying.

And even if I wanted to stop, the man was a *force*. I hadn't thought he'd been holding back in the bar earlier, but now that we were alone, I could see that he had been. He jammed his hand between my legs, forcing them open, going straight for my panties that had spent the last fifteen minutes getting damp thanks to me being held against him, sexy music playing in the background. He tore my underwear down my legs and tossed them to the floor.

"You ready for me, sweetheart?" he asked, raking his finger up and down my slit, then sliding it inside me.

"Oh, fuck, yes, I am." I dropped my head back against the window.

We weren't in a limo, just a large sedan. Which meant the driver could hear us. Could see us. But I was so pent-up I didn't even care.

Holden pressed his finger deeper in me, to the knuckle, then pulled it back out, faster and faster. He added a second finger and I was clinging to him, clenching my teeth and trying not to climax after only three minutes.

"You going to come for me, sweetheart?" he asked, his voice right in my ear, dragging his teeth down my lobe.

"Not yet," I grunted, glancing at the driver.

"He doesn't fucking care." Holden ran his hot tongue down my neck and across my clavicle.

"I do." But Holden didn't stop pumping his fingers in and out of my cunt.

"So you don't want me to fuck you in front of anyone?"

"No." I shook my head and he quickened his pace.

"You don't want to come for me in front of anyone?" He added a third finger, stretching me to the limit.

"Oh, *God*," I groaned, biting so hard into my bottom lip I drew blood.

Holden lapped it up, shoving his fingers high and hard inside me, curling them forward.

"Oh, fuck, oh, fuck, Holden, it's so fucking good."

"I know it is. So fucking come," he commanded.

And I did. I tried to keep it quiet but that proved impossible. I gripped the handle above the door and let my climax run through my veins like liquid metal, burning my bones, running me so hot I was all but screaming. Holden didn't stop. He kept at me until I was completely done, my mind floating back to earth on a slow cloud, my pussy still pulsing when he withdrew his fingers.

He brought them to his mouth and licked each one clean, a move I found so damn sexy I swear I grew wet again. I couldn't get enough of this man.

I dove across the seat toward him, straddling his lap and kissing him deep.

He moaned as he swirled our tongues together and I pawed at his belt and zipper to try to free him.

"I guess you don't give a shit about the driver anymore," he chuckled, when I drew back to get his cock out.

I grinned at him, dropped to my knees on the floor of the car and took him in my mouth. He was already hard, thick and long and so pretty. I don't think I'd ever seen a cock like this. Perfect size, glistening at the tip.

I licked that fucker like an ice-cream cone, up and down and over and over, swirling the tip in against my tongue and taking him all the way back in my throat. He seemed to enjoy everything I was doing, my fist priming his cock in tandem with my mouth. He shoved his fingers in my hair but let me control all of it, until he started to get close. The car stopped and I knew we were at the house, but I didn't slow down, didn't hesitate or take him out of my mouth. And he didn't make me, either.

He tightened his hand in my hair, controlling the pace with precision, thrusting himself deeper in my mouth, coaxing me with his words to take him. To suck his big cock, to lick his balls, to take him deeper. I did everything he told me and, when he was ready to come, he shoved himself into the back of my throat and let go with a loud curse while I swallowed every bit of cum he shot.

When he was done, panting and boneless, he lounged in the seat relaxed and blissed-out.

I shimmied my panties back on and picked up my clutch. "Thank you," I whispered, giving him a soft kiss next to his mouth and moving to the door.

He grasped my wrist, his eyes flying open. "Where are you going?"

"Home—well, to my room." I inspected the house through the glass. "Oh, wait, this isn't the place I'm staying at, is it? Shit, they all look alike."

He put himself back in his pants and zipped up. "No, this is Reed's aunt's place. Where I'm staying."

"Oh, well, it's not far. I'm sure I can walk, right? Or have the car take me?" I asked, sitting back in my seat and pushing my hair out of my face.

Holden stared at me and I shifted my gaze back him. "What?" I asked.

"We done?" he asked and his voice went strange—dead and emotionless. He gave nothing away, his eyes distant again.

Wherever he went to retreat, he was back there again. He folded inside himself and cut me off, just as he had twice before, at the party and at the beach. Something caused him to do this, something I wanted to get to the bottom of.

I leaned closer to him and he searched my eyes with his, slipping a hand onto my cheek. I rested my face in his large palm. "I don't want to be done," I admitted in a whisper.

His eyes changed, lighting when he set his lips softly on mine. He gave me a chaste kiss then took my wrist between his fingers, placing my hand at his crotch. "I'm fucking hard for you, Marley. Again. I don't want to be done, either."

I let my hand linger on his shorts for a moment, noting that, yes, he was in fact almost completely hard. *Again.* Just minutes after he'd come. I gave him a soft squeeze. "Wow," I said, not meaning to stare but not being able to help myself.

"I don't know what kind of backwoods hicks you've been fucking down in Carolina, sweetheart, but I'm not near finished yet."

He moved over me, getting the door open and holding it for me.

"I'm going to ignore that backwoods hick comment because I want you to make me come again," I said, pointing a finger in his face. "But don't press your luck, buddy."

He laughed again, tossing me over his shoulder in a fireman's carry and smacking my ass hard. I yelped and gripped onto his belt.

"I'll keep pressing my luck. And you'll keep taking it. Trust me," he ordered, heading into the house.

We were clawing at each other by the time we reached his room, ripping off each other's clothes and falling onto the bed in a flurry of limbs and kisses. He went slower this round, raking his tongue and teeth over my whole body. I'd come twice more by the time he finished inside me, buried to the hilt and sheathed with a condom. We were sweating, exhausted and panting side by side. I told myself to get up, to clean myself up, to head back to my own room. But while I was telling myself all of that, my eyes closed.

And the world went dark.

Chapter Two

I heard a faint alarm in the distance, soft, then louder. I groaned and flipped over, reaching out to the side of the bed, trying to find my phone and silence it. But when I went for the nightstand, it wasn't there. And I fumbled farther, so far I fell right off the bed and onto the floor with a thud.

"Fuck," I said, my voice muffled in the plush rug beneath me.

I heard a masculine chuckle and took a deep breath, getting up on my hands and knees, realization dawning on me as I peered over at the opposite side of the bed to see a sleepy Holden, half-covered with a sheet, watching me.

"Not funny," I said and he laughed again. He took me in, stark naked and on all fours on the floor, and his eyes filled with lust.

"Don't you dare move," he ordered, hopping out of bed to the other side, condom in hand. The man moved like The Flash, and while the comic-book-reading geek in me was impressed, the wanton slut in me dying to get fucked again grew dripping wet. He slipped the condom on and got on his knees behind me, stroking his already hard cock a few times and sliding it up and down my slit. I turned my head and watched him move back and forth, his hair mussed from sleep, his lips puffy from last night's make-out session, several bites and a few small scratches from my fingernails on his skin, seemingly lighter and happier than I had seen him since we'd met. Yesterday.

"Hurry up and fuck me before I start to think about what a mistake this is," I confessed and he rammed inside me.

He groaned loud as I bucked back against him. "This isn't a fucking mistake, Marley. It feels too fucking good to be a mistake," he said, gripping my hips. He pushed further into me, then spanked me hard, the *thwap* ricocheting off the walls.

My whole body went nuclear. I had never had a man spank me — well, that was sort of a lie. I'd had a boyfriend do it by accident once. I had been so excited and aroused by it, I'd come on the spot, which had freaked him out.

Apparently, he hadn't been prepared to be with the kind girl who was comfortable being dominated. And I didn't know I could be that kind of girl. But I'd gotten caught up in the moment at the time and loved it.

But this — *this* was something else. Holden took control of me, reminding me that he called the shots, and I was more than okay with that. As a woman who always planned the next step in her life, letting myself go and having him take the reins felt incredible. And his physical manifestation of that? Striking my skin hard with a palm, enough to cause a tingle and a slight sting? *Wow*. I wanted more.

"Fuck, oh, fuck that's good," I purred.

"Yeah? You like my cock, Marley?" he asked, his voice low. "You like to be spanked?"

"Yes, oh, God, yes, I do. I fucking love your cock. You're stretching me so fucking much," I confessed, pausing a moment, then going on, "I want you to spank me more."

He flexed his fingers into my hips at my admission and let out a low growl. His cock pulsed inside me — he liked this idea. He hit me again, right where he had before, then massaged the skin with his hand.

"Fuck!" I shrieked, climbing faster and higher toward my climax.

"I'm going to wear this fucking pussy out this weekend. You understand me? This pussy is mine for the next four days and I'm going to be as balls-deep in you as possible."

I groaned and he moved faster and harder, digging his fingertips into my skin, the sound of him slamming over and over again echoing off the walls. He gave me one last spank, the hardest one of all. I knew he would leave a deep, rose-colored mark on my ass cheek. My clit spasmed — it and I both liked that idea.

He responded with another deep, long groan. "You hear me, sweetheart?" He straightened my body so my back pressed flush with his front as he continued to fuck me.

I nodded. "Yes."

"Tell me this pussy is mine."

"This pussy is yours," I repeated, my insides clenching with every word.

"I'm going to fuck this sweet cunt over and over. Because it's mine. Who does this pussy belong to?" he gritted out, winding his hand around my neck and holding my chin, curving my face sideways toward his.

"You, Holden. My pussy is yours."

"That's right, baby. That's my sweet cunt. All mine. And I'm fucking it good and hard so you can think about me inside you all damn day." He pistoned his hips faster and faster, tightening his hold on my neck just that little bit.

He found my mouth with his own and kissed me, circling our tongues together, contracting his hand on my neck, the possession and want in his fingertips going straight through me, sparking every nerve in my body until he squeezed just tight enough to set me off. The climax that had been building for what seemed like hours, taking over every thought in my brain and muscle in my body, roared ahead. I lived on another plane of existence. One where only pleasure existed and all I could think about was Holden Pierce and his incredible cock.

I compressed and let go, every doubt in my brain erased the second I clenched his cock inside me, convulsing around him, coming like a shot, shouting his name so loud I know the entire second floor could hear me and I didn't care. Not one bit.

He fucked me hard all through my climax and when I was done, he pulled out, guided me back onto my hands and tore the condom off to come all over my sticking-up-high-in-the-air ass.

He groaned and shouted just as loud while his cum dripped down my skin and along my legs.

"Fuck, you look good like that," he rasped, once he'd stopped and his breathing slowed. He stood, hustled to the bathroom and came back with a wet rag. He cleaned me all over, taking his time and teasing me, a wicked grin on his face. He appeared elated, airy. His mood rang crystal clear for a change — he had enjoyed what had happened as much as I had.

I swatted his hand away. "Don't get started all over again. I'll never get out of here."

He shifted back into the bed, fluffing a pillow behind his head. "Where are you going?"

"Boating. Right?" I asked, standing and tugging my dress over my head.

His body went stiff. "Boating?"

"Yeah, I thought we were all going out on Reed's sailboat today." I stared at him while I knotted my hair up on my head.

"I'm not going." He rotated his rippled and powerful core, then grabbed his phone off the nightstand.

"Oh. You're not?" I stared at him.

"Nope." He kept his eyes on his phone. It took every fiber of my being not to snatch that thing and smash it against the wall.

"Why not?" I asked, irritation growing in my voice. This is why I couldn't overthink this—the man was a human ping-pong ball. Every single time I wanted to unwind and share his good mood, his dismissive nature reared its ugly head and his lightness vanished.

"Because I don't want to."

I crossed my arms and narrowed my eyes at his petulant response. "So, that's it? You don't want to so you're not going to bother?"

"Yep." He tapped away on his device.

I moved around the other side of the bed, climbing onto his lap and easing the phone from his hand.

He let out a deep sigh and glanced up at me.

"Do you not like boats?" I determined to get to the bottom of this.

"Not really."

"Do you want to tell me why?"

He ran a hand through his hair, exhaling a breath. "Nope. Not right now."

"Will you tell me sometime in the future?" I asked, trying not to sound hopeful, trying to keep things in the 'now' and not get caught up in there being a 'sometime in the future' between Holden and me — the only way I would get out of this without driving myself to insanity.

"Possibly. If you let me fuck you again before you leave, possibly might become most likely."

"You're employing sexual blackmail, huh?" I braced my hands on either side of his shoulders and dropped down closer to him. "Maybe this will be the first time in your life you don't get your way, like you said you always do."

He tossed me onto my back with ease, grasping my hands and holding them over my head to press his large frame against my small one. "I'm getting my fucking way, Marley. But you will, too," he promised then dropped his mouth to mine.

He made fast work of getting me going, grinding his naked thigh between my legs, pushing his knee up against my core for me to wriggle and clamp around him. He dragged his mouth languidly down my neck, across my chest and to each nipple, to leave faint sucks and bites then dip his tongue farther down until he lapped my skin between my legs.

"Holden," I whispered, driving my fingers into his hair. "Wait."

"I'm not waiting," he said from between my legs.

"I want to come on your cock."

He stilled then surged up and pressed his erection against me. "Baby, you've drained me dry. This isn't going to go quickly."

I gave him a wide smile. "Well, you gotta hurry, because I have an hour. And since you're abandoning me, I won't have you with me to make our excuse for being late." I was trying to be flippant, to throw him off the scent that I felt genuine disappointment knowing he wouldn't be around today. Not just because of the way he made my vagina feel, but because when he had been *present*, I sort of kind of liked him. Maybe even more than kind of.

He snagged a condom from the nightstand and rolled it on, pushing inside me hard and to the hilt.

"Oh, God." I tightened and nearly came as soon as he slammed inside.

He flipped us back over so I sat on top, gripping my hips and bouncing me up and down on his cock, faster and harder, grinding up against me every time we touched.

"Faster," I ordered and he complied. "Harder." He did that, too.

I dropped my mouth to his neck and sucked and he moaned. I'd learned last night that he liked that spot quite a bit.

His morning stubble scraped against my cheek but even that felt good. It all felt good. He started going faster than before and the moment I told him I was coming, he grasped my ass and slammed into me, over and over. One orgasm bloomed into two and he kept going as if he would never stop.

His body started to coil, the rigid muscles of his abdomen clenching, his biceps bulging with tension and the thick cords of his neck pulsing under his skin as he unloaded in me with a considerable groan. I wasn't quiet with Holden, and he wasn't quiet with me, his voice a boom so loud I swear it shook the window panes.

We were sweating and panting, coming down from the ultimate high. I leaned over to his ear and whispered, "You sure you don't want to go on that boat?"

He held my face in his hands and looked at me. "I'm not going on the boat. But I will see you later, yeah?"

I nodded, tucking away my feelings of being let down. We'd had one night together. I didn't have any right to be disappointed.

"I have a lot of work to do," he added, seeing the expression on my face.

"It's all right. I'll see you soon," I said, my voice bright.

He gave me a grin that didn't quite reach his eyes, but I took it and climbed off him.

I re-dressed with him watching then shot him one more smile before I walked out.

I remembered the water had been on the left when we'd come to this house for dinner yesterday, so with the water on my right, I headed down the sand. I have to say, though, prettiest walk of shame I've ever done. The waves were calm and the sky a perfect blue with wisps of clouds here and there. The sand felt warm on my toes and I lost myself in my own thoughts while I came up to a house that appeared somehow familiar and, thank God, still had the tent and plank floor set up.

Holden had distracted me with sex. I had wanted him to let me in, to find out what he suppressed behind those gorgeous brown eyes, but he had deflected with the best of them. He used his sexual prowess to make me acquiesce and I got kind of pissed at myself for having been so easy.

But I couldn't start thinking about this right now. If I started, I wouldn't stop. I would be frozen in place while my mind warred with itself over the decisions of the last twelve hours and how they related to the big picture of my life, how to conform myself and Holden to fit together. And we no doubt didn't, so I would most likely go mad trying to make it so.

I walked up the dune to the back porch and sneaked inside the house.

"Hey! There you are!" Elle said from where she and Nanette sat at the counter in the kitchen, a large spread of food in front of them. "Did you go for a swim this morning?" she asked, giving me a full-body scan.

"Uh, sort of." I didn't want to explain that I'd gone swimming in dick, a few times over. "I'm starving." I collapsed into a chair and dropped my heels and bag to the ground.

"Everything is amazing," Elle said, her mouth full of Danish.

Nanette focused on me. "You smell like dude."

"I smell like dude?"

"Yeah, like cologne and semen," Nanette expanded and I near-choked on my glass of OJ.

"You can smell semen on me?" I asked.

She narrowed her eyes. "I can smell something dude-ish." She tore off a piece of croissant. "Spill it."

"I went home with one of the guys from the wedding party. That's it." I gave a casual shrug. I hoped I sounded convincing. I doubted it.

"*You did?*" Elle screeched, gaping at me.

"It's not a big deal." The words came out false, wonky and strange. I had wanted it to be. But Sloane had been right—Holden lived life as a workaholic who would rather spend the day on his phone than with me on the boat. Holden had issues buried so deep I don't think he even knew how to deal with them. I doubted he would give them up to me, not after a weekend in

Martha's Vineyard. That kind of thinking was downright illogical.

And when all that sank in, I felt even more foolish for thinking that being impulsive would clear up the confusion in my life and satisfy some itch I didn't know how to scratch. Nope, it didn't do that. In fact, I felt itchy and weird everywhere now. I also felt lonely, dismissed and used. Just like with Ben and now with Holden. But this somehow felt *worse*.

"When are we setting sail?" I asked, trying to change the subject.

"Who was it?" Elle questioned, her voice low. "Which guy from the wedding party?"

"Holden Pierce," Sloane said, coming down the steps and into the room, the picture of seaside perfection in sexy romper and beach cover-up, her jet-black hair in a short ponytail and sunglasses perched atop her head.

"Oh, okay," Elle breathed.

I looked at Elle. "Wait, you didn't go home with Slater? You guys were all over each other at the bar."

"Yeah, but I'm not going to sleep with him! I barely know him! That's just stupid. And he'd never want me again," she added, oblivious to what she'd just said as she ripped the paper off a muffin and took a bite.

I swallowed hard, the glass in my hand shaking. "Yeah, stupid."

She froze. "I didn't mean that you —"

I held up my hand. "No, I made a mistake, fucked up. You're right. Stupid." I swallowed and stood. "I gotta go get ready. When do we leave?"

"Half-hour," Nanette replied, her voice cautious.

I nodded and breezed past Sloane, forcing a tight smile. "Save me a croissant." I hustled up the stairs and didn't cry until I reached the bathroom. I was proud of myself.

My love life had always been a series of disappointments, mirroring my childhood. Every time I was naïve enough to get my hopes up, someone or something would come along and remind me that I wasn't destined for a great life — rather, a mediocre one. *Average. Just like everybody else.*

And sometimes, not all the time — because I was happy, more than not, regardless of being broke, tired and lonely — it got to me. And that blatant, cold rejection I had endured this morning did now. Sure, deep down I knew I had been careless, but the way he'd watched me, the way his body had felt against mine, how his fingertips glided across my skin, how his lips pressed against mine — it had seemed like something more.

But I'm a girl, right? This is my fate — to make something out of nothing and hate myself for it.

I let the tears stop on their own, then I put on my bathing suit, not a bikini like Nanette had been hoping for, but with cut-outs on the side so it looked racy and fun, although destined to give me the most random tan lines ever.

I slipped on my flip-flops, blow-dried my hair enough so it didn't drip down my back and twisted it into a knot on the back of my head, skipping my makeup. What was the point? We were going to be tanning and sitting on the water, so I deemed makeup unnecessary. I threw my sunblock and lip balm in my bag and headed down the stairs.

I found all the girls whispering when I cleared the steps, then stopping dead once I came into view.

"I'm surprised you didn't send a mass text about my late-night activities, Sloane," I challenged as she looked at me like the cat that had caught the canary.

"Whatever. Was it a secret?" She bugged her eyes out at me.

"No."

"Okay, good, then can we talk about his dick size? Because I've always heard that he is enormous and —"

"Ava Lynn Burcar! You are getting married in forty-eight hours to another man!" Elle smacked Ava hard on the arm and cut her off.

"So? Just because I'm on a diet doesn't mean I can't look at the menu, right?" Ava said, batting her eyelashes at me and waiting for my answer.

"No comment." I shoved my sunglasses on my face and headed for the door.

"You're no fun!" Ava called after me. Sloane fell into step beside me.

"Is he coming today?" she asked as we walked to the cars.

I shook my head. "No. He said he has to work."

"Not surprised."

I glanced at her, but she had those mirrored shades on and her eyes gave me nothing.

I became determined to enjoy the day regardless of the addled thoughts bouncing around in my brain. "I've never been on a sailboat before," I told Ava.

"Well, it's not what you'd call a sailboat," Ava replied.

"I thought we were going sailing?"

"Oh, we are."

Chapter Three

A freaking *yacht*. That's where we were spending day two, on a luxury cruise liner that spanned half a city block. The gargantuan ship encased a large cabin tucked under the hull which had everything that could outfit a luxury home, and more. A seventy-inch flat-screen TV, two large and decadent bedrooms, a kitchen with gleaming granite countertops and heavy oak cabinetry. Everything shone bright and new, with top-of-the-line appliances and buckskin seats, textiles and wood trim that screamed *money*. They had also laid on a huge spread of food and drinks, along with several people aboard to restock the boat, steer the massive ship in the water and cater to our every whim.

We weren't to do anything but recline and enjoy another luxurious and fairytale location.

"*Wow.*" I tossed my bag onto the white leather booth table and slid into a comfortable seat.

"I know, right? It's nicer than our apartment." Elle took it all in.

"Oh, yeah," I agreed, digging in my bag for my sunscreen.

"Hey, I'm sorry about earlier."

"Don't be." I shook my head at her, knowing at once what she meant—the benefit of eighteen years of friendship. "I'm okay. Honestly." Little white lie. I would be okay and Elle didn't mean anything by what she said. And who knew? Maybe she was right. Maybe I had been tossed aside once the guy had gotten what he wanted on day one. It wouldn't be the first time it had happened to me. Not even the first time this *month*.

Determined to enjoy the sole vacation we were going on this year, I needed three things to make it happen—drinks, sun and Bon Jovi.

Sloane indulged my hair metal guilty pleasure and let me rock out to as much Mötley Crüe and Van Halen as I wanted. And the guys were on board—literally and with the music selection since they were all there with us, sans Holden, and Cece, who had decided to stay back and nurse a hangover—as well as lick her wounds since Mitch had rebuffed her every advance the night before.

And with Cece and Holden absent, Mitch stuck close to me. We lay on the bridge of the boat and chatted, taking selfies and posting them to our Instagram accounts with the hashtag made for Ava and Reed's wedding festivities—#AvaandReed4ever. Kind of dorky, but it made Ava happy so we did it.

And as the afternoon wore on and we ate a little and drank a little more, Mitch got more handsy, more assertive. He took a picture of himself kissing my cheek and posted it, then one of him kissing my shoulder and posted that. Then one of him kissing my neck and he posted it with the hashtag #isshehotorwhat?

He got a lot of thumbs-up for that one, several of his friends chiming in and letting him know that I was indeed hot, and asking if I was his 'weekend slam piece'.

We were seated in the circular cushions at the back of the boat, eating again and nursing another drink when Mitch showed me the post and comments.

"Guys are just so gross." I dipped a chip in salsa and took a bite.

"It's not gross! It's a compliment!"

"Oh, yeah, someone implying I'm your booty call for the weekend is super complimentary."

"He just knows I don't have a girlfriend," Mitch said, glancing at me from the corner of his eye.

"I don't, either," I replied, elbowing him and he laughed.

"Didn't Elle say you were dating your boss? I heard her, yesterday when you guys got in." He slung an arm around the back of the couch behind me.

"We've gone out a handful of times. It's not serious."

"And what about Holden? Last night?"

I lifted an eyebrow at him in response, taking a long sip of beer. He didn't expect me to talk about this, did he?

"Never mind," he said, reading my expression. "Holden's not your type."

"Oh, so you know what my 'type' is?" I faced him, challenge in my eyes.

"I'll say this. I know you're the kind of girl who wants to be handled with care. You're not someone a guy should use and toss away. You're a keeper, Marley, and I'm guessing you also want to be kept." He twisted a piece of my hair around his finger, then tucked it behind my ear.

I searched his eyes. "You don't know me well enough to assume that, Mitch," I whispered.

He stayed close to me, his arm settling lower, flexing his hand on my skin above my ass. "I think I know enough to know I wouldn't fuck your brains out loud enough for the entire house to hear then leave you alone all fucking day."

My cheeks went pink with embarrassment. "Yeah, well, maybe I wasn't any good at it." I bent my arm to grab my beer.

He took my chin in his hand and turned my eyes back to his. "Don't do that. Don't make this about you. This is about Holden and nothing else. The guy has problems and they don't have shit to do with you. Don't take that on."

I didn't want to take it on, but I lived a life of compassion. The girl who wanted everyone around me happy, healthy and fed. A girl who'd maxed out two credit cards so she could give her best friend the weekend of a lifetime. The girl who went home every other week to clean her parents' place and put groceries in the fridge. The girl who spent forty-plus hours a week feeding kids and families because it didn't feel right to know that people went hungry.

And I had known that kind of suffering. I hadn't grown up with a comfortable or even average childhood. I had grown up in the middle of a mess without the basic necessities that make a kid feel loved, even wanted, in a household always teetering on the edge of destruction and rage. And regardless of that, I still wanted to help others, to help my mom and stepdad, even if I didn't understand my own blind devotion to them. Maybe I was afraid of more loss. Losing my dad so young, I'd grown up desperate to keep any family I had safe and healthy. I did the little I could to make that happen, which for my mom and stepdad always meant money. Maybe I thought that if I could control that little piece of my existence, if I could get them both on a sure footing, all the other searching I had done for myself would fall into place and I'd find all that had been missing had been the adoration and security of a good family. As soon as I had that, the pieces would fit together and I would find the true happiness that always seemed just out of reach.

Or maybe I had been born with a bleeding heart. One destined to be broken, over and over again.

Maybe Holden did have issues, like Mitch and Sloane had said. But did he need help to get those problems resolved? Did he want to work them out and needed support? Could I be the girl to help him do that?

Or maybe I was just so eager to get the love I thought I'd missed out on that I made something out of nothing with a man who just wanted a piece of ass.

"I need another drink." I stood and made my way into the cabin. My head felt heavy and the conversation and liquor had contributed — along with my brain running away with my heart again. I needed to stop thinking and start just tanning.

I found Sloane on the front end of the boat, slathered in oil and worshiping the sun.

"Hey." I dropped down beside her and handed her a cold beer.

"You're a godsend." She sucked half of it back in one sip.

This was *just* what I needed — girl time. Relishing the friendships that I cherished. I peeked around at them all and the good news was that even though *my* love life, as pathetic as it might be, imploded around me, Ava and Reed were in heaven. They were attached to each other all day, kissing, hugging. And Reed seemed just as smitten with her as she'd told me over our countless phone calls and text messages she was with Reed. *Lucky prick.*

This made me happy. Ava led with her heart and not her head most of the time and I had been worried that would get her hurt. Whenever we drank too much, Ava always woke up the next morning ready with the hangover cure we inevitably needed. If we were cramming for a test, Ava stayed up making us peanut butter and jelly sandwiches at two o'clock in the morning and quizzing us with flashcards. She lent her clothes, her time and her friendship without any expectations in return. She endeared herself as a delight and a darling to everyone who knew her and Reed seemed to know and appreciate the most important aspects of her. Reed would walk through fire rather than let her down, and I appreciated that one of the four of us had moved on to a good life with a better half.

Juxtaposed with that, Elle and Slater were like two teenagers who had the house to themselves while the parents were away. They were making out on every surface of the boat and around every corner we went to. He was glued to her side and if I saw Slater and didn't see Elle, she would appear as if by magic three seconds later. I didn't know if Slater was smitten, but he should have been. Elle had always been generous and kind, dodging critters while driving so she didn't hit them, bringing home stray toads and cats to find them good homes, buying scarves and hats for her students who couldn't afford them. Goodness streamed out of every pore in her body and I hoped that whoever she ended up with — even if it was Slater Riley — saw everything that the girl had inside her and let her gorgeous light shine. But something told me they were more like an affair to forget.

Sloane had been playing footsie with Ethan for a while as he lay on the other side of her, but I could tell she was just passing the time. I had seen this set-up before. She came off as uninterested enough to look bored but attentive enough to seem like she didn't want to stab herself in the eye. Sloane was honest and intelligent, two qualities that I knew intimidated men, and she preferred it that way. Ethan would never last with her, but I could tell neither one of them cared about that. Brooks eyed her a few times, and I could guess that was because Nanette remained as the sole member of the opposite sex on the boat, minus the staff, but she would never give it up for any man, especially not one like Brooks. Nanette lounged at ease, the picture-perfect beach-goth, resting on the back of the boat, head to toe in black with a large sunhat, reading William Burroughs the entire time and reapplying dark lipstick. Brooks had a pink shirt on. Even if he'd had a vagina, the guy didn't stand a chance with her.

As the afternoon went on, the pit in my stomach over my poor choices from the evening before eased. I watched the people I loved the most being happy, having fun and I found my way out of the grim disappointment I'd felt earlier. I was here and going to enjoy myself, Holden Pierce be damned.

Once the boat docked again, we had a few hours to rest and get ready for the Jack and Jill party. I needed a nap, so I rinsed off the sun and surf and crawled into bed naked, the waves and breeze coming in through my open window.

I passed out in no time flat, my mind at ease with itself at last. Well, maybe not at ease, but definitely too tired to keep the gears churning.

When I woke up, someone's face crowded between my legs, their tongue lapping against my core, and I moaned long and loud. I half-thought it was a dream until consciousness pierced my brain.

I gazed downward to see Holden's dark head of hair buried between my legs, darting his tongue in and out of my slit.

"Holden, wait—" He didn't listen. I tried to sit up and he threw an arm around my middle to hold me down. He slid a hand under me and grabbed my ass, thrusting me up farther into his mouth and he lit my world on fire.

God, he was good at this. And my halfhearted attempt to stop him dissipated once he really got going. He darted his tongue in and out, fucking me with it, using his mouth, his tongue, his teeth, his fingers— every weapon in his arsenal except his cock to make me come *twice* before he relinquished his hold on me.

"Fuck, you taste good," he muttered, licking his lips and looking up at me, uttering the first words he had spoken. I had spent the last fifteen minutes praying and thanking every god in existence while he worked his magic on me.

He sat up and undressed, shoving his shorts down his legs and kicking them to the floor. He threw his shirt over his head and across the room and dropped his full weight on me, taking my mouth with his and kissing me hard, gliding his tongue across my mouth and inside.

"Holden." I again attempted to stop him, pressing on his shoulders.

"You didn't fuck him, did you?" Holden pressed his hands to the mattress and hovered over me.

"Didn't fuck who?" I frowned, confused.

"Mitch. On the boat."

"Are you kidding me? *No!*" I exclaimed.

"Thank fuck," he breathed, dropping his mouth to mine again. He kissed me even deeper, holding my face in his hands and moving his mouth down my neck and across my breasts, kissing, sucking, biting and blowing on my nipples until I writhed beneath him. I blamed the haze of sleep, but it was just the promise of another orgasm.

"You want another one? You're getting greedy." He plucked a condom from his shorts and inched it on.

"You're *making* me greedy," I admitted, pulling him back down on top of me.

He grinned like a devil, watching my face and gripping his cock in his hand. "You said this pussy was mine," he said, slapping his hard cock against my labia.

I jumped, my body raising off the bed of its own volition.

"I don't care who hangs all over you," he went on, hitting me again with his dick, my pussy getting wetter and wetter with each word and each stroke, glistening in anticipation.

"Don't give a fuck who posts pictures of you sexy as all hell in that little black bathing suit." He kept a hold on his cock to push in just an inch then ease all the way out.

I whimpered in response. He smirked in reply, his eyes flashing with amusement. "This sweet cunt is mine, Marley." He pushed in another inch then pulled back again.

I slapped the mattress with frustration and groaned. I wanted him so much I was about to propel him onto his back and take over. I was trying to figure out how to use my momentum to overturn him when he drove hard into me, done teasing.

"You're mine." He gripped the back of my hair, balling the locks in a tight fist while he held on and started to pound so fast, so hard that I was crying out in no time.

"That's right, sweetheart. Take my fucking cock. Take it all and milk it with your sweet pussy." He dropped his mouth down to kiss me while I came. He pumped harder and my orgasm turned into a climax that went on for either five minutes or five hours, I had no idea since time stood still. Eventually, I collapsed into a useless heap of lust by the time he was done with me, groaning and shouting as he emptied into me, crying out while still holding me.

We were both panting, stark naked and sweating, and he gave me the sweetest, most sincere kiss I'd ever had in my life. His eyes were wide open, as though he knew he'd twisted me inside out and wanted to keep on doing it, because we were both getting off on it.

But it wasn't *just* our bodies. And maybe I was being foolish and wanted to see something that didn't exist, but I felt the closeness between us grow, and when he did pull out, easing his grip inch by inch from my body, I missed him at once.

I had *never* felt that. I was *fucked*. In more ways than one.

After the second-best sex of my life, we lay side by side, quiet for a while. Then he started to ask questions—all kinds of questions. What was my favorite movie? An obvious choice of any girl in her mid-twenties—the blockbusting undead romance of the last decade. He didn't seem very impressed by my hankering for pale vampires. Did I have any siblings? An older brother named Ross who worked as a mechanic—a godsend since my car was more often than not puttering out on me. Did I like my job? Some days, yes, and some days it felt like throwing a rock into the Grand Canyon—nothing I did made a difference, I could never feed everyone and there would always be more need than resources. I answered him, lying on my side with my head in my hand, and he did the same, listening hard to all my answers and asking more.

I asked him questions, too, but he gave curt responses then switched back to talking about me again. I discovered that he lived in New York, had a degree in criminal justice from Columbia and worked at his father's law firm. That was it. I didn't even know his middle name, didn't know where he'd grown up — nothing.

But time ran away from us, which meant I had to get ready and so did Holden. He dressed in a hurry, gave me a deep, fast kiss at the door and disappeared — and I kind of didn't know if I'd ever see him again. He felt like a phantom — present, engaged, focused on me one minute then distracted and running off the next.

I didn't know how much longer I could play his game before I ended up burned alive.

Chapter Four

The Jack and Jill party that night took place at a huge house on the beach. I thought we had already been residing and partying at huge houses on the beach, but it seemed a *huger* house had been deemed necessary.

It had a large, open ballroom floor, with a wall of French doors that faced the water. Inside, the space had been transformed into a glitzy casino with roulette, poker and blackjack tables—even a few slot machines. Dark velvet partitions cordoned off some of the space and plush rugs had been placed under chairs and tables. The place buzzed already, almost full with newly familiar faces by the time we got there.

Sloane had forced me to borrow another dress, this one a black fitted number off one shoulder, with a funky cut on the other that exposed lots of skin and came down just below my knees. She'd also gotten hold of a pair of Givenchy open-toed leather heels in my size with silver rivets across the ankle. I hadn't asked how she'd gotten them. I didn't think they had ever been worn and both pieces together must have cost almost a thousand bucks. I just told her I would be careful with them.

She'd scoffed at me in response, waving a careless hand and telling me that was unnecessary. "Go ahead and set them on fire if you want. Makes no difference to me." *Ah, the life of the vulgar rich.*

A man in a tuxedo greeted us at the doors, assuring us all the proceeds went to the charity of Ava and Reed's choice and asking us how many chips we wanted.

"Five thousand dollars." Sloane handed him her debit card.

He scanned her card in a machine and looked to me next.

"Um, a hundred?" I squeaked out.

He gawked at me a moment, incredulous, and I busied myself with finding my wallet in my bag.

"Five thousand for each of us on my card. Thanks," Sloane said, sending him off while I still searched.

"What did you do that for?" I gaped at Sloane.

"Because you can't give a hundred dollars to charity," she deadpanned.

"Slo, I *work* for a charity. Some people give five bucks. Some give a freaking quarter. It's not that big a deal if I don't gamble all night. I'm just here to have fun," I said as she snatched two glasses off a tray of champagne floating by.

"So, we'll have more fun with ten grand." She took a sip from one, handing me the other.

"Sloane, the clothes, the money—it makes me feel weird."

"I don't care."

"Well, you should! We're friends and I'm telling you it makes me feel strange. I had a perfectly nice dress for tonight." I smoothed down the dress I was in that made what I had brought from home look like a dish rag.

"Uh-huh. Well, now you have two perfectly nice dresses to take back to Columbia with you." She tipped her glass to me. "Drink up. Not arguing about this."

I took a long drink of champagne, knowing full well none of this would make it into my luggage and would be returned ASAP to its rightful owner. But I kept that to myself. Someone walked up behind us and slithered an arm around my waist. I expected Holden but got Mitch instead.

"You look incredible," he whispered in my ear and I smelled the bourbon on his breath.

I moved backward a bit, out of his grasp, since I'd had another man's tongue on my clit just a few hours ago. "So do you." I gave him a once-over. "You clean up nicely."

He drew me back into him. "I still smell like your suntan oil. And salt water." He dropped his mouth to my neck and I mouthed to Sloane for help.

"Hey, Mitch, show me to the blackjack table. I've forgotten how to play," Sloane ordered, leading him off.

I shot her a wry, grateful smile and blew a stray hair from my face. Just as I started to move forward again, someone else wrapped an arm around my waist. This one I *knew* was Holden. That cologne, that godforsaken cologne that I recognized, knowing full well when this weekend ended, I would troll department stores until I found it and bathe in the stuff.

"Mitch done using you to get his dick hard?" he asked, placing an almost imperceptible kiss behind my ear.

"I think he's drunk," I replied, trying hard not to lean into Holden and heave a wistful sigh. I didn't succeed.

He chuckled, his chest vibrating behind me. "He's not drunk enough to stop trying to fuck you."

I turned in his arms to face him. Dear lord, did he look good. He wore a pair of slim-fitted black trousers that rode low on his narrow hips. He'd paired them with a brown-red belt, a dark-gray shirt and a black tie. He looked like he'd stepped out of the pages of a magazine.

"Wow... You." I gestured to him. "You look — *wow*."

He hauled me into him again. "You *are* wow, sweetheart," he murmured.

His phone vibrated in his pocket and I hid the disappointment I felt. The night had just begun and already I had to compete with an eight-hundred-dollar piece of technology for his attention.

"I have to take this." He removed his phone from his pocket.

"Of course. Sure." I plastered on a smile. I don't know if it was convincing but I doubt he did, either. Even though I felt like we knew each other better, the fact was that we didn't. He didn't know the difference between my real smiles and my fake ones.

As I stood by the door and watched all the rich people I knew mingling, all elegant and refined, joking around and drinking expensive champagne like it was water, I felt uncomfortable. I had not been born into this world. It would never *be* my world. And the longer I stayed there, the more obvious it became. I felt as though I wore a neon sign that said *trash!* with blinking pink arrows. Maybe I blended in, but deep inside, I didn't feel like it. I felt like an outsider, a misfit.

Maybe the fact of the matter was that I *couldn't* compete with an iPhone — it was worth more.

Sloane waved at me as she settled into a card game and I headed over, trading my empty glass for a full one on the way.

"Do you know how to play?" she asked when I glided into the seat beside her, Mitch on her other side.

"Gotta get to twenty-one, right? Not over or you bust, and not less than the dealer?" I confirmed, setting my clutch on the table while Sloane shoved a stack of chips at me.

"Exactly. You play cards?" Mitch asked, a smile across his lips.

"My stepdad does." I didn't mention he'd also taught me how to play every card game imaginable when I reached ten years to see if I could count cards, and gambled away all the money my mom had saved for Ross and me to go to college. She had only managed to set aside four thousand dollars, but one weekend in Atlantic City when I had just turned fourteen and it was toast.

"You know how to play poker?" Mitch asked.

"Pai Gow, Caribbean Stud and Texas Hold 'Em," I replied.

Mitch stared while Sloane smirked at me. "She's a girl that's full of surprises."

Someone took the seat next to me and laid several stacks of chips on the table. His arm came around the back of my chair and I rotated to that side as Holden looked at me. "You need something to bet with, sweetheart?"

"No, I've got her," Sloane told him, the double meaning not escaping my attention.

We placed our bets on the table then the dealer set out cards in front of all of us. I peeked at mine then tossed another chip on the table.

"Minimum bet is one hundred dollars," the dealer said.

"That's a hundred dollar chip?" I hissed at Sloane.

"Yes. A hundred is the minimum everywhere tonight."

"Jesus Christ." I shifted in my seat and swallowed.

"Don't worry if you lose, honey. I got you," Mitch said and threw a wink my way.

Holden didn't say a word, didn't react, just sat relaxed and jovial with his arm still around my chair. He didn't seem the least bit concerned about Mitch or his advances. Or any of the other mysteries that had plagued him on and off this weekend. Maybe the phone call had been from a voodoo witch doctor who'd exorcised all his demons via Siri.

I had two jacks in my hand, so I bet another hundred when it came around. Then Mitch raised it to a thousand and I chewed on my lip. *Shit.* This was why I didn't play games of chance — too many factors, too many possibilities. And the metaphor of my life choices, which were literally seated right beside me, didn't get by on me.

"I fold." I tossed my cards to the dealer and sat back.

"You had two jacks!" Sloane announced to everyone.

"Holy shit, Slo — you're cheating! You're not supposed look at my hand!" I said.

"Yeah, well, I'm bored. And you could cut the sexual tension between the two of you with a knife." She nodded her head toward Holden. "My eyes wandered."

My cheeks flushed with warmth when Holden let out an unabashed chuckle.

"You should've stayed in," Mitch commented as the dealer flipped over nineteen.

"Yeah, well, I said I knew how to play. I didn't say I was good at it."

"She plays it too safe. Always has." Sloane flicked a glare at Holden. "Until now."

He seemed to enjoy that comment, too, a wicked smile growing across his face.

"Let's go play the spinning wheel thingy." Sloane stood.

I went to get my chips and she studied me. "No, me and Mitch are going. You're going to stay put and bet all of that and lose it. Maybe then you'll get it out of your system, MJ." She glanced at Holden then walked away.

"MJ?" Holden's voice fell on my ear and I watched Sloane and Mitch disappear into the crowd.

"Marley Jackson," I said. I wanted her back. I felt naked and raw here, in public, Holden's arm still around my chair.

"What's your middle name?" he asked.

I spun toward him in my seat. "What's yours?"

"Frederick."

"Why Frederick?"

"What do you mean?"

"Is it your dad's name, your mom's bowling buddy — why Frederick?" I pressed.

"In my family, the firstborn son always takes the maiden name of his mother as his middle name. My mom's maiden name is Frederick. My grandmother's maiden name is Cavanaugh, so my dad is Richard

Cavanaugh Pierce. My great-grandmother's name was Morley, so my grandfather is Nelson Morley Pierce."

"That's kind of nice," I said, not having expected him to be so open. "What if you marry someone whose last name is Fuckrudder. Or Dahmer?"

"I've never met a girl named Fuckrudder or Dahmer," he said with a laugh.

"You could. You could meet and fall in love with her and have to name your kid Henry Fuckrudder Pierce."

"Yeah, I'll keep that in mind." He paused. "Jackson isn't a bad name."

My body went taut and he noticed, his body responding in kind. "Don't do that," I whispered.

He stared at me.

"Don't play games like that with me. We met yesterday. You have no intention of marrying me. You don't even plan on this going off this island, do you?"

"I haven't thought that far ahead." He moved his thumb in circles on my bare arm.

"Yeah, well I have. Because I do that. I map everything out. I've always done it. It's how I live my life. Because if I don't do that, and I don't have every possibility considered before I take any action, I get blindsided and end up under someone's shoe." I glanced under the table. "And I have a feeling that thousand-dollar Gucci loafers are going to hurt worse than anything else." I shifted the chips left on the table toward him. "I'm not much of a gambler," I said and walked off.

I'd had a weak moment. He'd shown up in my room, his mouth on my lady parts, and I'd let him do whatever he wanted. But now that we were in the light of day, I could see the game he was playing, literally and figuratively.

First thing he'd done when he'd gotten here was take a phone call, much more important than spending the evening by my side, even though he had been balls-deep in me two short hours ago. He'd teased me about something serious being between us when he had dodged a simple question about sailing earlier. It was all bullshit—he was just doing his own thing, in his own world, and I existed as a mere pawn to him, a part of a game like all the others in this room. And it fucking hurt.

I spent the next hour alternating between Ava, Sloane and Elle. Ava grew nice and numb as the night waned on and Reed parked himself at a poker table while she kept drinking and gabbing with everyone who crossed her path. Elle spent Slater's money as if it was going out of style and Sloane kept trying to get me to spend hers.

After thirty minutes of her shoving chips into my clutch at the craps table, I agreed to go to play a few rounds of poker. I took a seat beside Tish Martindale and Holden's mom, with Ethan on the other side of me.

"Hey, babe." Ethan planted a wet kiss on my cheek. "Where's that bony friend of yours?"

"Sloane is playing roulette. She likes the noise it makes," I said, whirling my finger in a circle.

"She's a good girl, that one. Funny as fuck."

"Yes, she is funny as fuck." I said, setting my chips out and noticing Tish staring at me with a sneer on her face.

I gave her a wide smile. "Hi. I'm Marley."

"Like the dog," Ethan added.

"I know who you are," Tish said, over-enunciating every word.

"Ava's friend from college," I filled in, assuming that's what she meant.

"Yeah, and the wedding party mattress, by all accounts." She snorted. "First Holden then Mitch. Now Ethan? Aren't you a prize?" She bowed away from me toward Mrs. Pierce and my mouth hung open. She was talking about the woman's kid! Gross!

But Mrs. Pierce gave me a dirty look that rivaled Tish's. "Common trash," she muttered under her breath and my face burned hot. Seemed some people *did* see the neon sign I'd convinced myself I carried across my chest.

"You in?" the dealer asked me.

I pushed all the chips toward him and nodded. "Yep. All in," I answered, wanting to get this over with as soon as possible. I wouldn't jump up and scurry away like I wanted to, but I could speed things along to expedite my escape.

Unfortunately for me, I had a winning hand. Which meant I doubled whatever I had shoved at the guy, which turned out to be three thousand dollars.

Then I won another hand. And another. By the time ten minutes had gone by, I'd won twenty-five thousand dollars, settled in front of me in plastic chips, and the extreme dissatisfaction of Mrs. Pierce and Tish.

"Are you *cheating*?" Tish snapped at me.

"No." I shrugged. "I'm just lucky."

"Not in all things, darling." Mrs. Pierce swept her eyes over me in a dismissive flicker. I wiggled in my seat and wanted to evaporate. *Wow, the woman was colder than the Antarctic Peninsula.*

"Ignore the old bitch. No one can stand her," Ethan whispered in my ear and I glanced at him, slowly smiling.

He shifted his drink over to me for some liquid courage and I played another hand — and won.

"Jesus Christ, did she stack the deck?" Tish asked in a loud voice, slapping her hand on the table.

"How?" I asked her.

"I don't know how you sneaky little bitches work," Tish shot back.

"Maybe I just know how to play." I offered a fake smile.

Ethan stood to go and I went to beg him to stay as my support system, but Holden glided into his place.

"Heard you're winning." He scanned his eyes over mine, unreadable.

"At poker," I said then tilted my head toward Tish and his mother.

A smile grew wide across his face and lit up his eyes. "That's good to hear." He flung an arm on the back of my chair. "Deal me in."

We were all given a hand and I exchanged two cards on my turn, upping the bet.

"You sure? I have a pretty good poker face," Holden said to me.

"I already know that, hotshot," I murmured back, tossing chips into the center of the table.

He glanced down at his mother. "You winning at all tonight, Mother?" he asked and I could tell that when Ethan had said no one liked Mrs. Pierce, he'd included Holden in that.

"I'm doing just fine. Regardless of the company," she sneered.

I won another hand and Tish threw down her cards in protest. "It's not fair!" she cried. I think she even stomped her foot.

"Life isn't fair," Holden told her, taking a long sip of drink. "You, of all people, should know that."

She narrowed her eyes at him. "That's not nice, Holden."

"No shit." He finished his drink and called the waitress over for another. "I'm not trying to be nice. You're not." He nodded his head toward me.

"Oh, I'm sorry. Did I hurt your little girlfriend's feelings?" Tish batted her eyelashes and faked a childish voice.

"I'm not his girlfriend," I piped up, but Holden didn't respond to it.

"Hurt her feelings all you want. She's the one that I'm going home with later," he announced.

I whipped my eyes to his and held his gaze. "Don't put me in the middle of *this* game, Holden," I hissed at him.

He stared at me a moment then slipped his hand onto my neck and squeezed it. I took it as an apology.

"You're so crude, Holden. Mind your manners. Your mother is present," his mom spat at him, venom lacing each word. Which I found ironic considering she herself had had an almost identical conversation with Tish about her son's sexual conquests moments ago.

"When have you acted like a mother? Ever?" he asked.

Mrs. Pierce gaped at him, her mouth hanging open.

"She did carry you for nine months, Holden," Tish pointed out.

"No, she didn't. She didn't want to ruin her figure. Both Spencer and I were via surrogates," Holden replied, glass in hand. And he held it so nearly, I could see the whites of his knuckles.

I bounced my gaze between Mrs. Pierce and Holden and I could tell he was being one-hundred-percent honest, including about why. I slipped my hand onto his thigh.

He took it from his leg and brought my knuckles to his mouth, kissing them with gentle lips. "You realize that's the first time you've touched me."

"No, it's not."

"Yeah, it is. You touch me after I touch you. You've never touched me first."

He was right. I hadn't. Because I calculated and strategized carefully. Always anticipating my next move and making the safe choice, a pattern I couldn't break, even when I thought I had.

I lay my hand on his face and drew his mouth to mine, kissing him and licking the seam of his lips, then sat back. "Now I'm not going to be able to stop touching you."

His eyes searched mine. "Make that a promise."

"I promise," I said and kissed him again.

I heard Tish and his mother stomp off but didn't even bother to watch the show. I had the distinct impression that if Holden had problems in his life, those two women were at the helm. He held my face between his large hands and tilted my head to deepen the kiss, longer than was probably sensible, considering we were in a room full of people.

"Come on," he said, his voice rough with want, hauling me to my feet and leading me through the crowd. It played out like a rerun from last night at the bar, but his pace slowed this time, much more purposeful. He took me out of the room and into the hall with the bathrooms, locating an unused coat room, since the humidity raised the temperature to eighty degrees outside, even after sunset.

He pushed me up against the closed door and locked it, shimmying my dress up over my hips and winding my legs around his waist.

"All I've thought about since I left you this afternoon is being inside this pussy again," he admitted, unbuckling his belt and shoving down his pants with one hand while the other held me up.

"Not *this* pussy. *Your* pussy," I reminded him and his eyes shot to mine.

"Don't say shit like that unless I'm inside you," he ordered. "Are you on anything? Birth control?"

I nodded.

He wasted no time slamming his dick hard into me, no condom on, and straight away started to pump in and out, harder each time. "You going to be a good girl and ride my cock and make me come?" he asked, tightening his arm around me.

I nodded furiously. "Yes, yes, yes."

"I'm going to come in this tight pussy, and all that cum is going to drip out onto your thighs. And you're not to clean yourself up, understand?"

I nodded, already losing myself to the incoming climax, spurred by the voices on the other side of the door and knowing we could be caught at any moment, along with his punishing pace.

He stared at me as if I was the only other being in the universe right now. "I want you to feel me on your skin while you're out there drinking and laughing with your friends and anyone who gets near you will know who the fuck you belong to. You're going to smell like me and taste like me. Because you're fucking *mine*, Marley Jackson."

Oh, God, I'd already started coming. The veracity of his voice, his words sent me tipping over and I banged my head against the door behind me when my apex blasted through me, trying not to yell but barely managing it. He raced up right behind me, bellowing his orgasm in my ear and pumping longer than he ever had, spilling deep inside my cunt and all along my legs.

He held on a long time before he dropped me to my feet. One of my shoes had been kicked off and my hair no doubt stuck up all over.

I did what I could to get myself together when he gathered up his pants and smoothed out his shirt.

"It's Mae," I murmured. "My middle name is Mae. Marley Mae Jackson. A good ole backwater name for a good ole backwater girl." I put a deep twang in my voice.

"Marley Mae. I like it."

"Uh-huh. I sound like one of the Beverly Hillbillies." I yanked open the door and peeked out into the hallway.

He chuckled behind me as I stepped out of the room and he closed the door behind us. He put a hand on my lower back and guided me back toward the casino room.

Things were still going strong and I found Ava passed out in a corner, snoring away.

"Shit. I'd better get her home. Where's Reed?" I asked, glancing around the room.

"Pai Gow table. I'll get her in the car and you tell Reed." He scooped Ava up as though she weighed nothing and carried her toward the doors.

I walked up to Reed and tapped his shoulder. "Ava's passed out. Going to take her home."

"Oh, shit. Should I go with you?" he asked.

I shook my head. "Nah. She's dead to the world. I'll put her in bed and have her call you when she gets up."

He wound an arm around my shoulders and kissed my forehead. "You're a good girl, Marley. Thanks for being here."

"No place else I wanna be, Reed," I told him, meaning it.

Elle and Slater were making out at the side of the building, oblivious to anything around them. "Hey!" I called and they lifted their heads up. "Ava's passed out. I'm going to take her home."

"Oh, we'll go," Elle said, almost sprinting for the car and diving inside the door Holden held open.

"You sure?" I asked, when Slater crawled in after her.

"We're sure. Night." Slater slammed the door and leaped on Elle in the back seat.

I snickered once the car pulled off. "Okay, well, that's done."

"You want to take a walk?" He nodded toward the beach.

"Okay," I said with a smile on my face.

He knelt down and took my shoes off, one at a time, then set them by a shrub with my clutch. He took his shoes off, too, set them next to mine then held out his hand.

I shot him a skeptical look. "You're being very romantic right now. I didn't think you had it in you."

He wound our hands together. "Guess you bring it out in me."

"Uh-huh. You want a blow job on the beach, don't you?"

He threw his head back and laughed. "Hadn't even crossed my mind."

"Liar."

We wandered down the shore, the water lapping between our toes and up to our ankles. A companionable silence expanded between us and the sky looked incredibly clear, with a bright half-moon above.

"I fucking hate this island," Holden said after a time, his voice low.

I glanced over at him, his hand still in mine. "Why?" I asked.

He took a deep breath. "I'm not friends with Reed — he was friends with my brother, Spencer. That's why I'm older than all these guys. Didn't go to school with them, but Spence did. All the way from elementary to college. He and Reed were never apart. If you saw one, you saw the other. It annoyed the fuck out of me. Five years ago, Spence got into law school. I had already been there a year and he and Reed, Ethan and Brooks came out here to celebrate. Stayed at Reed's parents' house, got wasted and went sailing. Middle of the night."

My stomach clenched. Spencer wasn't here. He hadn't been slated to stand up for Reed at his wedding this weekend. Holden stopped walking and stared out at the waves. "My brother fucking drowned five years ago because he was drunk and fell off Brooks' boat."

"*Holden.*" I shifted closer to him to clasp his hand. "I'm so sorry."

"I grew up and apart from Spencer. He was younger, a pest. Pain in my ass. When we were kids, we hung out. But then I got older and…"

I waited.

"I felt like shit when he died and tried to — I don't know — keep up the life he would've wanted. He loved these friends and he loved this fucking island. He would've been the life of the party all weekend. But I can't do it. It's not me."

"Your brother wouldn't have wanted you to be him."

"You don't know that."

"If you were gone, would you want your brother to live his life in your place?"

He regarded me for a moment. "No."

"So, why do you think he would?"

"He had been accepted into Yale Law. I was already there, and I couldn't fucking do it. Couldn't stomach it. And I felt like shit—he wanted it, I fucking had it and pissed it away. So, now I'm here trying to make up for it." Holden's words were rushed and I could tell he wanted to blurt this out, get it over with.

"You have nothing to make up for. It's your life. Don't live it for him. Don't live it because he's gone. No one wants you to be anything but who you are." I put my hands on either side of his face. "I know what it's like to lose yourself when someone dies. It happens to everyone. You just gotta find yourself again."

"I don't know who the fuck I am anymore," he admitted in a low voice. "To my mom and dad, Spence and I were accessories. We weren't loved. They had us because they wanted some kind of stupid fucking legacy. And now I'm the only one left to carry it on."

"What kind of legacy do they want for you, Holden?"

"They don't want it for me. They want it for them." He nodded his head back toward the casino and I dropped my hands. "They want me to marry a girl like Tish and buy a house on the island and spend all summer commuting back to my shitty job in New York. Just like they do."

"How do you know that's what they want?"

"Because they shove it down my fucking throat every chance they get."

"You don't owe them anything, Holden," I said, moving closer to him and clutching his biceps in my hands. "You don't. If I lived my life like my parents, I wouldn't be here. I wouldn't have gone to college, or moved to Columbia. I'd be taking up residence in a double wide with my high school boyfriend Travis and spitting out a half-dozen kids."

"I can't see that for you."

"Neither could I. So, I'm knee-high in student loan debt, late with my rent to my creepy landlord, maxing out credit cards to be here this weekend, because it's not the life I want, either. I'm not going to get stuck in Angler's Haven like they are."

"My dad told me that if I don't man up and marry Tish or some girl just like her then I'm out of a job at his firm."

"So what? You just said you hate your job in New York."

"Yeah, but it's what Spencer would've wanted to do." He swallowed hard. "He would've worked for my dad. He would've toed the family line."

"You don't know what Spencer would've wanted. He's not here. You'll never know. So you have to live your own life, Holden. For you. Not for anyone else."

"I knew he would've wanted to make a fuck of a lot of money," Holden said, running a hand through his hair.

"I thought you had a fuck of a lot of money."

"I do."

"So how much more do you need, honey?" I asked, stroking the side of his face with my thumb.

"Fuck, you're a good girl. How are you such a fucking good girl?" he asked, gripping the sides of my dress.

"I'm not *that* good. I did just fuck you in a coat closet," I said and he chortled.

I lured him to me and hugged him, resting my head on his chest.

"It sucks that I could never be in love with someone like you," he said, his voice quiet.

It was like throwing a bucket of water on me. I tried not to tense, but I couldn't help it. I tried not to let my eyes well up with tears, but they did.

"We should go back," I said, my voice catching as I twirled away.

"Marley, wait," he said, grasping for my hand.

"I'm getting tired, Holden. Going to be a long day tomorrow." I shot him a smile and started walking back. He followed, a few steps behind.

He didn't say sorry. He didn't offer an explanation of his words. He let them sit there between us, dark and thick, just like the ocean we were walking beside. I could drown beneath them, let them suffocate me.

I know it was stupid to want someone to fall in love with me after two days together. But damn if saying it out loud like that, making the whole thing real and forcing me to look at us and what we were and weren't, didn't fucking sting.

I was a fling to Holden, a weekend 'slam piece'. And that is all a girl like me would ever be to a man like him. Now the stickiness between my thighs didn't feel sexy. It felt like shit. *I* felt like shit. And we still had three days to go.

Chapter Five

I languished in bed the following day. The house had fallen quiet early that morning, just a few random footfalls outside my door — a pair I'm pretty sure belonged to Slater Riley when he exited my roommate's bed after eight a.m. Soft voices traveled up the side of the house and into my open window, whispering in cadence with the waves on the choppy water. I knew I shouldn't get used to a life like this, but *damn*, it would be nice. More than nice — a dream come true.

I had never let myself be the young girl who believed in happy endings, waiting for her Prince Charming to rescue her from a tall tower. Instead, I worked hard and followed the rules, knowing that Cinderella didn't exist — there weren't any palace balls being thrown in Angler's Haven on weekend nights. I had to build a life to be proud of, and I could only do that with careful precision.

I'd arrived at the Whitakers' home *alone* last night, leaving Holden in the casino and taking a town car with

Ethan back to the houses. He had been beyond shit-faced and puked out of the door. I'd even had to help him up to his room. I'd taken off his shoes and socks and put a large bowl beside the bed just in case he threw up again. I did not want to be the maid in there the following the morning.

Holden hadn't crawled into my bed and woken me again. He hadn't texted or called up to my window like Romeo. I assumed he'd gone home and to sleep and I was a faint memory. Because that was what I should be—this wouldn't ever work out long-term and long-term was how I needed to live my life. From now on. Get my head out of the clouds and forget all those useless fairy tales.

Although what he'd said last night had hurt, he'd just been honest. And honesty was what I needed so I didn't get lost in this fantasy world and want to stay here. I didn't belong. I would *never* belong.

I eventually made my way downstairs, covering a yawn as I reached the breakfast spread in the kitchen, similar to what had been laid out yesterday.

"Morning." I took a place beside Cece at the table.

"Hey." She swallowed a sip of juice. "I heard some shit about you last night."

I frowned. "Heard what shit about me?"

"Tish Martindale went off on Holden at the roulette table, claims he was using you to get to her. Said you were just some white trash hick here to get your hooks into a rich man."

"Cece, *Jesus*," Nanette scolded when she walked into the room, dressed in a black silk robe.

"I'm just telling her what happened." Cece shoved a pastry into her mouth. "Tish slapped Holden across the face and everything."

"She's delightful," I muttered and poured myself a cup of coffee.

"She's a fucking pill. Always has been. She outed me to my parents after she saw me fingering Jessica Moore at junior prom," Nanette said.

"What a bitch!" I said.

"Total bitch," Nanette agreed. "My parents were fine with it. But you know, would've been nice to tell them on my own. She also posted pictures of me making out with Sarah Shaw to her Facebook page with the hashtag #grossdyke. It was trending."

"Oh, my God. She needs a beatdown," I decided.

"Your accent comes out when you get mad. It's adorable," Nanette told me and I laughed.

"It's always out. What a total cunt. You should shove her into the wedding cake tomorrow," I said.

"That's not a bad idea."

I swore I could hear the wheels turning in Nanette's brain.

"Hey, ladies." Elle skipped into the room, bright-eyed and bushy tailed.

"Hey, Elle. Didn't figure you for a screamer." Nanette took a coy sip of coffee.

I stifled a laugh, best I could, and Elle's face went red. "I'm not always a screamer," she said in a small voice.

I mouthed *She's always a screamer* to Nanette.

"He's a maniac. And his dick is humongous." Elle used her hands to show us.

"Wow," Cece breathed, staring at the eight-inch space Elle had created.

"Please don't let you all be talking about my brother's dick." Sloane walked into the room with her fingers in her ears.

"Just Elle is." I smirked and Elle flipped me the bird.

"Am I the only one in this house not getting laid?" Sloane asked. Nanette, Elle and I said nothing.

Cece raised her hand. "I'm not getting laid."

"I am. Reed just left," Ava said, walking into the room in a silk nightie as the front door closed behind what I assumed was her fiancé.

"Nice. Right up until the wedding night." Sloane held out her hand for a high-five and Ava smacked it loudly.

"I'm not going to go without. Well, I have to tonight. But then we're like legal and all that." Ava got a cup for coffee.

"Do you think it'll get boring once you're married?" Cece asked.

"I hope not." Ava scrunched her nose.

"I think it depends on the man, not the circumstances," Elle said. "With Slater—"

Sloane held up a hand. "Nope. No talking about sex with my brother. Not on my watch." Sloane poured Baileys into her coffee cup. I held out mine and she dropped a large dollop in.

Elle pouted and crossed her arms. "Not fair. Ava can talk about her sex life. And we all heard Marley's sex life yesterday."

"And in the broom closet last night," Nanette added.

"It was a coat room," I mumbled, taking a healthy sip of joe.

"Geez. No wonder Tish got pissed. Her and Holden were supposed to get married this year," Cece informed us.

"How, when they were never even engaged?" Sloane queried.

"We all know it's going to happen. They're perfect for each other," Cece replied, her tone matter-of-fact.

I didn't know Holden Pierce or Tish Martindale well, but I could state without a shadow of a doubt that they were not 'perfect for each other'. I kept this to myself.

"Well, seems not, since he's with Marley," Ava said in support, giving me a wide smile.

"Uh, we're not really together. Just um, kind of a fling. It's flung. Like cow dung," I said into my coffee cup.

Sloane snorted a laugh into her drink.

The rest of the girls stared at me, waiting for me to go on.

"How big did you say Slater's dick was again, Elle?" I deflected.

We talked about penis size for the remainder of breakfast, though Sloane insisted that Elle employ a pseudonym for her brother, and we settled on — wait for it — Peter. Not surprising — we were all a little hungover and not very creative.

After that, we went to our rooms to get ready for the spa day, which included us, Mrs. Whitaker and Mrs. Burcar, Ava's mom, who insisted we call her Stephanie. I had gotten a third credit card just for today and handed it over to the desk girl when we checked in.

"Oh, today has already been taken care of," she informed me.

I glared at Sloane. "Not cool," I said through gritted teeth.

She held up her hands "Hey, this one's not me."

I turned back to the girl behind the counter. "Who paid for it?"

"Um…" She glanced at the book in front of her. "Mr. Holden Pierce."

I blinked at her. "He paid for my manicure and pedicure?"

"And your massage, facial and any other service you might require," she informed us all, her tone gleeful.

"Well, um, that's super nice." Elle stepped up behind me.

"I can split yours," I offered, knowing she was in the same boat I was, new credit line and all.

"Oh, Mr. Pierce paid for everyone in the party," the girl said and we all stared at her.

"Oh, that Holden. Such a sweet boy. Tish is one lucky girl," Mrs. Whitaker gushed as she headed for a massage.

"Heh," I managed in response.

"Damn. Holden's got game." Nanette threw me a glance. "Guess things aren't cow dung after all."

Sloane watched my face when I stood for a moment, confused. "You should thank him."

"How?"

She dug into my bag and extracted my cell. She held hers up and programmed his number into my phone. "Ava made me put everyone in the wedding party into my phone in case one of the guys is a no-show moron tomorrow. You're welcome." Sloane dropped my phone back into my bag and headed off for a manicure.

Cece and I were side by side for pedicures and I half-listened to her telling me about some guy named Jamie she'd started dating back in New York, how she was pretty sure he'd fallen madly in love with her. It hadn't stopped her from trying to bed Mitch all weekend, but I decided not to mention that out loud. I did think it, though.

It took a while, but while the girl was painting my toes a pale pink—the sole color Ava allowed, though Nanette got a pass to get glittery black, I texted Holden.

This is Marley. Thank you for the spa services. For all of us. Really nice of you.

The response bubbles appeared almost at once. I would have been flattered, but Holden's attachment to his phone was greater than his to me.

You're welcome.

A minute or so passed before he wrote again.

You having fun?

I'm stuck next to Cece. She hasn't come up for air once. She just keeps talking. I now know what she wants to name her future children.

I added a gun emoji and he typed back.

lol

Holden, I heard what happened last night.

What happened last night?

With you and Tish.

Nothing happened with me and Tish.

She didn't scream at you like a crazy person, call me a white trash hick then slap you across the face?

Oh that. yeah. She did.

You all right?

You think she could really inflict any damage? I'm insulted.

I meant more your brain than your brawn, tough guy.

I'm fine. My dad bitched me out after but that's nothing new.

About what?

My purpose in life.

Tell him you want to become a burlesque dancer. Anything you say after that will cushion the blow.

Lol. You give great advice. And great head. The perfect woman.

I didn't respond to that. I was far from the perfect woman—he had said as much himself last night. And the night before. And the night before that. Somewhere along the way I had missed the pattern where Holden all but implied through his words and actions that I would never be good enough for him. And when I say I *missed* it, I mean I ignored it, saw those russet-colored eyes and that tortured soul and jumped on his dick.

I existed as an embarrassment to all of womankind.

After the pedicure was finished, and my manicure, wax and facial complete, I sat waiting for my massage when my phone dinged in my bag. A message from Holden?

When are you done there?

No idea. I'm guessing less than an hour because I'm on my last treatment.

Which is?

The massage.

Nice.

Massages creep me out, to be honest. I'm only doing this because Ava insisted on it.

Why do they creep you out?

I guess I feel weird about a stranger's hands all over me.

You didn't feel weird about it Wednesday night.

I really hope this isn't that kind of massage.

Lol. That makes two of us. What's up after the massage?

Back to the house to get ready for the rehearsal.

The rehearsal is at 6. It's not even noon.

Well, then I guess I'll have plenty of time ☺

Ditch the massage and come out with me.

I chewed my bottom lip. This felt like he was asking me on a date. Was he asking me on a date?

I'll take you on a date, he added, seeming to read my thoughts.

I glanced around the empty waiting area with its fountain in the corner. I was in a standard-issue bathrobe, but my clothes were tucked in the locker room just a few feet away.

If I can make a clean getaway, I'm in.

I darted for the locker room and peered around corners. The only people in there were strangers to me, so I hustled back into my shorts and tee, shoved everything else in my bag and scurried to the front doors.

"Hey, can you let the girls I came in with, Ava's wedding party, know that I didn't feel well and had to skip out?" I asked the woman at the desk.

"Sure. What's your name?"

"Marley."

"Oh, yeah, Holden's girl."

"Oh, uh, no—I'm not uh, his girl," I stammered.

"Oh." Desk girl frowned. "Sorry. When he came in, he said he was paying for all *your* services today then he added everyone else. Figured you were his girl."

"Uh, no," I repeated, just as the doors pushed open and Holden strolled through them, Ray-Bans on his face and day-old stubble on his chin.

"Hey, you coming?" he asked.

The desk clerk beamed at me and I hurried after Holden, shoving him out of the door and following him through it.

"You almost blew my cover!" I told him when we were on the sidewalk.

He chuckled. "Just tell them you're going out with me."

"I can't ditch out on girl time to hang with a dude. That's breaking our chick code."

"But you are."

"Yeah, but I don't want them to know that. Now hurry." I pushed him and he laughed, walking to the town car.

He opened my door for me and climbed in after me, giving the driver an address to a lobster place on the beach.

"You like seafood, right?" he asked.

"I grew up in a town called Angler's Haven. Of course I like seafood."

He slipped his sunglasses off, tucking them into the collar of his T-shirt. "You look good. Pretty," he said, sounding shy all of a sudden.

I wiggled my fingers at him. "Pretty in pink. On my toes, too." I lifted a foot to show him.

"Nice. What else?"

"I got a facial." I patted my cheeks.

"No comment."

"Ha ha," I deadpanned. "And a wax."

"Wax, huh? What kind of wax?"

I glanced up at the driver. "Do you want to see what kind of wax?" I whispered.

"I really, really fucking do." He laid his hand on my thigh.

"Start lower," I murmured and he moved his hand down to my ankle.

"So, your legs." He ran his fingertips over the skin of my calf and my knees.

"Yes."

He moved even farther up. "Your whole leg." He padded his fingers against my thigh.

"Yes." My breath hitched.

He took my face in his hands. "Anything here?"

"Maybe." I tipped my head to the side and he gave me the softest of kisses.

"Arms?" he asked, taking his finger on a leisure path across my skin from shoulder to wrist.

"Underarms. But I'm ticklish." Which didn't stop him from nipping the skin behind my arm.

He walked his fingers down to the button of my shorts, then snapped them open. He skimmed his hand over my panties then under them, oh so slowly. His mouth was just centimeters away from mine, and I panted as he slinked a finger along my slit.

"They did a good job," he murmured against my mouth.

"Yes, they did." I swallowed hard.

He moved his finger in a lackadaisical, circular motion and I got wetter as his movements increased. The car stopped and the driver pointed out of the window.

"We're here, sir."

"Go around the block a few times." Holden didn't take his eyes off me.

The man complied.

"Everyone always do what you tell them?" I gasped.

"I don't know. You going to come for me when I tell you to?" he asked in a husky voice, gliding a gentle finger inside me.

"Yes." I drove my fingers into his hair and pulled his mouth to mine. He didn't hurry his movements, swirling our tongues together, and my body drew tighter with each pass of his hand.

"Don't come yet, sweetheart. I want this to last," he ordered.

I swallowed and nodded and he kissed me again, pressing his finger even harder against my core, making me writhe against the seat. He kept at that delicious, perfect spherical movement, hard at times, then lighter. Tight, slow loops, and wide, hard orbits. Occasionally, he would slip a delicate finger inside my cunt, then pull it out and rub my clit again and again, until I thought I was going to burst. My body heated and I squirmed in my seat.

"Stay still, baby. You want to come, don't you?"

I nodded, my breath coming in spurts.

"Maybe we should go eat, then I'll let you come," he suggested and smiled against my skin.

I pinched his arm in response.

"Okay, I'll let you go soon. But not yet." He bit my nipples through my shirt then pushed it up and exposed my stomach, licking along my abdomen.

I groaned and tensed, wanting so much and so hard to let go.

"You close?" He wasn't stopping, still moving his fingers in their gorgeous, revolving cycles.

"Yes," I gasped.

"You want to come, sweetheart?"

"Yes," I hissed.

"You ready to let go all over my hand?"

I nodded, clamping my eyes shut and holding off my climax.

"Who does this pussy belong to, Marley?"

"You. You. It's you, Holden. It's your pussy. All yours," I said through gritted teeth.

"Then fucking come for me," he ordered and in that instant I was there. I came so hard I clawed his shirt, driving my hips up hard against his hand, rocking the car with my motions. God, it felt incredible. I didn't know it could feel like this. I didn't know that a man giving me orders would make me go off like this. I'd never had it, and now I didn't know if I could live without it.

After the car stopped a second time and I collected myself, Holden climbed out and ushered me into the Gunwale, an old house renovated into a restaurant. The majority of seats were upstairs, on a long balcony that had been built out almost right to the ocean.

We waited a little while for a table and he told me about Tish's slap, which had been spurred on by Mitch finding out about our tryst in the closet and letting the cat out of the bag.

"Why would he do that?"

Holden gave me a raised-single-eyebrow stare, having to lift his sunglasses to do so.

"I still don't get it."

He put his hand above my head on the beam I stood against and leaned close to me. "Sweetheart, Mitch wants inside your cunt so bad he's willing do whatever it takes. And that means fucking with me."

"I barely know him."

"Yeah, well, that didn't stop *me* from wanting you, did it?" he said and stood straight, crossing his arms over his chest. He wore a navy polo shirt and blue plaid shorts, and the fabric on the short sleeves of his shirt was straining over the muscles on his arms. My gaze lingered on them for a moment and I think I started drooling.

"But, I mean, you didn't leapfrog over someone else to do it, and, you know, try to make their life miserable," I said. "Does he know about you and Tish?"

"There is no me and Tish."

"I mean, does he know about Tish wanting there to be a you and Tish?"

"Everyone knows about that. It's not a secret. It's also not a secret that I don't give a shit about her."

"Why doesn't she get the hint?"

"Because of all the zeroes in my bank account, sweetheart."

I frowned. "How does she even know about all the zeroes in your bank account?"

"That's not a secret, either."

The hostess came to bring us to our table and we followed her upstairs and out to the veranda, to sit at a small wooden table and pick up our menus.

"Everything looks amazing." I glanced at the food on the tables around us.

"Everything is. Spencer used to love this place," Holden said and I think the admission jarred him. He sat still a moment after he'd said it and I clutched his hand in mine.

He squeezed back, just for a moment, then let me go. I peered over the menu then set it down. "What would Spencer get?"

"Lobster roll. Always. And crab cakes," Holden replied with a sad smile.

"I'll get that," I told him as the waitress came up. We both ordered a local craft beer on her recommendation and she brought us waters and clam chowder to start.

"We don't have places like this in Angler's Haven." I took a spoonful of soup.

"No?"

"No. The local specialty is fried sea bass. It tastes like sewage and grease fire."

"That's tasty."

"Everything at home is so—small. I mean, things here are quaint, right? Cozy. Charming. Everything at home is dingy and worn-down."

"Maybe it looks that way because you've always lived there."

"No, it looks that way because it is. Because people are poor and they don't give a shit about a working lawn mower when they need food on the table."

His eyes found mine. "Did you worry about food on the table?"

"Constantly. One summer, I ate bologna and bread for every single meal, every single day. Even breakfast."

He stared at me.

"My stepdad would come home from the racetrack and I could always tell if it had been a good day or a bad day by what was in the grocery bag he was carrying. Bad day meant a loaf of almost moldy bread and off-brand peanut butter. Good day was meatloaf and mashed potatoes."

"That how you know how to play cards? Because your dad gambled?"

"My stepdad. And, yes, he taught me how to play cards. My real dad died in a motorcycle accident when I was six."

"Shit, Marley. I'm sorry."

"It's fine." I waved a dismissive hand. "Barely knew the guy. From what my mom told me and what Ross remembers, he wasn't that different from my stepdad, but he drank his paychecks instead of betting on horses."

"That why you took your job? To help kids like you were?" he probed.

"In part." I swallowed a gulp of beer. "I wanted to work for the Department of Agriculture. I got offered a job right after graduation. But I chickened out. It required a lot of travel and was based in DC. I couldn't do it."

"Why not?"

"Because I'd never been more than two hours from home prior to becoming eighteen, and even then I only traveled with Sloane, Ava and Elle. And my parents—they're still working and still struggling. Which means I have to help them out, too."

He frowned. "Why does it mean that?"

"Because they're my parents."

"They didn't take care of you when you were a kid. Fuck 'em."

"That's easier said than done, isn't it?" I raised an eyebrow at him and his jaw flexed. He understood my intonation—it was no easier for him to tell his parents and their expectations of him to fuck off than it was for me, or most anyone.

That relationship was always a complicated one, in poor families and in rich ones. There were so many strings tied to the past, winding their way around in twists and turns, stretching out into the future, so that unraveling it felt like a daunting and impossible task. So I did what everyone else did. I kept moving forward and making decisions based on those strings — and getting more tangled in the process.

"And if I did leave, it would all fall on Ross," I continued. "As it is, we're more or less the only reason they have any food at all. I put them on the list at the food bank, but they won't show up to get their boxes. Which means Ross or I have to go get it and haul it over to their house and put it all away. They're too proud to take a hand-out."

"Even if it's for their kid, right?"

I shrugged. "Yeah, I guess."

"Marley, you were the president of the Agriculture Club."

"Agronomy."

"Whatever. You were the head soil judge. If you want to work with farms or fucking dirt or whatever it is, you should do it."

"I'm not that brave, Holden. I'm not good at jumping off into the unknown."

"Fuck yeah, you are. You're here with me, aren't you?"

"Yeah, well, if the Department of Agriculture could guarantee daily multiple orgasms, I might consider it," I said, just when the waitress walked up.

My face burned red while she set down our plates. "I would, too, honey. Two more beers?" she asked, taking our empties.

"Yeah, thanks." Holden tried and failed to hold back a grin.

"Very funny," I said and he barked out a loud laugh.

Once he'd stopped cracking up at my expense and taken a long look at me, his eyes grew serious. "Don't not do something because you think you'll regret it.

Because you'll just end up regretting that you never took your shot."

I thought over his words as I took a bite of lobster roll. "Wow, this is amazing," I said, my mouth full.

"Spencer always talked with his mouth full, too."

I swallowed. "You act like you're so cool, a total bad-ass, unaffected by anything. But you didn't think your brother was just a pest. You loved him. You remember the things he loved. And that's the best way to live your life for him—to just remember him, Holden. Not try to be him."

"So, all I'm getting from this conversation is that we're both really fucked up," he said after a moment's pause.

I laughed out loud. "Yeah, but that's pretty typical. I don't think I would trust someone who isn't really fucked up. They'd be like a cyborg."

"An alien."

"Yeah, like invasion of the pod people or whatever." I mimicked a weird alien walk from my seat and he laughed and shook his head.

"You're fucking adorable, Marley."

"I have my moments."

We kept the rest of our meal to more boring topics such as the weather, the wedding tomorrow, how I'd never learned to swim…

"I just can't believe that. I mean, you're twenty-six," Holden said. He'd insisted on paying the bill and we were heading out of the restaurant.

"Hey. I'm still twenty-five for two more days. Watch it." I nudged him as we walked.

He grabbed my hand and we walked a bit longer, passing by the car.

"You want to go back to the houses?" I asked, stopping and tightening the connection on our hands.

He thought for a moment. "No. I want to go shopping."

"Okay. For what? Tacky souvenirs like plastic snow globes and refrigerator magnets?" I teased. He didn't let my hand go. And I loved it. I'd never thought hands were an erogenous zone. It hadn't been a favorite of mine. But with my small hand clasped in his larger one, it felt sexy. It felt brave. It felt like all the things I always thought I'd failed to be. It was as if the things I lacked pulsed out of Holden, emptying out through his skin and into my body, giving me the confidence to believe I could be something more.

"Nope, a bathing suit." He ducked into a shop that had clothes hanging in the window. Most were T-shirts with slogans such as *Edgartown – a drinking town with a fishing problem!* screenprinted on them in bright, outdated colors, or *Vineyard Life*, bearing an embroidered silhouette of a woman lounging on the beach with a drink in her hand.

"You don't have a bathing suit?" I asked as we meandered around the racks of clothes.

"Not with me."

"Okay, what kind do you like?" I held up a bright green Speedo. "Too much?"

"Not enough." He flipped through the rack in front of him.

I wandered around and fingered a cute eyelet cover-up in a pretty lilac color, and a pair of rubber flip-flops that would cost two bucks at home but cost twenty-five here. I picked up a wooden six-pack holder that had a vintage feel and *Martha's Vineyard* stamped across the side in a funky font. I flipped it over and the price tag on the bottom said fifty dollars.

"Jesus," I muttered and Holden came up behind me.

"What?" he asked.

"It's fifty bucks. I thought about picking it up for Ross, but I'm not spending that." I glanced around to make sure no one was listening to me spell out how fucking poor and cheap I was.

"I'll get it." Holden reached past me and plucked it from the shelf.

"No, don't do that. It's not a big deal," I blurted out.

"Marley, I closed the deal on three properties when we got here on Wednesday. I'm netting about a quarter of a billion dollars for them. I think I can buy your brother a beer holder."

I stared at him, not understanding what he'd said. "What do you mean three properties? Like houses?"

"No. Mixed retail spaces. In Manhattan and Queens." He turned toward the cashier behind us.

"You buy buildings in New York? Is that what you do for your dad?" I asked, hurrying after him. He had never said in so many words what his job entailed, only that he didn't like it. He'd started sharing here and I didn't want to miss it.

"No. I do legal investigation for my dad. I buy and sell real estate for myself." He set a handful of items on the counter. "You want a water?" He reached past me and pulled two bottles out of the fridge.

"I don't understand," I told him, my eyes focused on his profile.

He faced me. "I work for my dad doing investigative work for his cases. Someone claims a hit and run, or divorce filing, whatever, I research it. If it's on the up and up, we take the case and we use the evidence in our favor. The real estate stuff is a hobby."

"*A hobby?*" I blinked at him. "You just made a quarter of a million dollars on a *hobby*?"

"*Billion*, Marley. Quarter of a billion. You never seem to get that one right."

My stomach twisted in knots. If I'd thought I had a chance with this guy, I'd been dead wrong. I was not like him. I knew that. I didn't come from his world. I knew that, too. But to have it laid out like that, to feel the truth staring at me in the face… It jarred me. I felt stupid and small and simple.

"Marley." Holden's voice plucked me back from my reverie. "You all right?"

I swallowed. "Yeah, yeah. I'm fine," I lied. I wasn't fine. I wasn't going to be fine. I needed to go back to the house, stay in my room and just come out for the required events. I was *way* out of my element here.

Sloane had money — I knew that. Ava's family had always been pretty well off, sure. But Holden represented something else entirely. I owed five hundred and eighty dollars in already late rent and I had no idea how to get it by Wednesday to pay our shifty landlord. And in three days' time, Holden had made two hundred and fifty billion dollars without even having to be in town. With what Holden had just made, he could pay my rent for me four hundred and thirty-one thousand times over. My rent was precisely point zero zero zero zero zero two percent of what he had just made. I wasn't even good at math but I knew those ratios didn't favor me.

Fuck. I had to forget about this or I would lose it. And I didn't want to lose it. I had two and a half more days here so I had to keep it together. Afterward, I could go home to my shabby two-bedroom dump with Elle on Sunday evening and we could freak out about it there.

I took a deep breath, forcing myself to settle a bit. "What's all this?" I asked, glancing at the pile the clerk was bagging up.

"We're going swimming."

"Oh, we are?" I stared up at him and into those deep brown eyes with the thick lashes — and the happy-go-lucky air in them right now. "I can't swim," I reminded him.

"I know that, sweetheart." He wound an arm around my waist. "I'm going to teach you."

He took the bags of stuff he had bought, handed me one and led me out of the door.

"Where are we going swimming?" I asked, when we headed down the boardwalk.

"Beach." He pointed to the sign.

"The public beach? Isn't that, I don't know, crowded?" I wanted to say, *"Beneath a rich-ass motherfucker like you,"* but I didn't.

"Probably." He shrugged, shifting the bag to his other hand and intertwining our fingers together again. "But there's plenty of ocean to go around."

We got to the beach and he dug through the bag, drawing out a few items and holding them out toward me. "This is for you. Go change. I'll meet you by the showers." He took the other bag from my hand and headed off.

I glanced down at what was in my hand. It was the eyelet cover-up I had looked at — and the smallest bikini I'd ever seen in my life.

I went to the changing rooms and did what he'd told me to, winding my hair into a knot with a tie from my purse and trying and failing to make the fabric on the orange dental floss bathing suit cover all my parts. It *barely* did. Holden had done that on purpose. I was grateful he'd at least bought the cover-up, too. I was going to be neck-high in the water before I took this thing off. I put on some lip balm and the sunscreen he had also bought, tossed it all back into the plastic bag and headed out to meet him.

He stood near the men's room, wearing a pair of long board shorts with sharks on them. He looked good as sin standing there and, as I walked over to him, my steps faltered.

Yeah, he was out of my league. On so many levels. Even his calves were muscular and sturdy. The man's whole physique screamed power and money. I couldn't help but notice the lingering stares he got from the boys, girls, men and women alike who passed by him.

I had to remind myself we were only temporary — and that we both knew that. So I might as well ignore the wealth dripping off him and just have fun. I had already managed to put aside the ratios that spelled out in no uncertain terms how disastrous this would be in the real world, so I just had to keep doing that. I mean, wasn't this what I'd wanted? What I'd told Sloane that night at the bar — leave the mundane behind, to stop planning my next move? To live on impulse, if just for a few days? And, fuck it, I had struggled to do that up until now. Right now, I was living in the moment. From here on out, I was just going to *be*.

"You forgot to get me a bathing suit," I said, reaching him.

"I thought I handed it to you." He searched through the bag he was holding.

"Oh, you did. But there's no bathing suit to this bathing suit. It's just a ball of fluorescent twine that someone *pretended* was a bathing suit."

He gave a slow grin, trying to peer over the top of my cover-up.

"Oh, no. No, sir. No one is seeing this little number until I'm in the water. And even then, it'll only be for the fish." I set my mouth on his for the briefest of touches. "Thank you for the gifts, honey."

He stared at me a moment. "You're welcome, sweetheart," he almost whispered.

Everything around us fell away and I kept my eyes on him. "But now I know you're not an asshole. So the jig is up, dude. And, you haven't had your phone out for hours. So, you don't need that thing, either."

His mouth made a slow upward curve. "Come on," he said, taking my hand and leading me toward the beach.

We managed to find a small space halfway toward the water. He laid out a large, new blanket and a couple of towels he'd bought. Then he handed me a second bottle of sunscreen and pointed to his back.

"I expect a tip after this." I squeezed lotion into my palm and rubbed it across his well-built shoulders.

"You'll get the tip, baby. Then all of it."

I laughed, loving how he'd grown lighter than I had ever seen him. I'd thought he had shed some of the stress and anger he'd carried with him before, but seeing him like this now, the smell of the ocean, the voices of children laughing, the feel of the heat on our bodies—I could see that *this* made Holden Pierce happy.

I don't know why. In the span of the three days I'd known him, he had made more money than I could even dream of. But with us seated on a gingham-printed blanket and dressed in a couple of cheap bathing suits from a souvenir tourist trap, he was blissful. Positive. A new man.

The workaholic I had first met had vanished. He didn't bunch up his shoulders or get wrinkles of tension near his eyes. He seemed light as air, more attractive than I had ever seen him. And he'd practically been a Greek fucking God before.

I dropped a gentle kiss on his shoulder blade and he twisted to peer at me. "All done," I said, my voice cracking a bit. I wanted him happy like this all the time. I wanted him to discover this contented, peaceful enjoyment and bottle it and unleash it whenever he found himself without. But the saddest part is that I didn't even know if he realized it was missing.

"You ready?" he asked, standing and yanking me to my feet.

"No."

"You'll be fine. I promise I won't let anything happen to you." His voice was now serious. I knew he was thinking about his brother again. And maybe that was why he was doing this — teaching me how to swim. Maybe he didn't want another family to live through the tragedy he had. The Good Samaritan, a superhero whose special power was teaching those who didn't know how to swim while leaping buildings in a single bound.

"I know that. I'm nervous about taking this romper off."

He threw his head back and laughed. "Come on, chickenshit. Let's go."

I took a deep breath, steeled my nerves against the flutters in my stomach for so many reasons and did what he told me to. I left the cover-up in a pile by the water and walked forward.

He was knee-deep in the waves when I reached him. His gaze made a lazy path from my feet all the way up to the top of my head and back down to my eyes. "Holy shit."

"I know. It's ridiculous," I said, yanking at the bottom of the string bikini top, trying to cover more of myself.

"You look fucking incredible."

"I think you mean 'nearly naked'?" I corrected him.

He wound his hand around my middle, resting his hand just above the dimples on my ass, which were very visible in this low-riding, high-cut bathing suit bottom. "No, I mean incredible. You're a gorgeous girl, Marley. But in this — fuck, I feel lucky you're here with me."

"You're being sweet again, Holden Pierce," I said, resting my hand on the top of his shoulder and staring up at him.

"Sorry." He scooped me up in his arms and at once dipped both of us right down into the water.

I laughed as he brought us back up, dripping wet. "Asshole," I muttered, wiping water out of my eyes.

"All right. Let's move farther out." He walked backward, slowly, the water rising up my frame. When it was halfway up my chest, he checked in. "You good?"

I nodded. I had been in the water before, of course, but never when it was over my head. We didn't have a pool at our high school, and the lake was for fishing, not for swimming. And my trips with the girls had been spent drinking in bars and tanning on the sand.

But Holden took his time. He moved us backwards in slow steps, deeper and deeper, and when the water climbed up to my chin, he had me lie on my stomach and he cradled his arms under me.

"Kick your feet," he said, backing up a little bit. The water rose only chest high on him because he was taller. I did what he said. "Kick them in alternating rhythm."

"Who taught you to swim?" I asked. He kept moving me in the water, his hold tight on me.

"My nanny. Consuela. Huge tits."

I shot him a dirty glare.

"Whatever. I was a kid. She gave me my first hard-on."

"How old were you?" I asked.

"When I got my first hard-on?"

"When you learned to swim, smart-ass."

"Five or six."

"Really?"

"Yeah, well, we had a pool. And a house on an island. Made sense to learn early. Spencer was even younger." He paused.

"Did he like swimming?" I asked, keeping my voice quiet.

He shrugged. "No idea. I did. Swam in high school."

"But Spencer didn't?"

He shook his head. "No. He played lacrosse."

"Would he have liked me?" I asked during a moment of shrieking vulnerability.

"Oh, he would've fucking loved you. Spent this whole weekend trying to get his dick in you. And you would've turned him down every time."

"Why?"

"Because he wasn't me."

"Arrogant jerk." I narrowed my eyes at him but he just grinned wide.

I followed Holden's directions to a T and kept kicking. Eventually, he let go of my body and just held my hands. Then just my fingertips. And voilà! I was swimming!

"You're doing it!" he said.

"I am," I sputtered. Water got in my mouth and I only just kept my head up but I was doing it! I could freaking swim! Then a wave came and pulled me under, but Holden brought me right back up.

I coughed out water. "I gotta work on holding my breath." I shook water from my face.

"Yeah. Pretend you're giving me a blow job. Don't breathe through your nose."

"I'm supposed to breathe through my nose when I give a blow job. I'm guessing you haven't given very many. That's a basic tenet of giving good head."

"Yeah, well, no, I haven't given any at all so I'll take your word for it." He was still holding onto me and I curled around his torso like a koala on a tree. "You want to try again?"

"I kind of like where I am right now," I admitted, glancing up at him from under my wet lashes.

He dipped his mouth down to mine and kissed me deeply. Some kids nearby on a raft made mwah-mwah noises at us, but I didn't care. I was wrapped up in Holden and he was wrapped up in me. When we parted, his eyes were clear. He looked open and refreshed, relaxed. I wanted this for him, for always.

In our short period of time together, I wanted to give Holden something he couldn't get with all the money he had — *solace*. I knew now the tumult and attitude he copped was from the riotous ideas and feelings running through him. I wanted to be his friend. I wanted to have wild, crazy sex with him in semi-public places. Fuck me, I even wanted to figure out a *life* with him. I wanted it to be good—for both of us. That flicker of a spark that had been building had consumed both of us and we were burning up inside and out for each other, just with simple smiles and touches.

We took a couple more passes at my attempts to swim and I did better each time. He even moved away from me for a bit, giving me some confidence to go farther.

Over an hour went by before we went back to our blanket, collapsing on the soft fabric, dripping wet. We dried off with towels and applied more sunscreen, resting and letting the sun dry all our skin. My eyes closed and I didn't even realize I had drifted off until I felt a shadow over me and fingertips along my skin.

"Hey," Holden's voice said above me, soft and gentle.

I blinked my eyes open. "Hey," I replied, my voice thick with sleep.

"You are really beautiful, you know that?" he asked, his voice low.

I swallowed. "You are, too, Holden."

"Not like you are, Marley. You're beautiful inside and out." He traced his fingers along my hairline, down my jaw and neck.

"You have beauty inside you, too, Holden. You just keep it hidden away. Why?"

He regarded me a long moment. "I don't always."

I knew the words were hard for him to say. He was revealing something about himself and, whenever he did, it didn't come easily.

"I don't want you to ever hide parts of who you are. You underestimate yourself. You don't hate this island, and you don't not give a fuck about Ava and Reed. You're protecting yourself." I sat up, my eyes on his. "But you don't have to."

"This isn't the life I want, Marley. I don't want the weekend trips and the nine to five. I don't want to end up like my fucking parents. I want something — more."

"You have something more. You're already worth more than ten of them put together. I don't know why you can't see that."

He laid a hand on the side of my face. "I don't know how you *can* see that, Marley."

"Because you're letting me," I whispered.

He stared at me a beat, then out at the ocean. "It's almost four."

"We have to go, don't we?" I asked as he dropped his hand from my cheek.

"Yeah, we have to go." His words felt black and heavy.

We packed up all we had — he watched my ass as I shimmied back into the eyelet cover-up — and that heaviness grew denser between us. We made our way back down the boardwalk to the waiting car and, by the time we eased into the seats, it was nearly suffocating.

"Today was nice," I told him once the car headed back toward Reed's aunt's, sliding my hand into his, hoping for that connection again. Looking for him to pass over to me the strength and hopefulness I yearned for.

"Yeah," he said, but with each lapsing block, his shoulders hunched over more, the pressure winding him tighter like a coil.

"Hey." I took his face in my hand.

"What's up?" Even his voice was tense.

"You know, I owe you a blow job."

He blinked and gave me a crooked grin. "Yeah?"

"Well, yeah. I mean, I told you all about my stellar technique, holding my breath and all. I should at least show you what I was talking about. I mean, for the sake of education," I said, untying his board shorts.

"Well, I had no idea you wanted me to play teacher, little girl."

I got on my knees in the seat and he smacked my ass hard.

I moaned and closed my eyes, enjoying the sensation of a little pain overlaid by wanting.

"Well, I want you to know what a good student I can be, Mr. Pierce." I took his already hard dick in my mouth all the way, keeping my eyes on him as best I could.

"Fuck, Marley," he groaned, dropping his head to the back of the seat and closing his eyes.

I worked him over with my hand and mouth, cupping his balls and giving languorous licks along the bottom of his long shaft. He jerked in my hand and I knew he wouldn't last, not after all the touching we had done all day, not after how close we had become.

I took him as deep as he would go, three, four, five times, then he grunted, spurting for what seemed like forever, groaning and pulsing on and on until he'd drained himself completely.

"Jesus Christ. I don't think I'll ever get sick of that mouth," he said, his eyes still closed, his head still back.

"We're here." I kept my eyes forward and forced my emotions down. I told myself to keep living in the moment, because if I thought about not wanting this to end, I would start to panic. "I'll see you soon, right?"

He picked up his head. "Yeah, rehearsal." He sounded as if he had almost forgotten.

"Yep. Wear your Sunday best, hot stuff. Try to impress me." I poked him in the ribs when he shifted over to climb out.

"Will do, sweetheart." He shot me one last smile, got out and headed into the house.

I only let one tear fall, wiping it away and taking a deep breath. I could do this. I knew I could. I had to, because I didn't want to let Holden Pierce go, and I wasn't sure how I could keep him, either.

Chapter Six

This time around, I didn't argue with Sloane about wearing one of her couture dresses. I wanted to look good and seem like I belonged. I knew it would take more than a dress, but I could pretend. At least for tonight.

While she showered, I skimmed through my choices, wanting something appealing and sexy — but not *too* sexy. There would be grandmothers present at the rehearsal and dinner afterward, so I didn't want to embarrass Ava.

I ended up choosing a hot pink structured lace dress because the sun had given me a healthy, dewy glow the last few days and it contrasted so well with my tan skin. It flared a bit at the waist and fell just above my knee, showcasing my long legs. My nude pumps matched fine with it, but Sloane insisted the champagne-colored heels I had brought for my bridesmaid's dress for tomorrow were better.

I ignored the price tag on the borrowed dress.

Sloane did my hair, not harping on about me having disappeared from the spa day because I'd been 'sick,' but not in bed at Reed's parents' house when they'd all gotten home, and only having arrived thirty minutes ago in a bikini smeared with sand.

But when Elle showed up in the room later, she didn't go so easy on me.

"Where the hell were you?" she demanded, slamming Sloane's door and stomping into the room to stare at me.

"Wow, I love that dress. Is it new?" I asked. I wasn't trying to squirm out of the inquisition she had geared up for here—I did love the dress and hadn't seen her wear it before.

"Um, yes. It's Nanette's. She let me borrow it." Elle smoothed down the fitted skirt of the bodycon bandage dress. I guessed both she and Sloane were going to be the hussified bridesmaids that evening.

"You look hot, Elle," Sloane commented, picking back sections of my long wavy brown hair with beaded pins.

"Yeah, I know," she said with a gleeful smile. Then she turned on me again. "Where were you?"

"Learning how to swim."

They both gaped at me.

"Where?" Sloane asked, peering at my face.

"Holden took me to the beach."

"Which beach? We were at the beach here and at Reed's aunt's and you weren't there." Elle put a hand on her hip and stared me down.

"The public beach, in town. We went for lunch then swimming. I swam!" I yelped in excitement, hoping to deter them from their meddlesome attitude with news of having overcome a latent fear. No such luck.

"Holden went to a public beach?" Sloane sounded appalled.

"He did. And we had a lot of fun. He taught me how to swim, then we napped on a blanket. We just got back here less than an hour ago."

"Wow. I mean, good for him," Sloane said.

"That's kind of—I don't know—sweet. *Romantic*," Elle added.

"He did dunk me on purpose a couple times. But we had fun."

"Holden was *fun*?" Sloane said the last word as though it tasted sour.

"Yes. He was a lot of fun. He opened up and we talked and—listen, I realize that this is pretty stupid."

"It's not that stupid." Elle picked at her dress, avoiding my eyes.

"But I like the guy. He's not just a workaholic prick, swear to God." I held my hand up. "He's a little bit, well, soulful."

"Oh, God." Sloane tossed her comb on the counter. "I've heard this line from you many times, babe. Some dude is a misunderstood puppy dog underneath his rough exterior and you're just the woman to bring him to heel."

"I'm not doing that here. I'm not," I denied. "I know this is just temporary. That it's a brief affair. I'm okay with that."

Both girls eyed me.

"Well, I'm as okay with it as I can be. And I'm not going to stop, because, honestly, the sex is incredible."

"Oh, tell me about it," Elle breathed and Sloane shoved her fingers into her ears.

"La la la, can't hear you," she said, rushing out of the room to get dressed.

"Slater is a freaking animal," Elle continued. "We've done it like three times already!"

I didn't tell her that Holden and I were working on double that. "That's awesome," I said with a genuine smile.

"He's so great." She gave a wistful sigh.

Yeah, both the Angler's Haven girls are in deep on the island.

We all chitchatted as we finished getting ready, Elle performing a masterpiece of winged eyeliner on me and Sloane pinning Elle's hair back in the same style she had done mine in. We hurried downstairs with just minutes to spare, to find the town cars waiting in the drive.

"Nanette said this dress is a knock-off. I don't know about that, but there's no way to breathe in it," Elle commented while we headed down the steps.

"Just don't breathe then," Sloane offered and I giggled.

I gazed forward and slowed my pace. Holden leaned against the back door of one of the cars, his phone in his hand.

When his lifted his head, the creases between his eyes eased and he smirked with slow intent. "Hey." He tucked his phone into the pocket of his suit pants without a moment's hesitation. He wore all black, with a long, skinny tie, and had his hair artfully gelled.

"You look so fucking handsome," I said before I could think better of it.

He snaked his hand out and yanked me into him as soon as I got within arm's reach. "Oh, yeah?"

"Yes. You do. You know you do." I laughed, bringing one arm around his shoulders, and he held me close.

"Still nice to hear, sweetheart." He kissed me, just beside my mouth, his lips gentle. "Don't want to mess up your lipstick."

"I have more in my bag," I murmured, closing the gap between us and kissing him deep. He tightened his hand around my back and dug his fingers into my waist. When I at last pulled back, he breathed hard.

"Fuck, you can kiss, baby," he said in a low voice, his lips just a whisper from mine.

"Ahem." Sloane cleared her throat in an obvious fashion behind us.

Holden detached himself from me, wiping errant lip-gloss from his mouth, and opened the car door. Sloane climbed in and I followed, but Elle had already climbed into the car in front of us with Slater.

"Hold up!" Cece hurried down the steps and ducked in through the open door before Holden had a chance. He closed it up and got into the front passenger seat.

"Oh, hi, Holden," Cece cooed when she saw him, flipping her hair back and putting on a pouty, aren't-I-so-fetching face.

"Hey." Holden didn't even bother to turn around. He drew his phone out of his pocket. Ha! He gave her the old brush-off-for-my-tech-friend move I had gotten just a few days ago. But I hadn't today.

"You look great," she gushed. He ignored her. She obviously hadn't seen the kiss we'd just shared, or if she had, I should be punching her lights out, cheeky little minx.

She didn't seem to notice or care about his attitude and just pushed her breasts up higher in her low-cut dress — the third amigo for the sexy-dress crew tonight.

"Where'd you run off to today, Marley?" she asked, still fiddling with her tits.

"I went to the beach."

"Which one? We all went down to the one here at the house and didn't see you."

"The public beach, in town."

She whipped her head to me. "Oh, gross. You mingled with the locals?" She gawped as though I had just said I'd eaten a shit sandwich for dinner.

"I did. They were all covered with green slime and had three eyes. It was awesome." I gave her a sweet smile.

She narrowed her eyes. "Well, I guess you would fit right in there," she said in typical fourth grade fashion.

"Fuck off, Cece. You're just jealous none of the guys on this island will touch your vagina with a ten-foot dick dripping with disease." Sloane gave Cece her best glare.

"You're not getting any, either, Sloane. I'd watch what you say," Cece countered with derision.

Sloane didn't reply and sat back, her face and body relaxed. I scrutinized my friend who I knew so well and pinched her thigh.

"Ouch!" she shouted and glared at me. Yep, behind those eyes lay a secret. And we didn't have secrets between us, which was exactly how I knew.

"You got something to tell me?" I asked.

Sloane shook her head once. "Nope. Not a thing."

"Uh-huh. You forget how well I know you, Sloane Makayla Riley." I pinched her again.

"Stop doing that!" She slapped my hand away. I did it again just for good measure and she laughed.

I just stared at her. She pulled her phone out then nodded at my clutch. I dug my cell out and she shot me a text message.

I fucked Brooks.

I gasped so loud I drew the looks of everyone in the car. I hid the screen of my phone against my chest and plastered on a fake smile.

When???

Last night. And this morning.

Really??? How? Where??? Why the hell didn't you tell me?!?!

Too busy fucking Brooks.

Bitch.

☺

How was it?

On a scale of 1 to 10, 233.

I coughed out a laugh and Cece sneered at me. I tucked my phone away and pinched Sloane again.

"Okay, stop. You're going to leave a mark." She plopped her Samsung back into her minaudière and pinched me back.

"Ow!" I exclaimed.

"Yeah, see? It hurts."

"You two are like toddlers." Cece rolled her eyes at us, fixing her enormous hair.

Sloane and I beamed back at her and Holden chuckled from the front seat.

The car steered to a stop in front of the church and the driver and Holden got out to open our doors.

Cece scrambled out and tried to grab Holden's arm. "Escort me inside?" she asked in a high-pitched voice, pressing her huge fake tits against his arm.

"I already have someone to escort, Cece." His voice dripped with sheer annoyance and he took my hand, helping me out of the car.

She harrumphed and flounced away, her heels scraping on the sidewalk as she went.

"Do you think Ava will be pissed if Cece has a black eye in all the pictures tomorrow?" Sloane asked.

"Whatever. She has makeup. She can cover it up," I offered.

Holden took my hand in his, bonding us together once again, and we headed toward the church. Ava and Reed were standing outside, talking heatedly about something, and Ava had tears in her eyes.

"Hey, Ave. You all right?" Sloane tried as we walked up.

"The wedding is off!" she screeched and ran into the church.

"Fuck." Reed scraped his hands down his face.

"What happened?" Holden asked him.

"No fucking idea. My mom said something about the flowers and Ava lost her shit. Then she got mad at me because I didn't lose my shit. She's wound so fucking tight she's gonna explode," Reed told us.

"It's a lot of stress. And you know Ava. She wants it all to be perfect."

"Yeah, it will be. And if it's not, who gives a fuck? It's just a wedding." Reed shrugged.

"Oh, god. I hope you didn't say that to her," Sloane groaned at him.

He gazed at her blankly. *Yeah, he said that to her.*

"Reed, this is Ava's big day. This is supposed to be the happiest day of her life. And you know she wants it to be for you, too," I said, my tone measured.

He stared at me. "What the fuck does that have to do with the flowers being wrong?"

"I'll talk to her. Just do her a favor? Tell your mom not to mention it again. Or anything else. Gently. One less thing for Ava to worry about." I patted his arm.

He nodded and I turned to go find Ava. "Gotta go," I told Holden.

Holden nodded, his eyes on me. I gave him a quick kiss on the cheek and Sloane and I hurried off.

"This is going to be bad. Should I get a fifth of Jack Daniel's?" Sloane asked as we headed inside the church to find Ava.

"Maybe just some champagne. Take the edge off."

"On it. I'm going to guess she's in the bathroom," Sloane said. Loud weeping came from the children's room at the back of the church. I pointed to it and Sloane nodded, heading in the opposite direction.

I tapped on the door and pushed it open a crack. "Ava, honey, it's Marley."

"I hate him so much, Marley," she said, as I stepped in.

"No, you don't." I dropped my clutch on a chair in the row in front of us then sat by Ava, winding my arm around her shoulders.

"I do!" she sobbed. "He's such an oblivious jerk!"

"Well, they're all oblivious and I don't think he means to be a jerk."

"He does! He doesn't know how to *not* be a jerk! I mean, his mom is such an evil shrew, saying my flowers looked like funeral flowers, and he just laughed! And kept laughing when I burst into tears!"

"Well, that's pretty stupid, I'll give it to him there," I said, rubbing her back in small circles. "But he doesn't know anything about flowers for a wedding *or* a funeral. I'm sure he laughed because he's nervous. Just like you are."

"No, he's not. He's been drinking and smoking weed all weekend. He's so mellowed out, he couldn't even get a boner this afternoon!" she shouted, the second Sloane opened the door and Ava's voice carried into the hallway.

"Whoopsie." Sloane slammed the door closed, ignoring the curious looks sweeping toward it. "I stole a box of church wine. It's all I could find." She also carried a stack of tiny Dixie cups she must have gotten from the bathroom.

"I hate Reed," Ava stated, wiping her nose with a tissue I'd snagged from the box behind us.

"Well, there's a lot to hate. I mean, he's hideous." Sloane poured a cup of wine and passed it to Ava.

"Stop it, Sloane. I know what you're doing," Ava said.

"He's not intelligent at all. Summa Cum Laude, my ass," I added.

"I'm serious, both of you. Stop." Ava knocked back the plastic shot of wine in one sip. Sloane straight away handed her another one.

"He hates dogs. I saw him kick one in the street just when we came walking in. Then set it on fire," Sloane continued.

"Oh, God, I miss Bear. The dogsitter sent us a pic of him playing in the sprinkler today, his fur all wet and matted. My little man. Reed showed everyone at the beach the pictures," Ava said, sucking back her second cup of wine.

"He's also been a total asshole to us this weekend. He didn't arrange for all the accommodations and food then take us out on his boat and be totally sexy while doing it," Sloane asserted.

"Okay, fine, Slo. I get it." Ava gulped down her third cup. "He's perfect."

"No, Ave. He's not perfect. But listen. Things may go wrong tomorrow, but the fact is, everything is beautiful. You and Reed — *that's* what matters. And he loves you more than anything on this earth. Fuck the flowers. Fuck his mom," I said.

"No, thanks." Sloane took a swig of wine.

"Everything is wonderful. We are all having such a great time. And Sloane even banged someone last night," I said.

"You what?" Ava screeched, holding out her cup for a refill.

"You loud-mouthed slut," Sloane shot back at me and I grinned over the top of my cup.

"Hey, you all okay in here?" Elle poked her head in.

"Ava called off the wedding because Reed donates too much money to charity," Sloane said. Elle slipped in and shut the door behind her.

"Shut up, Slo," Ava ordered, but she laughed a little — the wine must have been working.

"She's also had to fake every orgasm, including the one she had on the plane on the way here to the island when she told him she wanted to be a member of the mile high club," I went on.

"Stop, you guys. Seriously." But Ava started smiling and the tears began stopping.

"God, he has such a tiny dick, too, right? And he never goes down on her." Sloane handed Elle a small cup of wine.

"And her engagement ring is soooo small. Remember that unromantic way he proposed when he covered their whole apartment in New York in flowers and candles and got down on one knee? What a fucking loser," Elle joined in, taking a seat beside Sloane.

"And that date where he took to her to a Yankees game because she once said during a passing conversation that she'd always loved baseball and he never forgot about it and planned the whole thing where she met Chase Headley, her favorite player?" I added.

"Okay, you guys. I got it. Reed is pretty fantastic." Ava wiped under her eyes.

"No, I want to talk about the time he ditched a big meeting at work and rushed home because you broke your ankle. Spent two days at home taking care of you. What a dick." Sloane winked at her.

Ava sniggered. "Okay, so maybe I overreacted."

None of us responded.

"Okay, so I overreacted," she repeated.

"It happens. Don't worry about it. It's over, Reed's going to be fine and this wedding is going to be amazing." I wrapped my arm around her and hugged her to me.

"You think?" Ava asked.

"Of course it is! I mean, it's already been a great weekend," Elle said with an encouraging smile.

"Totally. I mean, we've all gotten laid and that hasn't happened since like junior year when we had that girls' trip to Edisto Beach," Sloane observed.

Elle whipped her eyes to Sloane. "You got laid?"

"She never tells us anything." I pouted.

"Was it Brooks? He told Reed he's been in love with you since you guys were teenagers," Ava said, her tone off-hand.

But Sloane's whole body went tense. "He what?"

"Yeah, I guess it's like a well-known fact that Brooks Vaughn has had the hots for Sloane Riley since middle school. Apparently, you were his first kiss. He's been pining big-time." Ava sucked back another cup of wine.

Sloane went green. "Uh, I gotta—um, pee." She raced out of the room.

"Nice one." I nudged Ava.

"What?" Ava asked, widening her eyes and placing a hand on her chest, fooling no one.

"You know Sloane is petrified of commitment. She won't even live in the same place for more than six months because she thinks it's putting down roots," Elle said.

"Well, it's not like Brooks asked her to marry him," Ava commented. "Though he did tell Reed he would someday."

"Don't tell her," Elle and I said both together.

"Okay, fine." Ava drew in a long breath. "I feel exhausted. And we haven't even had the wedding yet."

"I know, but trust me when I say it'll all be worth it soon. And Reed loves you, Ava. A lot." I squeezed her thigh.

"I know." She sighed.

"Let's practice getting you married. Then we can do the whole thing again tomorrow," Elle said with a bright smile.

Ava gave a full smile at last and went off in search of Reed with her tail tucked between her legs, Elle close behind for support. I stayed back to clean up the evidence of us imbibing Jesus' blood in cheap plastic goblets when the door to the room shut closed with a thud.

Holden stood there, his back against the door. "Ava all right?"

"Yeah. Crisis averted. Though I'm definitely going to ask her sister to see if she can get a hold of half a Xanax for tomorrow so this doesn't happen again." I bent over to pick up the rest of the cups Ava had tossed aside once she'd finished each one.

Holden came up behind me, smoothing his palms over my ass. "Damn, I love your ass."

"Oh, yeah?" I asked, still hunched over, my voice husky.

"Yeah. I want to fuck your tight little hole so bad, sweetheart." He pushed my panties aside and traced a finger from my cunt back between my cheeks.

"How bad?" My voice caught.

"Bad enough that I'm rock-hard and willing to do it in a fucking church. Right now." Holden dropped to his knees and shoved my underwear aside to lick a trail from my pussy to my ass.

"Oh, God, Holden. *Fuck*," I panted, gripping the chair and leaning deep.

"You want your ass fucked, Marley?"

"I've never— *Fuck*, Holden!" I gasped in a whisper as he prodded my asshole with his thumb.

"You've never let anyone fuck your ass, baby?"

I shook my head, glancing at him over my shoulder.

"Shit, I think I nearly just came in my pants." He stood, unbuckled his belt and plucked a condom from the front pocket of his pants. He'd even brought lube.

"We have to hurry. And be quiet," I said, but I didn't care if the whole fucking congregation of people heard us. All I could think about was Holden's thick cock buried deep in my virgin ass and my pussy dripped wet for it.

"Goddamn, you want this as bad as I do." Surprise and desire colored Holden's voice and he ran his dick over my slit, dampening it with my need.

"I do. I really, really do," I admitted.

Holden teased my opening first, pressing his thumb slowly against the pucker, then pushing it inside. He got all the way to the knuckle when he started to moan and his cock jerked against my pussy.

I peered over my shoulder again and shifted backward, wanting him to go on, to go deeper, not to stop. He didn't seem to have any intention of halting and after dragging his thumb in and out of me several times, stretching me open, he gripped his cock in his hand. He nudged his tip to my opening and pushed forward, forcing just an inch inside.

"Oh, God," I rasped, dropping my head and letting my neck hang down.

"You're so tight. Goddamn, Marley, it's so tight." He moaned, thrusting in another inch.

"Holy hell," I breathed, and he leaned over my back and ran his fingers along my clit. He tapped his fingers lightly against my cunt, then teased the wet opening with a long finger, running it all the way back to where he fucked my ass, then forward again.

"You like getting your ass fucked in a church, Marley?" he asked me, his voice in my ear.

"*Jesus*," I breathed, my pussy starting to throb, my body aching to come.

"You're such a good girl for everyone else and so dirty for me. I fucking love it." He pushed farther in me and drew out slightly, then back in. He fisted my hair around his hand and yanked it tight. "Goddamn, you're going to be the fucking death of me, sweetheart."

"Touch me, Holden. Put your fingers in my pussy," I begged, done with his teasing touch. He rammed two fingers in. I felt so full, so stretched. I had never had this sensation before and I was enraptured with it. "Oh, God, yes. Holden, I'm going to come. I can't stop it." I pressed backward, driving his whole cock into me, and I climaxed just at that moment.

It didn't take Holden long. A couple of deep, hard strokes inside and he came with a groan through gritted teeth. I looked back over my shoulder to see him still perfectly put together, just his dick out of the hole in his pants.

Once his movements had stilled, I stood, slow and careful, and he slid out of me, his half-hard dick bobbling between us when he wrenched my mouth to his, my back pressed to his chest.

He kissed me deep, circling our tongues together then pulling back. "Your pussy was mine, and now your ass is mine, Marley. *You're* mine." His eyes were intense, in the same way his words were.

He'd fucked my ass, in a church, yeah, but I wanted so much to believe it was more. That even though there had been a lot of sex between us, something else could be building along with it, and that his words mirrored that slow burn of emotion and concern, mingled with friendship and affection, converging in our mutual desire to get off and get close to one another. I wanted that with him in this moment more than I ever had.

I shoved aside my history as the daughter of a gambler and a schemer, the girl who'd grown up so afraid of becoming just like them that she organized every inch of her life, never leaving anything to chance. The girl who dated men with day planners and plausible goals in life. Who never let lust, love, or want come between her and a solid, predictable future.

Right now, I existed simply as a girl who had been fucked hard, in her ass, by a man she had known for just four days. Never mind that he was a man who would never commit to her, who would never be more than *this*—I had to let myself be her for just two more days.

Or I would fall apart.

"What's going on in that pretty head of yours?" he asked, brushing my hair back from my face.

"That I probably need to go to confession every day for at least a year to make up for this mortal sin."

"Yeah, well, that makes two of us." He straightened and tucked himself away. "But I'm not Catholic."

"What are you?" I asked, fixing my lace panties and dress.

"I was raised nothing. And I'm still pretty much nothing. You?"

"Lutheran. I think. We went to church on Christmas and Easter only when I was a kid. Then when I got old enough to decide not to, I stopped going at all. It all seemed so—"

"Fake."

"Yeah, fake. Not bad, just, contrived, you know? And with my parents doing so little to live Christian lives, it felt even more fake."

"Were they mean to you, Marley?" he asked, his voice low and cautious.

I regarded him for a moment and swallowed. "They could be. But really I just never got to be a kid. I was like a little adult, having to be the grown-up in a house of people who didn't want to be. I had to learn to cook at eight. I had to clean the house or we had bed bugs. I had to mow the lawn or we got fined by the city. I had to change Ross' diapers when I was only four years old. I had to sign the permission slips and pack my own lunches. Elle, she didn't come from much either, but that's because her father left her mom with Elle and her three sisters when she was just six months old. But Elle's mom taught her how to ride a bike and baked her birthday cakes and gave her Christmas presents. I didn't have that."

I told him all this with no emotion. I didn't have any left after years of lamenting my lot in life. *It is what it is. I can't stop it, and I can't escape it.* The only way out is to do what I had been doing—plan with care and live a conventional life.

"My mom has never baked a thing in her life. And my nannies taught me to ride a bike. They played catch with me. They bought, wrapped and gave me my presents as a kid. My parents were vacationing or arguing, who the fuck knows. For a while, it was me and Spencer against the world. Then I grew up, moved out and he was alone. Then—gone."

I took a step toward him and laced my fingers through the back of his hair. "The other side is never much greener, is it?"

He shook his head, his eyes boring into mine. "No, Marley. It's not."

"Hey, come on, guys, we're starting." Ethan burst through the door with a thud. He paused for a second. "Wait, were you two just banging?"

Holden ignored him, his eyes still on me. "You all good, sweetheart?" he asked quietly.

I put on a wide smile, blocking out everything else but him. His handsome face, his casual and sexy way, the feeling of his hands on my skin. "All good. Let's do this, Groomsman iPhone." I winked and he chuckled.

We joined the rest of the wedding party already assembled at the back of the church, listening to the priest going through all the steps of the ceremony. Holden kept trying to creep his hand under my skirt as the man spoke and, though I had just been a very bad girl a few minutes ago, I did have my limits and being groped in front of a man of God was one of them.

It didn't stop Holden from trying, though, a secretive smirk on his face. Eventually, I moved in front of Sloane. "Sinner," she whispered and I spit out a laugh.

Everyone glanced at me and I covered my mouth with my hand, pretending to cough into it. Sloane just laughed outright.

The wedding planner took us through all the motions of the procession itself, reminding us several times what time we had to be there and what our roles were. Nanette was in charge of Ava and the rest of us were in charge of the groomsmen.

"Fuck, yeah." Ethan high-fived Mitch—at least the priest was far enough away that he didn't hear him.

Pretty sure Ava's Nana Burcar did, though. She clucked her tongue at Ethan and made her way up to the front by the altar.

Holden and I were the first couple to rehearse and Holden kept me close during our measured, slow pace to the front of the church, nodded at the priest then went to opposite sides of the altar.

Mitch and Cece were next, followed by Elle and Slater. Then Ethan and Sloane, Nanette and Brooks. I tried to see if Brooks and Sloane shared a secret glance, a smile, anything, but neither of them gave anything away. They appeared just as distant as they had been the whole trip. I half-wondered if Sloane had made it up.

Then, just before Reed came out from the room behind the altar and took his place beside Brooks, I saw Brooks look over at Sloane. He quickly shifted his gaze away, but I saw it and, fuck, there was fire in it. Lust, sure. But also something else. They had connected. He was enthralled with her.

And I knew that would make Sloane run. She had a bad habit of getting close to a guy, and when he pulled her closer, she took off. She'd seen a counselor for years and I have no doubt he could shed light on her inability to commit. But I hoped she stopped doing it soon, because if a man stared at me the way Brooks had her, I would marry him in a second.

He was smitten. Anyone paying attention could see that. Maybe Holden had that same look in his eyes?

Nope, he had his phone out. And when Mrs. Whitaker scolded him for doing so, he slid it into his pocket. He smiled over at me, but there wasn't more there. His grin was open, infectious—I found myself smiling back. But I knew that smile was as far inside Holden as I could ever get.

And this weekend held the beginning and the end for us.

We went through all the details for the following day, then at last were excused to go get dinner.

"God, I wish we could skip this," Holden murmured, taking his place at my side to file out of the church.

"We can't skip it. It's the rehearsal dinner," I whispered back.

"Yeah, and we know how to eat. We don't have to fucking rehearse it," he muttered, running a hand through his hair.

"Well, I'm starving." As if on cue, my stomach growled.

"I just fed you five hours ago."

"Oh, I'm sorry. Do you only like women who eat once a day?" I teased as we reached the town cars.

"I like women who would rather suck my dick than eat a steak."

"I can't do both?" I raised an eyebrow at him.

"At the same time?"

"Down boy. This is still Ava and Reed's big weekend. And this is what Ava and Reed want. So, get in the car." I pushed him toward the open door.

His eyes darkened and I knew why. *Spencer.* His brother's absence haunted him, even if he wouldn't admit it himself. Spencer's friends were gathered around him nonstop, his parents expressed their hopes for him at every turn and the ocean itself reminded him of what he had lost to it.

His reluctance to engage made sense to me now, but I didn't know how to get him to try to enjoy himself. He climbed into the town car and I followed. Mitch clambered in beside me.

"Hey, kids." A joint hung out of his mouth and he dug into his jacket and pulled out a flask.

"You're prepared," I told him with a laugh.

"Like a fucking boy scout." Mitch puffed out a cloud of smoke and offered me the joint.

"No, thanks." I curled my nose and Ethan climbed into the front seat with the driver.

"Thank fucking god. I'm dying, man." Ethan spun around and grabbed the spliff before Mitch had a chance to offer it to Holden.

"It's Pierce's go," Mitch said to Ethan. Holden declined the outstretched joint and Mitch took a swig of liquor and offered me the flask.

"What is it?" I asked.

"Macallans. The good stuff." He grinned at me, dropping his eyes to the front of my dress.

I took a tentative sip and choked it down. "It's strong," I said and Ethan and Mitch chuckled.

"That it is, darling. Holden, you want in on this?" Ethan held the joint out for him.

He distracted himself again with his phone, and just shook his head once, not even bothering to lift his eyes.

Anytime it wasn't just the two of us, the man closed himself off like a clam. He retreated into himself, into his work and I had a feeling that Holden did this in New York, as well. This wasn't just because we were here—Holden no doubt avoided the real world by keeping his head down and burying himself in emails and phone calls.

"Holden told me that Spencer played lacrosse. Did you guys play, too?" I asked and all their bodies went static the second I said his name. Mitch's and Ethan's usual jovial and carefree faces fell, growing serious.

"Uh, yeah. We did," Mitch said, his Adam's apple bobbling when he swallowed hard.

"Did you play for the same team?" I continued.

"I did. Mitch played for another team. He went to Kent." Ethan nodded toward Mitch.

"How did you guys all meet?" I asked and Holden curled his fist tight as he kept his eyes on his phone. But I couldn't stop myself—I *wouldn't*. Holden wasn't the only one missing his brother. As hard as it might have been for him to admit it, Spencer had been a part of all their lives. They were all on the island beside the ocean that had taken his life. It couldn't be forgotten.

"Reed took an illegal hit from some douchebag from Kent and I ratted the guy out to the ref. After the game, Spence came over and thanked me, told me about some party they were going to that night. I tagged along," Mitch said. "Rest is history."

"What was Spencer like?" I asked.

Mitch glanced at Holden but Holden didn't move. Didn't react. Kept his attention averted, but I knew he was listening. "Uh, funny. You know? Kind of a goofball. Would do anything for a laugh."

"Stupid fucking pranks, always. Hair dye in the shampoo bottles, whoopee cushions in the cafeteria. The whole nine yards." Ethan laughed.

"And the guy had no game whatsoever. He always wanted to be wingman when we went out, and I'd see a hot chick and chat her up, tossing Spence to her friend. And within five minutes both girls would be walking out of the door because Spencer had told the friend her ass was fat or that he wanted to lick her skin off or some shit like that. Fucking awful." Mitch and Ethan laughed and even Holden smiled.

"Oh, man, I had this chick in the bag one time when we were at Harvard, and Spence comes rolling up to us and pretends I'm his boyfriend. Screaming at me, telling me I broke his heart—fucker even started crying on cue. The girl slapped me. Took off. And Spence just laughed his ass off. Told me that girls loved that *Will and Grace* shit so he'd thought it would work."

They were all cracking up now and I joined in. What a tragedy that he wasn't still alive, but I guessed, based on what they told me, he would've liked that he could still make us all laugh.

"Would he be pissed his friend Reed is settling down?" I asked, watching Ethan.

"Nah. He'd probably move into the spare room, though. Him and Reed were half in love most of their lives. Ava would have to share." Ethan chortled.

"Oh, that's for fucking sure. I think Spence planned on him and Reed getting married and living together, anyway." Mitch shook his head.

"You should say something, or have Brooks say something, about Spencer in his speech tomorrow," I suggested.

Mitch went rigid again and glanced at Holden, then at me. "I don't think that's a good idea, hon."

"If you guys miss him, I'm sure Reed does, too. Reed would have wanted him to be there. He should be, in some way," I said, my tone gentle.

The car crawled to a stop in front of the Promenade, a fancy restaurant inside the Royal Park Inn where we were having dinner. They were all quiet a moment, no one moving from the car.

"Yeah, babe. You're right," Ethan said in a quiet voice, his eyes on mine.

I gave him a smile and he climbed out of the car.

Mitch looked at me, then at Holden. "You're a lucky bastard, you know that?" he said to Holden, then pushed open his door and got out.

"Don't be mad," I whispered.

"I'm not."

"I don't want it to be like your brother didn't exist. He did. He meant a lot to these people. He needs to be recognized, somehow."

"You're right, Marley," Holden said, his voice caked with emotion.

I gave him a smile. "By the way, my ass is terribly sore. I'm going to need to sit on an ice pack during dinner," I said, lightening the mood.

He stared at me a beat then threw his head back and laughed. "I'll see what I can do for you."

I winked and got out, Holden close behind. He took my hand, tethering us together again in the way that I couldn't get enough of.

The tables were arranged in a line down a long courtyard, with trees and tall shrubs on either side. Candles flickered on the tables and huge vases of flowers sat squat on every surface.

"This is beautiful," I said in awe, pointing at the twinkling lights strung from branches overhead.

"You're with me, MJ." Sloane linked an arm through mine. "And so is Brooks, for some weird fucking reason. If you open your mouth, I will put my Manolo Blahnik down it, got it?" She raised a severe eyebrow at me.

"Yes, ma'am, I got it." I made a motion of zipping my lips then locking them with a key and tossing it over my shoulder.

She just snorted a laugh and took a seat.

Holden tugged my chair out and sat in his spot next to me, with Elle on the other side.

"This is so romantic." Elle slipped into her space as Slater sat beside her.

She'd hit the nail on the head. I could have choked on the romantic atmosphere this place employed — that this entire weekend had seemed to create.

"Last wedding Marley and I went to in Angler's Haven was on a Thursday night at a bar called the Rusty Nail, with hot dogs on the menu," Elle recalled.

"That place should be called the Tetanus Shot," I said into my glass of water.

Brooks skated into the seat beside Sloane and she blatantly ignored him, but he'd seemed to anticipate that and didn't appear bothered one bit. He pulled the bottom of her chair closer to him and tossed his arm around the back. She tensed but didn't stop him.

It felt a little bit like watching a chess match through dinner. Brooks would say something to her and she would inch away. Brooks would ignore her and she would lean closer to him. They bobbled back and forth like a ping-pong ball throughout the whole dinner while I watched on, amused.

Elle and Slater created their own little cocoon, only coming up for air once or twice to consume the food we had.

Holden talked to Brooks about New York real estate, the Yankees — guy shit. He kept me close to him and, by my second glass of wine, I was leaning farther and farther into him. By the time we were done with dessert, I was almost in his lap. I had my shoulder pressed against the arm he'd wound around me, and I could feel the vibrations on my back as he spoke across the table, his voice deep and rumbling.

"I like your voice," I said to him, interrupting him in the middle of a sentence.

He looked down at me. "You like my voice?"

"Yeah. It's deep and growly. Sexy." I fluttered my eyelashes at him.

He searched my eyes for what, I don't know. But then he settled on my mouth. "I like your voice, too, Marley."

"No, you like my mouth. Because I give good blow jobs."

Sloane choked on her martini and even Brooks chuckled. Elle and Slater were oblivious.

"You give good blow jobs. But I like your voice, too, sweetheart," he said.

"I like you," I blurted out.

He stared at me for just half a second, then slowly, slowly smiled. "I like you, too."

"Good. That's settled. Can we get out of here and go fuck again?" I asked, again too loudly, and stood.

Sloane threw back her head and laughed, slapping her hand on the table as Brooks chuckled and shook his head.

"You're a lucky man, Pierce," Brooks said.

"Yeah, Mitch told him that earlier, because we'd just had anal sex in the church," I informed Brooks in a stage whisper.

Sloane tumbled out of her seat, laughing, and Brooks had to catch her before she hit the ground. I watched a look pass between them, but that could've been all the booze I had drunk. At that point, everything seemed like a flagship for love.

Holden pulled me into him. "I'm getting you home. I think you've had enough tonight."

"It's church wine! Jesus' blood has a high alcohol content," I told them all.

We wove our way through the tables and I called out a loud and embarrassing goodbye to Ava across a crowd of people. I'd torpedoed my plan to wear something more conservative so I didn't stand out—I felt like pretty much a total idiot by the time we were in the car.

"God, those people hate me." I depressed the window all the way down to let the air waft over my face.

"What people?" Holden asked, still keeping me close to him.

"The rich people. The *you* kind of people." I poked his side.

"Those aren't my kind of people, Marley. If they were, I wouldn't be right here."

"Don't break my heart," I said in a rush, before I could even run the words through a filter first.

He blinked at me. "I won't."

I had no idea if he meant it or had even had time to think about what I'd said. But his confirmation was enough for me. I launched myself at him and wriggled in his lap, winding our tongues together and trying to get closer and closer to the man I was falling for.

He shouldn't be the kind of man I wanted. My destiny didn't include a life like this. But I felt myself falling deeper and deeper for the guy with the cocoa eyes.

We pawed at each other, getting desperately riled up, but didn't take off any clothes. We just grabbed and gripped and scored each other. We couldn't get to the house fast enough and Holden didn't bother letting me walk on my own. He wrapped my legs around him and didn't even take his mouth away while we fumbled into the empty mansion, up the stairs and into his room. We took delightful detours on the way, against the wall as he ran his hands all the way up my dress and took off my underwear, shoving it into the pocket of his pants. When we hit the stairs, he laid me down on them and ground his hips into mine, his hard dick pressing against my now bare core. The fabric of his pants chaffed against my clit, but I loved that sensation. That pain mixed with the promise of pleasure — I couldn't get enough of it.

Once we cleared the stairs, Holden stopped at the wall just beside his door, discarding my dress and leaving me in just my bra for him to grope and bite my nipples through the lace. The dress pooled at our feet as he shoved the door open and we toppled through it. We didn't make it to the bed. Holden took me right there on the carpet behind the door, releasing his cock at last from behind his zipper, sheathing himself with a condom and shoving his pants and boxers down, not even getting them all the way off before slamming into me. He pounded ruthlessly until I came with a shrill scream that I'm sure would have scared the neighbors if they'd heard me.

But Holden wasn't done. He had me coming twice more before he finally did, jerking his cock all over my tits while I watched, licking my lips, sprawled out on the bed, my tits in my hands and my pussy sore and happy. Then he took me to the shower and cleaned me up and made me come once more with his hands. This time he went slower, as though a panic had passed and now he wanted to take his time, worship every inch of my skin, and I loved the chance to reciprocate. I would never get enough of this man and I didn't know how to extract myself from him in two days and say goodbye.

* * * *

I woke up a few hours later, blinking across the darkness, my mind still in a fog. I had a leg thrown over Holden's, my thigh hiked up between his legs and my head tucked under my hands, facing him. My eyes met his, and they were wide open, watching me.

"Hi," I croaked, my voice thick with sleep.

He reached a hand out and traced my lips with the tips of his fingers. "Hi," he murmured in reply, his eyes following the movement of the finger he was moving feather-light across my mouth, cheek and face. "You're breathtaking."

My whole body melted and I shifted closer to him without even thinking about it, closing the small gap between us.

He cupped my face and brought his lips to mine. "Mitch was right. I am lucky," he whispered.

I raised myself upward and pressed my mouth to his, then settled my cheek against his chest. I wanted to say something, to hold the feeling of this moment in my brain, to let it wash over me with warmth and sweetness.

But my eyes closed of their own accord and I fell asleep again.

Chapter Seven

I woke the next morning, wedding day morning, with a pounding headache. I swear it was the Jesus wine. Cheap box wine always made me feel like I'd been run over by a garbage truck.

Holden had departed, having left a note to tell me he'd gone for an early run and had gotten me a Gatorade and some Advil and signing off with a smiley face. *How fucking adorable.*

The moment we'd shared in the darkness a few hours earlier came back to me, and heat glowed across my chest and through my veins as I remembered the intensity of his stare, the softness of his touch, the tenderness in his words. There were depths to Holden Pierce that I hadn't even begun to understand but I wanted to, more than anything.

But right now, I had a best friend to marry. I managed to stumble back to the Whitakers' in my second morning walk along the beach but this one having gone much better than the last. I'd gotten a note with a smiley face this time.

The house bustled with a flurry of activity with hairdressers and makeup artists working their magic on anyone who needed it, including a panicking Ava.

"I got her the Xanax. She won't take it," Nanette told me the moment I came in, dropping my shoes and bag by the back door.

"Hey, Ave. It's Mrs. Whitaker day! You doing all right?" I asked in a sweet voice, coming up to where she was getting her hair curled in the dining room.

"No. My face is blotchy. And I can't find my garter." She sniffled, tears running down her cheeks.

"Well, the makeup girl will take care of the blotchiness—"

"She already tried! This is what I look like after she put on makeup!" Ava cried.

Oh. Yikes.

"You know Sloane has magic foundation. I'll find it. And I'm sure your garter is in one of your bags."

"It's not. I searched through everything. Twice."

"I'll find it," I vowed. Nanette came up behind me with a pill and a cup of water. "Hey, do me a favor. Take this."

"*No!*" Ava shouted, scaring the hairdresser so much she jumped.

"If you don't stop crying, your face is gonna stay red, honey. You take this and, trust me, the face will calm down." I walked with caution toward her and handed her the pill and the water.

She sucked it back then snarled at me. "Find the garter." He voice took on the tenor of a possessed demon during an exorcism. I hoped this pill worked fast.

"Will do, Ave. On it." I scrambled away before her head started swiveling one hundred and eighty degrees on her neck and she puked up pea soup.

I got to her room and threw out everything she had in bags, rifling in drawers and under the bed, combing every inch of that room—and still nothing. "Shit," I muttered, texting Reed.

You have the garter by any chance?

He wrote back a few minutes later. *No. Is it missing? Is she freaking?*

I wasn't going to put this on him. Today happened to be *his* day, too.

Just found it! Sorry for the mix up! I lied.

Shit. I went to my contacts and dialed Holden.

"You left." He sounded out of breath. He must've just got back to his room from his run.

"I did and we have a minor crisis brewing here. I can't find the garter. Reed doesn't have it and it's not in Ava's room. I've looked everywhere."

"What the fuck is a garter?"

I rolled my eyes, even though he couldn't see me. *Men!* "A garter is the elastic piece of lace and ribbon that brides wear on their thighs. They take it off and toss it to the eligible bachelors in the room and supposedly the one who catches it is the next one to get married."

"That sounds ridiculous."

Agreed. But nevertheless, I remained determined to make it happen.

I took a breath through my nose. "I need help. I gotta do makeup and hair and girlie nonsense here and my head is still fucking killing me. Can you go find a garter? There's gotta be some store in town that would have one. I don't care if you just find a ribbon and lace and I can find a way to make one. Ask one of the drivers or maybe Google it if you can't."

"Marley, I've built a billion dollar real estate portfolio. I think I can find a garter."

"Oh. Okay." I straightened my spine, realizing I might not have to beg. "So you'll do it?"

"Of course. Anything else?"

"A picture of your dick would help. That's for me, not Ava," I added.

He roared out a laugh. "I'll see what I can do." He hung up.

Okay, one task complete. On to preparation. He did send me a dick pic. It was beyond hot.

The bridesmaid's dresses were a dove-gray color, with a fitted lace bodice and a tulle overlay. They were cinched with a ribbon at the waist and a deep vee at the top that had tulle around the back in wide strips. The dresses were hung up, ready and waiting for us, pressed and tailored. I slithered into mine easily once my makeup and hair were done. A jeweled chignon twisted my locks off my neck, like all the girls', and my makeup was smoky and subtle. Being pampered, given countless orgasms and dark maroon lipstick worked well for me.

I shoved a bagel down, determined to eat something before the day started because I knew I wouldn't be able to again. I had been a bridesmaid many times. It was a thankless job that felt a little bit like foraging for survival in the wild. You were tossed into a sea of strangers in an expensive and tight-fitting dress and expected to survive the day. If I ever got married, I planned to elope. I couldn't do this to my friends. It felt like Chinese water torture in a seven-hundred-dollar dress.

I choked down some juice as Elle walked into the kitchen with Holden close behind.

"Oh, hey." I breathed a sigh of relief when I saw him. "Did you get it?"

He stared at me a beat. "Yeah. Got it." He held out a little pink bag.

"Thank you. Hope you didn't have to carry this far and it destroyed your manhood," I teased, closing the distance between us and taking the garter out of the bag. He had done well—the design seemed very typical but pretty enough. I just hoped Ava didn't flip when she noticed it wasn't the one she had brought with her, but the Xanax had to have kicked in by now.

"You look beautiful," Holden murmured.

"Oh, um, thank you," I said, all of a sudden shy. No idea why I was shy—the man had come in my ass less than twenty-four hours ago.

He lifted a gentle hand to my face and stroked my cheek, then kissed my forehead. "I'll see you soon, sweetheart," he murmured. He lingered his gaze on me for a moment, until I gave him a small smile. He returned it, then walked out, seeming to have forced himself to, when he had wanted to stay.

Elle, Sloane, Nanette and two hairdressers who had been in the room watching us all exhaled at the same time.

"Holy shit, that man's sexy," one of the hairdressers said.

"He even had *my* lady parts wiggling — and I don't like men," Nanette added.

"I may have been wrong about Holden Pierce. He sure seemed like he knows what he wants now," Sloane threw in.

I wanted to explore this idea more, but Ava came breezing in. "Hi, girls! I'm so excited!" she exclaimed.

Yeah, the pill had kicked in.

I gave her the garter and she either didn't notice or didn't mention that it didn't look like the same one. She had a big goofy smile on her face and gave me a wet kiss on my cheek. "I love you so much, Marley. You're my rock."

I hugged her tight. "Love you, too, honey. Can't wait to see you get married. So happy for you and the luckiest man on the island."

"Don't make me cry!" she admonished, wiping her eyes.

"Okay, the photographer is here. Picture time!" Stephanie announced.

Then, it began. Not the wedding — we still had two hours for that. The pictures began. I love Ava, I do. But she made that photographer take at least ten thousand pictures of us all over the island. Then, it was like paparazzi inside the church. I barely had time to say hello to Holden prior to being shoved down the aisle to the *Canon in D*, and more pictures were taken. Then the ceremony went on for ages, the church packed and stuffy, and we took more pictures after.

Thankfully, for that part of the afternoon, the guys had managed to get a couple of coolers of beer and some snacks, so while the family stood for photo after photo after photo, we took the edge off with cold beer and junk food, which was apparently all the guys managed to pack. After we'd shoved down the smelliest and manliest food I had ever eaten, we were called over toward the backdrop for a dozen or so more pictures, then herded back out, then back in and out and in and out nonstop. I felt like cattle. I wanted never to take a picture again.

Then Ava told us we had to post to Instagram all the fun we were having, so we pasted on fake smiles, took selfies and did that with her required hashtag. When the ceremony finally happened and we were tucked inside the reception at the Harbor Hill Hotel, I relaxed. Then a flashbulb went off in my face and I swear I had post-traumatic stress disorder and jumped and screeched.

"You okay?" Holden asked, sliding into the seat beside me and putting a steadying hand on my leg.

"I can't take any more pictures, Holden. I can't do one more. I feel like they're stealing my soul." I grabbed the lapels of his jacket and yanked him to me in desperation.

He chuckled, resting a hand on the side of my face. "It's okay, sweetheart. Almost done. Just a few more for the dances and —"

"No, no more. I can't do it. All I see are spots. Your face is just blob after blob of Technicolor dots. You look terrible," I whimpered.

He eased my hands off his jacket and into my lap, squeezing them. He rubbed my back in comforting circles and I took a deep breath and a sip of water. Then another camera shutter went off across the room, and someone called out for Holden and me to move closer together for a picture and I nearly lost it.

"Come on, sweetheart." Holden flashed a smile and put an arm around my shoulder.

Ava's little cousin Jacklyn squealed as she snapped a shot of us. "I'm posting it to the Internet!" she shouted and ran off.

"Okay, that was cute. Now I don't care about pictures anymore." I took another sip of water.

A long procession of speeches began, and Holden kept his hand on my leg, my palm up on my thigh and our fingers intertwined. He had found little ways to touch me all day, even though family and friends were crowding us, and I appreciated it. It kept me grounded and made me feel safe, cared for.

I knew I shouldn't have let my mind go there, but after Sloane's comment in the kitchen and Holden's attention throughout the day, I couldn't help myself. I wanted this for me. I wanted this to be *more* than a fling.

I didn't give a shit about his money. I could ignore his sometimes jealous and prickly attitude. I could love this man for a long, long time. And as the priest recited a beautiful benediction about putting the other's needs ahead of one's own and sharing all life's joys and tragedies, I wanted what Ava had for me, too.

And I think, God help me, I wanted it with Holden Pierce.

I twisted toward him for the toast and clinked my glass with his, and I swear I almost told him I loved him. But I managed to stop myself and just smile. He gave me that sexy smirk and took a sip of champagne.

Yep. I was in love with him. *Officially.* Just watching him drink a glass of champagne turned me on and made me woozy. *Shit.*

Brooks got up and gave a very frat guy kind of speech, delineating all the trouble he and Reed had gotten into at school and all the brotherly love they had for the other. Then Nanette gave her speech about what an awesome big sister Ava had been growing up, even when Nanette cut off all of Ava's dolls' hair and drew tattoos on their arms with a Sharpie.

After we'd all raised a glass and taken a drink following her speech, I scanned the room for Ava's dad, who was supposed to be next. But Nanette walked down toward us behind the table and handed the microphone to Holden.

I stared at Holden, standing in his place, and he cleared his throat. "Hey, I hope you don't mind, but I asked Nanette to give me a second when she finished to say a few words." His voice echoed through the speakers in the room.

I stared up at him.

"It's been five years since we lost Spencer and I know it's been hard for all of us," Holden started.

I grasped his hand and held on tight. He squeezed back and kept going, holding hard to my hand as though it was a lifeline. "And you know Spencer would have loved this weekend. Pretty girls, lots of champagne, a captive audience for him to play jokes on." The crowd tittered with laughter.

"He would've been really happy for Reed and he would've adored Ava, I have no doubt. And as Ethan said earlier, probably ended up living in their spare room," Holden continued.

"I didn't want today to go by without Spence being here. A friend told me he should be —" Holden glanced down at me and I could have sworn he might start crying. I had. "And I wanted to give you all the chance to remember him today, too. So raise a glass," Holden ordered, letting go of my hand so he could pick up his champagne and hold it aloft. "To Reed and Ava and my little brother. Miss you."

Well, there wasn't a dry eye in the house, including Reed. After we'd all toasted, Reed came down the table and yanked Holden into a long and tight dude-hug, which had even more people crying. Reed almost bawled when he told Holden he was glad he was here today, and Holden told him he had been honored.

Fuck, that did me in. Tears fell in brisk succession down my face and I couldn't wipe them away fast enough. Cece handed me a napkin and I thanked her — even *her* icy exterior had melted.

I had thought moments ago that maybe, possibly, perhaps I was falling in love with Holden. But that was not the case. I had fallen. *Hard.*

Holden handed the microphone to Reed's dad, who clapped him on the shoulder and gave him a nod, wiping away a tear from his weathered face.

Holden just nodded back and sat beside me, taking my hand again. He was shaking and I tucked his big palm between both of mine. "Proud of you, honey," I said, tears still falling.

He glanced at me with a tight smile and a small nod and took a deep breath. He didn't let go of my hand again.

Mr. Whitaker started, saying he didn't know how to follow that, but that he and his wife felt so privileged that Holden and his family were there with them that day, that they thought about and talked about Spencer often. He got choked up a few times then turned toward Ava and Reed.

"Today is about celebrating the joining of two lives. And Spence wouldn't have wanted us to dwell on this. So, I'll say how happy I am that Ava is joining our family and thank her for making Reed happier than we've ever seen him. We were all a little lost when

Spencer left us, but Ava brought light back into our lives. So thank you for that. And welcome to the fold, Mrs. Whitaker."

Okay, all of us were crying again, including Ava who hugged Mr. Whitaker when she broke down in tears. Once more champagne was poured, things returned to normal. Thank God. I don't think any of us could take much more. The photographer started prowling around again, too. *Ugh.*

We ate a delicious dinner, mingled a little bit, the girls all helping Ava pee in her titanic dress. I danced with Holden, the second time we had danced together, which I teased him about since he'd told me he didn't dance.

"I guess you're the exception to that rule then, Marley."

Swooning.

We were moving closer and closer as the night wore on and stealing secret little moments to make out rapidly before we had to go back to the fray. I went hunting for him after another bathroom break with the bride and heard his voice coming from the sitting area at the front of the hotel, in a small parlor area under a windowed atrium.

"This can't go on, Holden. You're being ridiculous." A different voice. Female. My steps slowed.

"Nothing is going on, Mother." Holden's voice, deep and irritated. *Shit.* This wasn't good.

"Anyone with eyes can see the two of you groping each other. It's uncouth."

"No one is paying any attention to us. It's Reed's wedding. All anyone cares about is him and Ava."

"She's poor white trash, Holden. Everyone at this wedding knows that. She is not the kind of woman for you. She would never belong in our world."

My steps stalled to a stop, just outside the door, my heart hammering.

She was talking about me, I knew that, just as I knew that I was falling in love with her son. And she was right. *I am poor white trash. I don't belong in their world.*

But maybe, just maybe, Holden felt differently. Maybe he had cast aside any doubts he might have had and plunged headfirst into the feeling he had when we were together, that calming bliss that overtook him moment after moment in each other's presence. Fuck his job. Fuck his reservations. Fuck his reluctance to let go of everyone's expectations for him, including himself. He would tell her that what he really wanted was *me*.

"Listen, Mother—"

"You listen. I know you're upset about Spencer. This girl is just a distraction for you. You've done whatever you have with her because this was hard for you here." She made a snorting and disdainful noise. "But this does not go on off this island, do you understand? This ends tomorrow."

"I have no intention of it going any further," Holden said, point blank, his voice robotic and rehearsed.

My head felt heavy.

"Tish is a nice girl, Holden, and if you keep holding her at arm's length, she will find someone else. Then who will you have? No one. She comes from a good family, she has an education, she wants children. You need to think about those things."

"Tish is the type of girl I should settle down with. You're right. Are we done now?" he asked, his voice still a monotone.

"You need to listen to me," she hissed.

"Trust me, Mother, I am listening. I agree with everything," he said.

At that, I turned and hurried down the hall. *Holy fuck, that was harsh. Devastating.* My heart actually hurt and I felt a pain in my chest, pressing against my skin and trying to crawl up my esophagus. I banged into a stall in the ladies' bathroom and emptied the dinner I'd just had into the toilet. All of it, appetizers to dessert, all puked up. My hands were shaking. This felt worse than any hangover I had ever had. I had been drunk on love then rammed into sobriety with a fierce, verbal shove. I stood and stepped out of the stall, into the curious gazes of Elle and Nanette.

"Oh, god, Marley, you okay?" Elle rushed to me.

"I'm fine," I said, pouring with sweat. I had to get hold of myself. So a boy I liked didn't like me back? It had happened before. In seventh grade I'd asked Todd Clementine to the school dance and he'd said he was going with Melissa Tretter because she 'had big knockers and a better personality'. Holden hadn't been responsible for the first rejection I'd felt. I'd had experience at being tossed aside for someone better. But this hurt deeper because it had run deeper.

Nanette wet a paper towel and held it to the back of my neck.

"Thank you," I murmured, wishing not for the first time in my life that I was attracted to girls. Maybe life would be easier.

"You should head back to the house. The last thing you want is to feel sick when you have to travel tomorrow," Nanette suggested.

Girl had a point. I had to get on the ferry, then a bus and onto a plane, all before ten a.m. The clock read quarter past eleven—I should just go back to the house, shower, cry and sleep. Yes, that sounded like a great idea.

"Yeah, I will. I'm going to." My hands still trembled as I washed them, then as I wiped my face with a paper towel. At least they assumed this was illness and not that I had fallen head over heels for a man who had used me to get through an emotional weekend without his dead brother. A man who, at thirty years old, allowed his mother to dictate the path his life should follow. The flu was a cleaner excuse.

I told them I felt better and would find my bag and a car, and say my goodbyes to Reed and Ava.

I stepped out of the bathroom and found Holden standing in the hall, holding a glass of liquor, a pensive look on his face.

"Hey," he said, brightening once his eyes met mine.

I swallowed down rising bile. "Hey. I, um— I think I had one too many." I forced a wonky smile and wiped my forehead with the back of my hand. "I'm going to head back to the house."

"Best news I've heard all day." He slugged back the rest of his drink and slammed his glass on the side table next to him. "Let's go."

He wrapped an arm around my back and led me into the reception hall. I hesitated for just a moment then went forward with him.

Why? I didn't know. Maybe because my self-esteem had just been tossed down the toilet along with tonight's up-chucked filet. Maybe because, even though I had heard every word he and his mother exchanged, in the back of my mind I held onto a faint hope that he didn't mean it. Maybe because after fighting my good sense all weekend, I'd finally got what I was so afraid of and I was still standing, so fuck it. *Might as well do what I do best and detonate it all.*

Holden and I said our goodbyes to Ava and Reed, the Burcars and Whitakers, and I got my clutch and went toward the circular drive where the cars were waiting.

I prepped myself mentally a couple of times to ditch Holden at this point. But all my mind focused on were how his hands felt when he traced them across my skin. How his tongue felt inside my mouth. How many times his dick and mouth had made me come.

And how I had fallen in love with a man I could never and would never see again.

As soon as we got to the waiting car, Holden kissed me, hard, and I was grateful for the breath mint Elle had handed me in the bathroom.

We had *one* day. Not even a whole day. Just twelve more hours together then it was over. And I felt weak and sad and I let him make me feel better. I let his touch be the balm against the hurt he had inflicted without his knowledge.

I kissed him back, and just like it always did, it veered out of control. We stumbled into the car and made out the whole way back to the house. Just kissing, but incredible, the best it had ever been. Every nerve in my body was on fire and I felt as though my head would pop off my body.

He held my face as if he cherished me, kissing me soft and slow, fast and hard and all the ways in between. When we got to the house, he stripped my clothes off, piece by slow piece, and we seemed to last for hours. We were sweaty and quiet, not needing our dirty talk or playful ways to get off.

I came on top of him, grinding myself down on his dick while he surged inside me, coming at precisely the same time. Then we lay down and when he was hard once more, we did it all over again. We didn't fall asleep for hours and when we did, it was out of sheer exhaustion.

My heart and my body were worn down. It was all my fault, I knew that. And I feared I would never recover.

Chapter Eight

The next morning, I tried to get ready to leave without making any noise. My mind clearer than it had been, I was angry and hurt and I wanted to get the fuck out of there, fast. I had done half my packing yesterday, but I still had some clothes and toiletries to get into my two bags. I had hung all the items Sloane had let me borrow on hangers outside her bedroom door. I didn't want any charity — from anyone. My bridesmaid dress rested on the chair by the door and I'd tucked it safely inside my suitcase when Holden rolled over and breathed deep, his eyes opening.

"Hey," he croaked, looking over at me.

"Hey," I replied with a tight smile.

"What are you doing?" He sat up. The sheet fell down around his waist and I tried not to stare at his sculpted form. But this was the last time I would see it, so I drank him in for just a moment then shoved my things in my bag.

"Packing. I gotta get the first ferry out. Our flight leaves at eleven and we still have to catch the Jitney."

"I have my plane here. I'll take you back to Columbia later today."

I rotated slowly on my toes and blinked at him. "You have a plane?"

"Yeah. I have a plane. It's parked on the island. My parents aren't leaving so we can fly out whenever we want."

He had a plane. A fucking *plane*. Yeah, maybe if he'd told me this after I'd met him Wednesday afternoon when I'd forced him to carry those champagne bottles, I would've steered clear. Then we wouldn't be here right now. *He owns a goddamn airplane!*

His mom was right. I didn't belong in their world. They had private planes and beach houses. I had second-hand thrift store luggage and a bus ticket.

"I have tickets from JFK." I zipped up my bag.

"So? Get a refund."

"I bought them outright. No insurance. Couldn't afford it," I added the last part in a pissy voice. He didn't seem to notice.

"Okay, well, it doesn't matter if you don't get on the plane. Just stay. I'll get you home whenever you want."

"I work tomorrow."

"So do I. I'll get you back tonight," he countered, still not noticing my attitude or ignoring it.

A knock came on the door and I called out, "Come in!"

Elle stepped in with her bags in hand. "Hey, you ready?" she asked, keeping her eyes averted so she didn't peep at any nakedness.

"Yep. All set." I fastened my second bag.

"Marley, wait." Holden wrapped the sheet around his waist and stood.

"I really can't wait, Holden. We gotta go." I moved toward the door where Elle stood, waiting and watching.

"I— Fuck. I had a day planned. For you." He glanced at Elle then back at me.

"Well, I'm sorry. Nothing I can do."

"Yeah, there is. I'll fly you out later if you want to."

"No. I can't. I can't risk it. We need to leave." I braced myself, leaned in and gave him a quick kiss. I fought through the anger. I fought through the desire. "Thanks for everything this weekend. Take care," I said and rushed toward the stairs.

"Marley— Hell. Just wait one minute," he called but I kept moving, grateful for the waiting cab.

We were back to reality already—no more town cars. No private planes. No ocean views. Home to Columbia and our deteriorating apartment along with my foreseeable, monotonous future.

No billionaire love affairs for this girl anymore. One had been enough to last me a lifetime. The hurt he had inflicted would live inside me forever.

Holden still called after me when I closed the door to the cab and it lurched forward. He raced onto the steps of the house, his pants up around his waist, but nothing else. He watched the car drive off and when we reached the street, I burst into tears.

Elle listened to all of it, every word that exploded from me as I told her what I'd heard him and his mother saying to each other the night before. How I had fallen in love with a man I couldn't have and that as soon as I'd realized it, I'd regretted it.

And it didn't escape me that I had been very wrong when I'd thought Elle would be the one with a broken heart on our journey home.

"Oh, Marley." She let me cry on her shoulder through four separate modes of transportation. By the time we were back at our place in Columbia, I had worn myself out from the weekend and the tears. I went to bed as soon as we hit the door and didn't wake up until midnight.

I stumbled to the kitchen in the middle of the night to get a glass of water and dug into my carry-on for my phone.

I had three messages — all from Holden.

Come back. I want to be with you today.

Did you leave yet?

Happy birthday, Marley.

Yeah. Happy birthday, Marley.

Chapter Nine

I felt hungover the next morning, back in the real world, though I hadn't had a thing to drink. The travel, crying and residual anger from the episode at the wedding had my head feeling stuffed with tissues. I made it to my office with a minute to spare and tried to dive right into work, but my cell phone rattled in my bag. I looked at the display — *Holden*.

Well, here we are. *Off* the island. What I had been dreading because I couldn't predict it. I didn't know what was going to happen with this man so I had avoided thinking about it, then fallen in love and run away.

All my worrying and uncertainty this weekend had been pointless. I'd ended up right where I'd started — back at work, mapping out all the trucks' stops for the week and making lists of all the food that needed to be packed inside.

I silenced my phone and let it go to voicemail. I would listen to the message later, after work, with a bottle of wine and ice cream at my disposal.

It was afternoon by the time I even glanced up from my computer after dealing with the emails from the week prior and scheduling all my drop-offs through this Friday. Ben stuck his head into my office without knocking.

"Hey, you got a second?" he asked.

Fuck. *Ben*. We hadn't spoken since I'd left work last week and I hadn't even given him a second thought most of the weekend. His hump and dump wasn't even on my radar anymore. I had been so preoccupied at having gotten the brush-off and now my heart had been shattered by something that had meant so much more and had perpetrated so much more damage.

I took a deep breath. I'd guessed we were going to just ignore whatever had or hadn't happened between us. That was how he had been performing, so I decided to join him and chalk our little something up to a whole lot of nothing.

"Yeah, sure." I put on a smile and followed him out of my office and into his. He shut the door behind us and leaned against his desk as I sat in a chair in front of him.

Ben was a handsome man. A total do-gooder type who'd gone into the Peace Corps out of college and participated in Teach for America. He always crowdfunded some kind of altruistic cause, and tried to get all of us to go to rallies to save whales and native lands and everything that needing saving.

With his mop of curly brown hair and crooked mouth, I wished I'd felt with him *anything* like I'd felt with Holden, not just gone through the motions because it had seemed like the practical thing to do to be with a man like Ben. But my heart had had other plans. My heart had decided it was going to implode on impact. *Thanks a lot, heart.*

"We need to let you go, Marley," Ben said.

Silence loomed between us.

"Um, what?"

"We are letting you go. You need to turn over all work materials to me and get any personal effects from your desk right away."

I blinked at him, not sure I'd heard him right. "I-I don't understand. You're *firing* me?" I asked, my voice going up while my brain tried to put the words together in a cohesive thought.

"Yes, Marley. We decided as an organization that your behavior on social media this weekend did not represent the mission of Richland Hope." His voice sounded practiced and short.

"My behavior this weekend?" I sat there, thoroughly confused. *How does this weekend have anything to do with my job?*

"Posting photographs of yourself in a bathing suit on a yacht doesn't look good for us, Marley. Partying it up on some swanky island with booze and men is classless. You are one of the faces of our cause and that kind of superficial materialism doesn't sit well with the board."

"Wait, the *board* wanted to fire me? Because of an Instagram post?" I started to panic. This was *not* in my life plan. I could *not* be jobless two days from rent day.

"Because of *several* Instagram posts," he corrected with an eyebrow raised. "Seems you didn't have any trouble making new friends, did you?"

My synapses were firing in all directions — what was he saying? "Wait, are you — are you *jealous*?"

He scoffed. "Hardly. I'm just — let's say — *stupefied* that you moved on so quickly after we consummated our..." He paused, searching for the right word. "Relationship."

"Relationship? *Relationship*?" *Oh, that motherfucker.* He was pissed I hadn't been pining for him! He'd shown the board the pictures because *he* was angry I hadn't become a blubbering mess of goo when he'd ghosted me, so he'd painted me as some kind of vapid hussy and requested they fire me. He had *used* me to satisfy some kind of carnal itch then decided I was expendable — in all facets of his life.

"You can't do this to me, Ben. I have rights," I protested through gritted teeth.

"You're an at-will worker. And the board has taken *my* recommendation on this," he sneered at me, smarmy and satisfied. He knew *just* what he was doing. He had befriended me, worked his way into my life romantically, then, when he had delivered on a mediocre sexual escapade, he'd taken off and hadn't felt comfortable with me viewing our relationship as nothing more than a one-night stand.

"I do a good job here — a *great* job. My performance reviews have always been impeccable. I work overtime, I fill in when you need me — I'm a good employee." My chin started to quiver. *Oh, no. Oh no no no no no.* I would not give Ben York the satisfaction of crying while he canned me.

He remained implacable. No wonder the sex with him had been mediocre. All the passion he'd felt was fake, a farce to look like a guy who cared about his community. He had no passion. Ben York was an asshole, just like all the rest of them—my dad, my stepdad, Holden. They were all the same. *Give them what they want and they'll shower you with love and affection. Take away something and you're pond scum. Shit on the bottom of their shoe.* Replaceable with a redhead with a big bank account and bigger boobs. Just like Melissa Tretter in seventh grade. Not one thing had changed since I'd been twelve years old.

"Clean out your desk, Marley. You know, on second thoughts—" He picked up his phone. "Yes, security? I need a former employee escorted out of my office. Now."

"I have proof, you know. Text messages from you and me, planning to meet up. I could tell the board we slept together. I could show them the things you sent me." Yeah, his messages had been tame compared with the cock shot I'd gotten from Holden—which I had double deleted on my phone. I wasn't that stupid. But they definitely implied an affair. I didn't want to threaten him but he had backed me into a corner. I had to protect myself and my job, the one thing that stood between me and utter destruction right then.

He scoffed at me. "Good thing that's a company phone. So, you won't be taking it with you when you leave."

The door came open and Bert, the old gruff security guard who'd told me he loved my chocolate cookies and always got a big tip from me on holidays, came through the door.

"Let's go, Marley." Bert took my arm as though I was a common criminal. As though I hadn't just fawned over pictures of his new grandson only that morning.

I jutted my chin out in defiance. "I need my purse."

"I'll get it to you outside. Leave the building now, Marley," Ben said, crossing his arms over his chest.

Bert yanked me through the hallways of our buildings, my coworkers all coming to their doors and staring and whispering, making me feel even worse. No one said goodbye or cast out disgust over the unfairness of it all. No one gave me a hug or stomped into Ben's office and demanded answers. They all watched my eyes fill with water, shame and regret. I had so many regrets swimming in my head I couldn't pin down just one long enough to wallow in it. They all swarmed over me like bees buzzing in my ears, humming out the disappointment in me, the disappointment I felt in myself.

I'd taken this job to be smart. I'd done it well. Not my dream job, or what I had always wanted, but I'd held a certain fondness for feeding young children, for obvious reasons, and I'd settled for what I didn't *want* so I would always have what I *needed*. And now, I didn't have that, either.

Security deposited me outside and left, then returned several minutes later with my purse—my phone not inside.

I guessed I'd never know what Holden's voicemail message had said.

I managed to make it home, even though I cried all the way. I had just enough money in my purse for a gallon of caramel delight ice cream and a cheap bottle of fizzy wine. Therein lay a metaphor about my life, but I was too tired and too upset to dig it out.

I lay on the couch, the TV on in the background while I drowned my sorrows. This sucked. This really, really sucked. I hadn't planned for this, which had always been my forte—planning. All my savings had been wiped out by the wedding extravaganza. I didn't know what to do to make ends meet until payday.

I thought about calling my brother—if I'd had a phone, of course, but Ross had less money than I did. He had been saving up to open his own small mechanic shop, and I would never allow him to bail me out with the money he'd worked so hard to put away. He had a dream—he deserved to make it.

I knew Elle couldn't help me—I don't even think she had ice cream and wine money in her purse. She'd been digging through couch cushions for gas money this morning before she'd gone off to her summer tutoring jobs.

I was one-hundred-percent fucked. All my preparations for life's uncertainties hadn't done shit. All my guarding my heart against disaster this weekend hadn't worked, either. I had failed in all aspects of my life.

I could try my parents—Lord knew they owed me. But I didn't have a freaking phone! My mom did love Facebook, though, so maybe she was online.

I fired up the old laptop Elle and I had had since college and logged into my account. All the pictures I'd been tagged in from this weekend had thumbs-up and little hearts by them, with comments from friends and family about how great I looked and how much fun it seemed as though I was having. Heh. If they only knew.

My mom was indeed online so I sent her a message.

Hey, Mom. How are you?

I had texted when I got in yesterday so she knew I was home safe. For all my mom's faults, she did love me. She did worry for me. She just didn't do anything to stop my worries by taking care of her own life.

Gr8 Marley Mae! Did you see that cat video I posted? Lol lmao rotflmao!

I'll have to check it out. Ma – I got fired today.

OMG! WTH? How not fair, baby.

It's really not fair. And my rent is due day after tomorrow.

I waited for her to pipe up and maybe make an offer. I'd hinted pretty hard there.

Maybe you can get an extension?

We already have. It's five hundred and eighty dollars. And we have to pay it Wednesday.

I waited for her to write back.

IDK. Bill spent our first of the month $$ at the track. He had a great tip! Didn't pan out tho. ☹

Yeah, sure he had. He always had a great tip that didn't pan out. And the date was June sixth. They had lost an entire month's resources in six fucking days. Which meant if *I* didn't get some money and fast, *they* were going to go hungry. And as much as I shouldn't care, as much as I should let them struggle the way *I'd* always done, I just couldn't. I wasn't built to let someone get steamrollered by life without holding out my hand to pull them out of the way.

All right, Mom. I gotta go. I'll come by later this week.

Can't w8! Luv U!

Love you, too.

FML. What was I going to do?

* * * *

Elle didn't have any answers, but she did drink the wine and eat the other half of the ice cream.

"I'm so sorry, MJ. You didn't deserve this. Ben is a giant prick. And bad at sex! He can't get away with this. You've always been so dedicated there!" She dished out some great platitudes and it perked me up a bit.

Then she got a call from Slater and disappeared into her room to giggle, I'm pretty sure, get out her vibrator and have phone sex with him. Lucky bitch — she had a *phone.*

I had one credit card with a thousand dollar limit left. I hadn't put anything on it, so I used that to get a phone. It was stupid, I knew that, because I wouldn't be able pay the bill when it came because I didn't have a job.

But not having a phone didn't seem very safe. We hadn't signed up for a house phone and I needed to make the trek to Angler's Haven pretty soon and that stretch of highway could be unkind. I needed to have something with me.

Not to mention I now had to put job-hunting on my life's agenda, and I couldn't tell employers to mail me a letter if they were interested — I had to have a phone number for them to contact me. I spent all day Tuesday updating my résumé and combing over job sites. A few were promising but I doubted Ben and the board at Richland Hope were itching to give me a glowing recommendation so I probably needed to do something shitty. Waitressing. Motel maid. Retail clerk.

But even those jobs were few and far between. All the popular job sites and the local paper had a couple of advertisements, but by the time I called, they had twenty applicants ahead of me and I fell to the bottom of the list. I *was* offered a job right away at a Hooters knock-off restaurant by a slimy, mustachioed manager — my last resort.

I spent all week searching, calling, emailing, following up. It was fruitless endeavor that left me feeling even more defeated than I had been before. After an agonizing week, Friday, pay day, arrived and I could be done hiding out from our landlord in the bowels of our apartment at my computer.

I went by the bank between dropping off applications and found that my paycheck was four hundred dollars short. I called Ben's office on my new phone.

"Ben York," he answered.

"Ben. Marley." I stood in the parking lot by my car, staring at the print-out of my bank statement in one hand and a handful of bills in the other. I didn't have enough to make rent if I paid my other bills and helped out my mom.

"Marley, all calls from you need to go through HR."

"Why is my paycheck short?"

He paused a moment. "You need to speak to HR."

"I'm not fucking calling HR, Ben. You've had your dick in me." I was done being delicate. The situation called for brutal honesty. "Why is my paycheck short?" I asked again, over-enunciating every word.

"Because you weren't paid for your little jaunt to the Vineyard, Marley. We don't pay staff to booze it up and screw around."

"I had vacation time! I took *paid* vacation time for the trip to see my best friend from college get married!" I exclaimed.

"You didn't have enough vacation time in your bank. Sorry." He sounded as smarmy as fuck right then. I wanted to stomp into his office and smack him across the face.

"You can't do this to me, Ben." I fell against my beat-up Hyundai. "I need that money. You know I do."

Ben was not ignorant of my family troubles. We had shared all about ourselves before we'd even started our brief tryst together, when we were just colleagues and friends.

"Can't help you, Marley." He paused. "I'll keep your parents on the monthly food box list. But that's only because they qualify."

"Yeah, well pretty soon *I'm* going to qualify."

"You should've thought of that before you went off and posted to the world what a vapid gold-digger you are. You know, Marley, I always knew I was too good for you. I mean, I obviously went slumming. I regret that now. I thought you were the kind of woman who could make a man like me proud. But you are not that kind of woman. You're just the girl who gets fucked." With that parting shot, he hung up on me.

And the hits just keep on coming.

I guessed I should've fought harder. I should've hired a lawyer if I could have afforded it, or sent a strongly worded letter to the board of Richland Hope, though I didn't want to sully the name of a good organization just because some dickbag asshole worked there. I should've done something to try to save my job or at least save face and what tiny bit of my dignity I had left.

But Ben's words rung in my ear just as Holden's mother's had and, by association, Holden's own — *I'm the kind of girl that gets fucked. He's too good for me. I was a distraction. I didn't belong. I'm not the kind of woman to make a man proud.*

As much as it hurt to hear, it sounded true. All of it. And an expensive attorney couldn't change that.

As I had always known, but forgotten somewhere along the way, Marley Mae Jackson wasn't meant for a fairy tale. A happily ever after. Not in the cards for the poor little girl from Angler's Haven, South Carolina.

I made my way to my and Elle's landlord's office, armed with four hundred bucks and hoping to God the man took it easy on me. And didn't unzip his pants like he'd been known to do to my poor roommate when implying how we could make up the 'difference.'

He sat in his office, mounds of Indian food in front of him, and glared at me from atop his dated glasses. "Yeah?" he asked, picking his teeth with his fingernail.

"Hi, Mr. Vindap. I know we're late. And I don't have it all. But I have four hundred. And I promise I'll get the rest by next Friday." I stepped in and set down the bills in a pretty fan design, hoping to distract him with all the fancy greenbacks so he didn't press.

He stared at me a long minute then grunted, "All right."

I didn't look a gift horse in the mouth. I thanked him and *ran*. Whew. One thing down. I had other bills that needed attention, so those were tended to. Then I pocketed the rest to help my parents.

I thought of Holden's words — '*Fuck 'em. They didn't take care of you so why bother taking care of them?*'

But Holden's once-wise words rang hollow now. He'd been a dick searching for a hole. And anything he'd said between coming on my tits or in my ass was moot. I had just fulfilled a purpose for him. Just like with Ben. Just like with almost every person I had encountered in my now twenty-six years.

I sat on my bed that night, staring at the dented walls that had housed my meager belongings for half a decade. Elle and I had moved in right after college when we'd gotten jobs in Columbia. I'd had a part-time job bartending and had spent my mornings answering phones at an advice hotline, connecting people with local resources. It hadn't paid much, but I'd liked it and managed to get a chunk of student loan debt down with my tips.

Then I'd gotten the job at Richland Hope and I'd thought I was making a difference there. I had families I'd known for almost three years, those that came before the Christmas holiday to get their turkeys, who showed up during the summer to get food from the trucks at the county fair, thanking me with tears in their eyes. I'd made some friends at work and went for drinks to blow off steam and complain about mounting paperwork.

I had built a life for myself, a life I was proud of. A careful and meticulous life, and one I'd thought was full.

But it wasn't full. It was empty, just like my closet. I had five pairs of jeans and six pairs of shoes. A winter coat with holes in the pocket. And I had just spent a week trying to find a job that could barely afford to let me buy a new one. For the first time in my life, I had no idea what I was going to do next and that paralyzed me.

I called Sloane that night. Thank God Elle had most of the contacts I needed in her phone, and I had texted a few friends and my family my new number. Sloane had texted back asking how I was and giving me some grief about leaving the island without saying a proper goodbye but I hadn't wanted to get into the why and everything else at that time. Sloane would try to fix it. And my life couldn't be fixed right now.

She answered on the second ring. "Hey, babe!"

"Hey, Slo." I forced a smile into my voice. "How are you?"

"I'm good! You know, living the dream." She laughed. "I'm thinking about getting a cat. What do you think?"

"I thought you were allergic."

"A hairless one."

"They creep me out," I told her, shuddering. "They're just skin."

"You're just skin."

"Yeah but I wear clothes so you can't see my genitalia."

"True, true."

I smiled. Sloane always made me feel better, even if it was just a tiny, miniscule bit. "How's things in the Big Apple?"

"Eh, the usual, you know. We hired some new girl and she's got teal-colored hair and speaks in a fake British accent. I'm either going to hate her or ask her to move in with me. I don't know yet."

I let out a low laugh.

She was quiet a moment. "What's going on there?"

"Nothing."

"Nothing? Literally nothing? Are you sitting in a vacuum of space surrounded by white noise and blackness?"

"No. I'm sitting in my room."

"It's a Friday night. Why aren't you and Elle out drinking beer at the bar you like or swiping right on some bearded lumberjack on Tinder?"

"I, um—"

"You're working, aren't you?" she said with a groan.

I swiped at a stray tear that fell, forcing myself to speak in an even way. "No. I'm not working."

"Are you crying?"

"No."

"You're lying."

"Slo—"

"Don't lie to me. I can tell through the goddamn *phone* you're lying."

"I got fired," I told her, wiping my nose.

"What? When?"

"Monday. When I got back. Ben said he saw the pictures that Mitch posted and that I didn't fit in at Richland Hope anymore."

"Wait— He fired you because of Instagram photos?"

"He said I didn't represent the image of the organization."

"The image of the organization? Marley, you work your ass off for them. You have for three years! You kicked ass in college, carrying a full course load and working part-time, then you graduated and worked two fucking jobs, then started there and got promoted within six months! How can they fire you?"

"Because I was stupid enough to fuck my boss and he told the board that I was a vapid, superficial, materialistic hussy. I think he was looking for a way to get rid of me and I fucking gave it to him. He was done with me, in more ways than one." I wiped away falling tears.

"That motherfucker. I'm gonna kill him."

"Yeah, well, he also docked my pay. Because he is, in fact, a motherfucker."

"Oh, babe. You need money?" she asked in a flash.

"No. I don't. I'm fine. The kicker is that all the open jobs here require me to wear clothes that are three sizes too small. There's not much else, honestly. And trust me, I've looked. I just—I can't do it right now. I will. Just right now, I can't." I broke down into sobs.

"Come to New York, Marley. Right now. Come and visit me. We'll get this all sorted out," she said, her voice gentle again.

"I can't."

"Why not? What's keeping you there?"

Girl had a point. I mean, I could do that, right? I could run away for a little while. I'd spent seventy bucks on a phone, so I had over nine hundred dollars left on the credit card. I could pay for a ticket and a few things in New York for a week or two—I'd figure out how to pay the bill later when I forced myself to take the job at the Hooters knock-off place with Mr. Mustache Manager. But right now, escape sounded better. Escape sounded like survival.

"I don't know, Slo. I need to find a job." I hesitated.

"Well, New York is hiring," she said with a snort.

"Where would I stay?"

"With me. Of course, with me."

I took a deep breath. "Okay." My voice sounded small.

"I'll buy you a ticket."

"No. No way. You're letting me stay with you, right?"

"Of course."

"Well, that's enough. I just need to find a flight, pack and stuff. And I need to drop off some money at my mom and dad's."

I heard her exasperation that said, *No you don't, Marley. You don't need to take care of them. They need to take care of you.* She had said it enough that I recognized the sound just by her breathing.

"I'll text you the flight details. Okay? You going to be working the next few days?" I asked.

"A little bit. But I'll give you directions for the Subway. And leave a key for you."

"Okay, good. Good. This is—this is good, Sloane. Just what I need."

"What you need is to let me pay for it."

"Absolutely not, Sloane." I used my no-nonsense voice. I didn't even know I had that voice inside me anymore. I'd figured the last week had made it dissolve along with my self-worth.

"I'm so sorry about the job, MJ," she said. "I know you loved it."

"I kind of did. I mean it wasn't soil judging, but it made me happy."

"Yeah, well we can't just sit around all day on our ass judging soil, can we? Starving people need food."

"Yeah. Yeah, they do."

"All right. Book a flight. Text me details. Dying to see you," she said. "I mean it's been a week and I miss your gorgeous and perfect ass."

I laughed. "Me too, Slo. Love you."

"Love you, babe." She hung up.

I took a hot shower, made myself some tea and considered spiking it with liquor to help me sleep, but we only had shitty gin and I didn't think that would mix well with chamomile lemon tea. I got out a book I had brought to read on my trip to Martha's Vineyard, but hadn't cracked open once for obvious reasons. Elle knocked at my door then poked her head in.

"Hey," she said, pushing the door open further and stepping in. "I smell tea."

"Yeah, I made the last bag. But get some water and we can share it," I offered.

She gave me a smile and disappeared, returning a few minutes later with a steaming mug of water.

She snuggled into the bed beside me, stealing my tea bag and squeezing the rest of the flavor out of it. She took a sip and swallowed. "It sucks."

I laughed out loud for the first time in days.

"I thought you finished that book while we were on the island." She gestured to the Jack Reacher novel sitting on my lap.

"No. I didn't get a chance because I was too busy getting fucked then getting fucked," I said with a loud sigh.

She shot me a sympathetic smile. "I heard you're going to New York."

I swallowed. "Wow. Good news travels fast."

"Is it good news?"

"It's not bad news. So that's a vast improvement around here."

"Well, I think its good news. But Slo — she seemed to think you were doing this out of desperation."

"I probably am." I exhaled a long breath. "There are no jobs here. The bagger at Valuland has a Ph.D. in Chemistry. Honestly, the one thing I applied for that seemed promising is that pseudo-strip club by the highway."

"Ew, gross. I met the manager there once. Super creep." Elle wrinkled her nose in response.

"Super-duper creep," I agreed.

"Listen, I know you, Marley Mae. Better than *you* know you. And you're blaming yourself for this. You didn't do anything wrong by going on vacation and posting pictures of it online."

"Yeah, well, there are some who would beg to differ."

"Fuck Ben York."

"I did. That's what got me into this mess."

"He'll get what's coming to him. Even if it's in the form of me slashing his tires."

"You say the sweetest things." I brought my mug to my lips.

"You're thinking that taking a chance and going to New York to find work is too big a step for you."

"It is a big step!"

"It's what you need to do, MJ. You have to get out of here."

I stared at her. "Elle — *you're* here."

"I know," she said with a humorless laugh. "And I've been trying to escape for years. And maybe — maybe I will this time."

I looked over at her, watching her take another sip of weak tea. "Maybe you will this time?"

She shrugged, "Maybe it's time we both stopped living in the past, being afraid to have a big life, and start taking chances."

I swallowed. "I took a chance, Elle. It backfired."

"No, it didn't. You heard something you shouldn't have and ran away. I think—I think you need to find out what Holden really meant."

"I know what he meant. I heard him. I was a distraction, that's all."

She shook her head. "I don't believe that."

"I do."

"Because you're a scaredy-cat, Marley. And you *want* to believe it so you can hunker down back into our safe little life here and not go out on a limb. Fuck that. *Go out on a limb*. If the tree breaks, I'll put you back together."

"You really think I should go? That I should—see Holden?"

She set her eyes on me. "I think you should start living life as it comes and stop worrying about what's around the next corner. You can't predict it. You can't know. So—just be brave. Hope for the best. And if the worst comes, I'm here."

I shifted my cup to my other hand and threw my arm around my friend. "I love you, Elle Belle."

"I told you to never call me that," she said, all mock anger.

"Yeah, well, you told me to live dangerously. And here I am."

She squeezed me hard, we finished our tea and she headed to bed, kissing me on the forehead and reminding me to be courageous—and flip on the coffeemaker before I left in the morning. *Roommates.*

I felt better, much better after bonding with my roomie, my oldest friend.

Then I remembered Holden's body curved next to mine in sleep, that morning I had woken up and he'd stared at me, so gentle, so sincere, told me I was breathtaking, that he was lucky. And I started crying again.

Chapter Ten

I managed to get a reasonable flight for noon the following day, so I had just enough time to head out to my mom and dad's and drop off a hundred bucks and pick up some groceries I'd grabbed for them before I left. They were, as always, home, waiting for it. And they were, as always, asking for more.

"It's all I have right now." I didn't bother to remind my mom that I had lost my job and had asked her for money earlier that week.

"Well, that's a damn shame. Thought you was a big-time city girl now with all yous fancy friends," my stepdad scoffed at me across the stained kitchen table.

"She lost her job, Bill. I told you that," my mom spat at him.

Bill swirled the toothpick to the opposite side of his mouth. "Well, then, how'd she get dis money righ' here, huh?"

"I had a final paycheck coming. And I needed to pay rent." I didn't owe this man an explanation *why* I couldn't give them more of *my* money when they should have their own, but I did it anyway, because my no-nonsense voice had melted away again.

"All them big ol' student loans you got ain't worth nothin' now, are dey?" my stepdad sneered at me.

The man may be an asshole, but he was right. And that bill was overdue, too. *Fuck.*

"She'll find a job, Bill. She got resources." My mom tried to defend me, but I doubted Bill knew what the word *resources* meant. "Thanks for the food, honey." My mom patted my hand. "We know you'll bring by more money when you have it."

Not "Could you maybe bring by more money?" or "We would so much appreciate it if you could bring more money by?" Nope. Just "We know," because I would. I always would.

I said my goodbyes and didn't mention my trip to New York because that would be a kerfuffle I was hell-bent on avoiding and stopped by Ross' shop to shove a hundred bucks into his grease-covered back pocket.

"What's this for?" he asked with a laugh.

"Mom and Dad. I'm going to visit Sloane and I just dropped off groceries and money to them. But I might be gone a few weeks and I didn't want it to all fall on you when they need more."

"Well, thanks, Marley. Appreciate it." He hugged me.

"Ick, now I'm covered in cooties."

He chuckled. "How was the wedding?"

"It was good. You know, the island is pretty. The ocean was pretty. I even learned how to swim a little bit," I told him with a small smile. I guess the trip hadn't been useless. If there should ever be a forty-day Noah's Ark kind of flood or I managed to go to a town that didn't use the river as a garbage dump, maybe I could use my new skills again.

"You did? That's great." He was genuinely happy for me, because Ross is a genuine guy.

Sometimes, I don't know how we got out of our house alive, let alone with the capacity to give a shit about other people. But there we were, giving so much shit that we were going broke taking care of everyone around us.

"Hey, man, that your hot sister there?" one of the guys called from inside the bays.

"Ignore him. He's already got two ex-wives and four kids—none of 'em with the ex-wives," Ross commented.

Yeah, that sounds about right for Angler's Haven.

"Ignoring. I'll call you soon. Love you." I gave him another quick hug and walked toward my car.

"You're a good girl, Marley. The best!" he said with a wave.

I waved back and smiled. Not the best—barely good enough for much of anything right now. But I was lucky enough to have a brother who would think the world of me, no matter what.

* * * *

The flight from Columbia to New York City sped and I managed to not get lost in the bowels of the city's Subway system. I had been there a few times to visit, but Sloane always had a new place so I was heading into the unknown. Not that I could remember and navigate the complex streets of New York from memory, anyway.

The sun shone bright and it helped to perk up my mood. Then I almost got mugged and my mood dropped again. I felt as though life was trying to test me. *Like, maybe if we push this girl just far enough, she'll crack.*

I fended off the would-be robber and got to Sloane's unscathed. She'd left a key for me with the girl at the front desk of her building, since she *would* live in a place that had a freaking front desk girl. I took the elevator to the fourth floor and let myself into her apartment.

The space, which was larger than her last place, had graceful, high ceilings and coved window arches. The floors were shiny beech, covered with deep, burgundy rugs and she'd had each room decorated with impeccable taste. It was very Sloane.

She'd made up the guest room for me and I crawled without hesitating onto the fluffy white queen-size bed and curled on my side. I didn't know what the hell to do with my life now. I didn't know what I had to offer anyone.

But I still had my friends. My beautiful, supportive, gorgeous friends. And right now, that would help me make it through anything. Just like they always had.

I had gone broke to watch Ava get married and I would do it again for any one of them. I had been blessed with three of the most stunning, generous, genuine women on the planet. In that way, I would always be lucky, because I would always have them.

And it didn't take long for one of those friends to arrive.

"Hello hello!" Sloane called, coming in.

I had almost dozed off and popped up when I heard her voice.

"Hey, babe!" she said with a wide smile.

"Hi!" I smiled back and she hugged me tight. Then I lost it. "Holden said I was poor white trash."

She went taut, her arms still around me. "He what?"

I stood back and her arms dropped. "The night of Ava and Reed's wedding. I found him talking to his horrible, aging-badly mother and she called me poor white trash."

"You said *he* called you poor white trash." She sounded confused.

"She did. He didn't argue. So, it's like he said it."

"Come sit down." She towed me over and onto one of the modern-style couches in her living room. "Go back a bit. How did you hear this?"

"I went searching for him and they were in the parlor room at the hotel. I stopped by the door and heard them talking."

"And she just straight up said you were poor white trash?"

"No, she said I was a distraction. That he had been using me to get through the weekend without Spencer there."

"That's not true, Marley. I saw him and you together. He cares for you."

I shook my head. "No, he doesn't. He said he had no intention of there being anything more between us than what happened on the island. He said he would look up Tish when he got back because she's more his type."

"He said that?" Sloane asked, stunned. *Welcome to my world.*

"She said I didn't belong with people like them. That we were being uncouth, running around with each other. And he said, and I quote, 'I agree with everything you said, Mother'."

"Wow. I mean, I just — I was really wrong about him. Well, I was right, at first. Then wrong, then kind of right?"

"Yeah. You were right." I said it with a sad laugh.

"Oh, babe." She wound an arm around me. "You are way too good for a man like Holden Pierce. You're out of his league, not the other way around."

"You're saying that because you love me."

"I'm saying that because everyone loves you, Marley. You're so good and sweet. And you help everyone who needs it. As soon as anyone has a problem, they always go to you because you always help them. No questions asked. No thanks necessary. You are a fucking diamond, my friend, and Holden blew the best thing he could've ever had."

"It felt so real with him, though. It felt — right," I said, sniffling. "I fell in love with him, Sloane."

She hugged me hard to her. "There's a better man out there, waiting for you. I know it."

I sniffed back more tears. "I need to get him out of my head."

"Great! I know just how to do it. Slater and the guys are meeting at some café for dinner. Let's tag along."

"Slater and what guys?" I asked.

"Mitch and Ethan. Come on, don't dilly-dally. Let's get you in some knock-out sexy romper and hit the town!" She popped up and headed for her master bedroom.

"I don't know. I feel weird," I admitted, ambling after her into her room.

"Why?"

"I mean, I just saw those guys. Glued to Holden. What if they ask about it?" I sat on the edge of her bed. Her opulent room had been decorated in pink and she had a huge princess bed in the center. Her closet mimicked the size of my room back home.

She snorted from behind the door. "They won't ask."

"How do you know?"

She poked her head out. "Because they all wanted to fuck you while we were there. So all they're gonna do is try to fuck you again." She ducked back in.

"Slater didn't."

"Yeah, well, Slater's the exception. And he won't give up any details about what's going on with him and Elle, no matter how many times I ask."

"They had phone sex. I know that."

She came out of her closet. "They're still talking?"

"Yep. Every day. At least once."

"Huh. Well, I'll be damned." She went back into the closet and came out with three summer silk rompers on hooks. "Pick one."

"Whichever one covers the most skin."

She tossed the opposite one at me and went back to the closet.

"He called me. Holden did," I told her and she peeked back out.

"When?"

"Monday. The day after we got back. Left a message."

"What did it say?"

I shrugged. "I have no idea. When I lost my job, they took my phone before I could listen to it."

"Just as well. He probably said something stupid like, 'Oh hey, have you seen my cufflinks?'" She put on a deep guy voice that made me giggle.

"I never saw him wear cufflinks."

"That's because you were always naked together," she called out from the closet.

I took a quick shower to wash off the travel grime and dressed in the navy floral-designed romper with the three hundred and ninety-five bucks price tag still on it. The girl was a clothes horse and I felt thankful again we were nearly the same size.

I slipped on my sandals, which Sloane allowed me to wear because I didn't have any other options, and she told me they worked. Then she said we were going shoe shopping the next day. I didn't argue, but I had a feeling she would be buying shoes and I would be window shopping.

We were meeting the guys at a place near where they lived in Brooklyn, so we had to take a cab. Sloane refused to use the Subway unless absolutely necessary or when Elle and I had insisted on our trips to visit because we were always going for the cheaper option. She told me she'd planned to splurge on a cab and I didn't argue. I didn't have it in me right then. And considering all the other things she wanted to pay for and I had refused, a cab ride seemed like a good compromise.

The driver let us off in front of a place called the Black Cat, and I recognized straight away Slater's dark hair and handsome profile seated at a table outside on a patio.

"Yo! I have a surprise!" Sloane announced as we walked around the fencing toward them and all three guys swiveled to look at me.

"Fuck, Marley!" Ethan said, jumping up and hugging me, spinning me around in a circle.

He set me back down and placed a wet kiss on my cheek. "Hey, Ethan."

Slater stood and gave me a kiss and a grin. "Good to see ya, babe."

Mitch gave me a wide smile, holding me a little too tight, a little too long, and giving me a kiss a little too close to my mouth. "You look radiant."

"That's because Sloane made us take a cab so I don't have Subway slime all over me." I stepped back and settled into the chair Ethan held out for me at the head of the table.

"I refuse to go sublevel." Sloane scrunched her nose in disgust.

"You here for a visit?" Slater asked, taking a long sip of beer.

"Yeah. Came to see Slo for a few days. Maybe a week or two." I forced myself not to think ahead. Not to freak out that I had an open-ended ticket back home. That even if I went back home, nothing existed much for me there.

Living in the moment, girl about town, flying by the seat of my pants — a new Marley Mae Jackson from now on! *Woo-hoo! Freedom!* I shoved down more bubbling panic.

"Nice. Best time to be in NYC, baby. In June. Before the garbage starts to stink." Ethan took a sip of draught beer from a pint.

"City gets so hot that trash just fucking bakes on street corners. It's sick," Mitch explained.

"Ew, gross." I shuddered.

"You get used to it," Slater insisted.

"No way. I can't get used to that. I grew up in a town that was surrounded by a lake that doubled as a toxic waste dump. I'm never living in a smelly city again," I said as the waitress walked up. I was already searching for excuses to run away back home like a scared little kid. How pathetic had I become?

She took a drink order and the guys ordered a few small plates to snack on.

"So, how's my girl?" Slater asked me.

"Is Elle your girl?" Sloane asked, a sly smile on her face.

Slater just shrugged, not giving anything up.

"She's good. Buying lots of batteries," I told him.

Slater furrowed his brow in confusion as Sloane bellowed, "For her vibrator, dumbass." She whacked her brother on the arm. "Because you two have been cyber-ing for a week now."

"Oh, yeah," Slater said, with a wave of his hand. "She's a fucking wildcat that one. Tight as a fucking drum."

Ethan fist-bumped him with a smile and Mitch chuckled.

Sloane covered her ears. "Gross. I didn't want to hear her talk about your dick and I really don't want to hear you talk about my best friend's vagina."

Slater just shrugged.

"Speaking of island love affairs," Ethan said and I braced myself for someone's question about Holden, "I got to watch Nanette scissor with some chick on the car ferry back to New York."

Whew, relief. And uh, kind of gross, Ethan.

"Did she know you were there or did you creep up on her with your phone out?" Mitch asked.

"She knew, oh, man, she knew. Girl picked up a total stranger on the ferry and they just started going at it in the back of a Beemer. It was *smoking*, dude," Ethan assured us.

"I didn't figure Nanette for the stranger-danger type," Slater commented.

"She is," Sloane and I both replied in unison.

"Kind of hot, I gotta say. I mean, I don't mind a little public action, you know. As long as it's consensual," Ethan told us.

"Its weirds me out." Sloane took the outstretched beer the waitress handed her. "There's too many cameras all over this city. Remember when that kid got kidnapped and they found him, like, three hours later using ATM and traffic cameras? Anything you do around here is captured forever in the cloud."

"Good point, Slo." Slater swallowed a sip of beer.

Ethan's face went gray. "Oh, shit."

We all laughed at his expense. Hard not to.

We sat and ate for a while. We talked about the fun we'd had that weekend. Mitch, of course, snapped a couple of selfies of us to post to Instagram.

"Careful with that. You got my girl fired," Sloane told him as she and I were heading out to another bar.

"What?" Mitch asked, darting his gaze between us.

"Her boss, and her ex-lover, saw the pics from the island and canned Marley on Monday. That's how she's here," Sloane explained and all the guys stared at me.

"Oh, fuck, really? Shit, Marley, I'm so sorry." Mitch grew ashen.

"It's not your fault. I shouldn't have been fired for it. Please, don't feel bad." I gave a dismissive wave.

"So, wait, you're not here to see Holden?" Slater blinked at me.

"Oh, there's a cab. We gotta go. See you dudes later!" Sloane saved me from having to answer that.

"Thanks," I told her as the cab drove away.

"Anytime. Now let's get wasted and forget all our troubles." She grinned.

We did for a few nights straight. Drinking a lot and eating late-night fried foods, which made me feel as though we were back in college.

When Sloane had to go to work on Tuesday, we slowed our pace. We switched to watching Netflix and eating takeout. We shopped in upscale second-hand stores and went to see a show on Broadway.

Every time we went out and did something spontaneous and fun, I expected to feel a backwash of regret, to have my subconscious kick in and tell me I was making another horrid mistake. But I didn't. I just went with it. I knew eventually I would have to go back, find a job and reenter the real world.

For the time being, though, I enjoyed just *being*. I sent my résumé out to dozens of food pantries and non-profits, and even had call-backs from a few. But I wasn't in a rush. I felt like if I went too fast, if I jumped into this with both feet first, I might regret it. So, I was moving slowly.

But I didn't miss home one bit. Or going a whole week without calling my parents or putting one single thing on my long-term agenda. It felt really good, freeing and peaceful.

And yet, underneath all the fun we were having, and the change of scenery I had desperately needed, I missed Holden.

We'd had so little time together and yet the intensity of it made me crave him. I felt like an addict who needed her next fix. I just needed a kiss, or a smile— *something*.

All his social media accounts were private, so I couldn't even properly stalk him and I flat-out refused to send a friend request. I hoped to God I never reached that kind of desperation — to try to be Facebook friends with a man who'd tossed me aside once his dick deflated.

I did sneak into Sloane's phone one night and find his contact info, and decided to grow some grapes and call him. It had been over a week since he had called me, but I could just call him back, right? It was the polite thing to do and I was nothing if not polite.

But I wussed out. I put her phone back and tiptoed to my room, lying awake and thinking about Holden. And, for the first time since I'd gotten there, crying myself to sleep.

Chapter Eleven

My tennis shoes squeaked across the marble floor of the wide vestibule and I had my hood drawn up to try to keep some of the rain out of my face, though it didn't do much. I was drenched from head to toe. And, knowing myself as well as I did, and counting on the string of *awesome* luck I had had as of late, I moved at a snail's pace so I didn't skid on the floor and tumble to the ground with a giant container of chicken noodle soup in my hands, and bust my femur.

I made it halfway across the floor, my hood still drawn up, my eyes on my feet, when a trio of bodies came toward me. I skittered to the other side of the floor to get out of their way, keeping my eyes focused on the floor, when I heard a deep voice.

"Marley?"

Holy fuck, I knew that voice. I knew that voice so well it shot a lightning strike in a straight line through my backbone that exploded in every vein in my body.

It was the voice of a man who sounded older than his years, deep and rough, lacking any enthusiasm at all.

I froze. I cringed. My stomach fell like a lead anvil into my soggy Keds.

With painful slowness, I gazed up to see Holden Pierce standing there, cell phone to his ear and wearing a button-up shirt with the sleeves rolled to the elbows, and tailored pants. He looked *just* as he had the first time I'd set eyes on him on the staircase at Reed's parents' house on Martha's Vineyard, three weeks ago today.

"Holden." I swallowed a lump of emotion creeping up my throat. What were the odds in a city this enormous? Eight and a half million people and there stood the man my heart wouldn't let go, two feet away.

There were two other guys with him, one older and one younger, both in suits and carrying briefcases, staring at me as though I were a bug under a microscope. I probably came across like a waterlogged hobo, my top with the holes along the collar clinging to my damp skin and the shorts I've had since high school bearing the marks of their years.

I shifted, shuffling my feet. *Why does the universe hate me?* "How-how are you?" I spluttered.

"What are you doing here?" he asked, ignoring my question about his general wellbeing, raking his gaze over my dripping form, confusion furrowing his brow.

"Uh, Sloane lives here. Fourth floor. She's sick with the flu so I got her some chicken noodle soup." I held up the paper bag in my hand as proof. I should've told him I planned to marry Prince Harry in a Central Park ceremony tomorrow. Anything to make myself seem less pitiful than I felt.

"I mean what are you doing here in New York?" he asked, his phone still at his ear. I heard a voice blast through the speaker and he hung up without saying another word, still gazing at me.

"Visiting Sloane," I semi-repeated.

"I saw—fuck—I saw a picture of you that Mitch posted, but I didn't think—"

"Yeah, it's me. I'm here." I raised my hand up and waved like a total dork. "We went to hang out with Slater and he was with Mitch and Ethan. So, huh, three-for-one special." God, could I make this any worse by acting as if I had never interacted with a human being before? I wanted the ground to open up and swallow me whole.

An uncomfortable silence passed between us while I fumbled for an excuse to get away. Or develop the courage to declare my undying affection for him.

"I called you," he said and I shifted closer to him when a family of four passed by behind me.

Even closing that tiny bit of space between us made my pulse quicken and my breath stammer in puffs. God, he was good-looking. I thought I'd remembered how I felt in his presence when I thought about him— dead wrong. Those dark coffee-tinted eyes, the thick lashes, the naturally striking face. He seemed taller somehow, maybe because I was slouching and wearing my embarrassment in my vertebrae, hunched over like Quasimodo. He *still* felt all-consuming. He *still* forced the air in my lungs to speed up. He *still* gave me that flash, the spark, the one I had so desperately ached to feel with someone my entire life—it was right *there*, like a goddamn livewire igniting and glowing inside my heart.

"Yeah?" I asked, scooting back as soon as I could to try to get some space between us again. To get my goddamn head on straight and remember all the things I should be remembering right then. How he had dismissed me to his mother. How I'd existed as a mere roll in the hay, a detour on my precision-drawn life plan, who didn't belong with a man like him. How he had said he could never fall in love with someone like me.

"Yeah. About a dozen times." He didn't seem mad. He didn't seem—*anything*. He talked to me as though he was in shock, his voice devoid of emotion. I remembered that Holden, too. The one who'd shut off, who'd removed himself from everything around him. And sadly, I even missed *this* version, not just the one who came like a gladiator and laughed at my jokes as if he had never heard something so amusing in his life.

"Well, I lost my phone." I shifted again, my skin and clothes still sending droplets of water onto the floor beneath me.

"You lost your phone?"

He seemed determined to not make my transition to not being a freak here any easier. I felt so painfully inelegant and jumbled right then.

"Yeah, well, I didn't lose it. I got fired and it was in point of fact a company phone, so even when I went to get a new one I had to get a new number and the thing I got is so basic I don't even know if—"

"You got fired?"

I nodded, swallowing. "Yeah. I did. My boss—uh, you know, my, uh, Ben, the CEO? Well, he saw the pictures Mitch posted from the island and said I didn't represent the Richland Hope mission statement. That lying on a yacht in a skimpy bathing suit didn't, um, jive with the image of a woman who ran a soup kitchen." I fought back the tears that threatened since this was all still so fucking raw. "And he's kind of right. I mean, I doubt it helped that I slept with him once, but I didn't have any proof of it since he confiscated my phone and they escorted me out like a goddamn felon." I lost the battle to hold back tears and a few leaked out of the corners of my eyes. "It was so embarrassing."

I have no idea why I'd blurted all that out to him. Probably because I still acted like a Martian that just crash-landed on planet Earth. A giant meteor could show up anytime now!

"That's fucking bullshit, Marley." He clenched his fists by his sides.

"Well, it *was* embarrassing. I mean, they didn't even let me go back to my desk – " I started to defend myself.

"Not that. Firing you. They don't have the right to do that."

"Oh. Well, I was an at-will employee. So, they could fire me for whatever they wanted. What really sucks is they docked my pay for the wedding trip and I ended up fucked. I applied for a ton of jobs, but Columbia's economy is like dead. I considered selling an internal organ."

Why did I continue to vomit all this information at him? I doubted he gave a shit. I mean, I was prepared to bet he'd already queued Tish up on speed dial per his mother's suggestion. Last I heard, he'd put her on deck as soon as he came back to New York.

"Anyway, I came up here to see Sloane for a bit. Get my bearings. You know." I lifted one shoulder in a half-shrug. "So, how are you?" Shit, I'd just blown my chance to skitter away by asking a direct question.

Truth was, I didn't want this to end. I didn't want him to walk away.

"Fine. Busy. Work." I could tell he was still trying to process all this. And maybe trying to escape and get away from this crazy New York version of me. The babbling one without an ounce of self-preservation.

And I stood soaking the floor beneath us from the rain. "I should get going." I took a step backward, but Holden moved closer to me.

"No, wait. I — shit — I'm supposed to go to a meeting. I'm buying this building." He turned toward one of the silent dudes with him.

"Oh, really?" I glanced up and around at the gaudy chandelier above us and the outdated wallpaper behind him.

"Yeah, owner called me out of the blue, said he heard I was in the market for locations like this."

"It's nice. Needs some modern décor maybe." I offered my opinion even though he didn't ask for it. "I mean, the wallpaper looks like snozzberries." I gestured behind him and he glanced at it then barked out a loud laugh. *Fuck, I missed that sound.*

The two guys who were with him were taken aback by his response and I wondered if he had ever shown amusement around them before. The reactions led me to believe that he hadn't. They were gawking at him as if he was a pod person.

He faced off with them and spouted off some legal and business-y words to one guy, promised to do something or other with some kind of doohickey to the other, then turned to me once they'd stridden away.

"Bye," I said with a clumsy wave to their backs.

The older guy kept moving but the younger twisted around and waved back. That made me feel a little better. Maybe I didn't look like the Hunchback of Notre-Dame crossed with the Great Gazoo.

"They're fun," I joked and his face split into a wide smile. Boy, had I missed that smile, too. I didn't even realize how much until I saw it again.

"Where's Sloane's place?" he asked, heading toward the bank of elevators.

"Four ten. And she has a leak in one of the bathroom showers. So, if you're buying this place, you should get that fixed for her."

"I'll get right on that."

"Are you really buying this place?" I asked, pressing the elevator button.

"Don't know for sure," he said, his hands in his pockets. "It's way overpriced. They want sixteen for it, but I'm not paying more than twelve."

I knew enough now to know he was talking about big money.

"Sixteen million dollars?" I couldn't stop myself from wheezing.

"Yeah, but it's Lower East Side. The resale just isn't the same for buildings like this. Lower East Side doesn't have the appeal it used to."

"Yeah, it's totally dead and lame here. Pssh. Game over, man." I faked a surfer guy accent and he chuckled, his eyes lingering on mine for a long moment. He seemed poised to say something profound, but thank God the elevator opened and we stepped in, all at once very close together in a very small space. He still smelled like him—that woodsy cologne that I had discovered is something called Clive Christian Number 5. I couldn't afford even a small bottle, but I did go to Nordstrom's in Charlotte once during my seemingly endless job search and spray it into my bag so I could smell it when I wanted to for a few days.

He pressed the number four and I gave him a small smile, fidgeting with the pull strings on my zip-up.

"You look good, Marley," he said, his eyes on me again.

"I look like a drowned cat." I shook the water out of my long ponytail.

"Just like I remember you."

"So, I always look like a drowned cat?" I asked with an eyebrow raised.

"No, you were wet. From the ocean. That's how I think of you. That day at the beach, just you and me. I think about that every fucking hour. What the hell happened, Marley?" he asked bluntly.

I swallowed. *I don't think I'm ready to do this. Not here. Not now. Maybe not ever.*

The doors skated open and I stepped into the hall, moving toward Sloane's apartment. "I need to get this soup to her, but um, I guess we could talk if you wanted to," I said, not daring to meet his eyes. Knowing if I did, I would break down and tell him everything.

That I had fallen in love with him. That I *thought* he was falling in love with me. But that I had heard the conversation with his mother in the parlor on the day of the wedding and I knew that I had been duped. And that I would never have him.

"Yeah, I'd like to talk," he said, close behind me while I unlocked the deadbolt with Sloane's keys. This man was going to annihilate me. I knew it.

I pushed the apartment door open and called out, "Hey, sick girl, I'm back." I dropped her keys into the ceramic bowl she had on the buffet by the entryway.

"In here. I puked up something green. I don't even remember eating it." Her voice sounded stuffed up.

"I brought, um, a visitor," I said, slipping out of my wet shoes and padding across the rug to the living room.

Sloane smiled until Holden came into view behind me. "Uh, what in god's name, is he doing here?"

"Sloane!" I admonished. I loved my bestie, but I didn't need her to pick up one of her 'defend Marley' crusades right now. My gut had already screwed itself in knots over this entire interaction and I wanted the rest of it to be as easy as possible—should that be an option. "Please, um, have a seat." I gestured toward the couch in the living room.

"Good to see you again, too, Sloane," Holden remarked, seating himself across from where Sloane had parked herself, covered in Kleenex and blankets.

She glared at him in response and I lifted the bag to show her the chicken noodle soup. "They only sell it by the gallon, it seems, so I'll get you a bowl. You need anything else? Water or ginger ale? I got some of that, too."

"Just water, thanks," she replied, her voice still icy as she stared across the room at Holden. I scurried to the kitchen. I had to get this done so Holden and I could have our *talk* then I could go back to being melancholy. I'd gotten pretty good at it. I should have hosted an online class to give tips and tricks on how to implode your life then wallow in self-pity for the rest of eternity. "So, how did you two run into each other?" Sloane asked.

"I was in the lobby. I've been thinking about buying the building. I met the appraisers to see what they think it's worth," I heard Holden tell her.

"My shower leaks," Sloane informed him.

"Yeah, I heard about that," he replied, a smile in his voice.

I got them both glasses of water, prepared Sloane a bowl of soup and brought it out to them.

"You want anything?" I asked, offering Holden the second cup of water.

"No, thanks," he said, his eyes on me when I handed Sloane the soup and put both waters on coasters on her table. I went over and sat next to him on the couch, as far away as I could without sitting on the windowsill. That seemed sort of insulting. I mean, we could share a sofa, for crying out loud. I wasn't that pathetic. Was I?

"I got a text from that bitch Rita at work. She said the whole office has the same fucking sick disease. Which means some asshole came in and spewed germs all over and now I'm paying for it," Sloane bitched, taking a tiny spoonful of broth.

"I didn't realize you worked, Sloane," Holden said.

"Yes, I work." Sloane narrowed her eyes at him. "Though I can occasionally extract myself from it. I'm not obsessed like some people, determined to make millions by the time they hit thirty."

"*Billions*," I corrected her without even thinking first.

Sloane continued to glare at Holden. "I'm surprised Marley never told you during your weekend love affair."

"Told me what?" Holden toggled his eyes between us.

"What I do for a living. Why I do it." Sloane looked at me. "You didn't tell him?"

"You know I would never do that, Slo," I said.

Her eyes softened. Then they hardened when she glared over at Holden. "I was sexually assaulted at Clemson. My freshman year."

She said it so with no trouble at all now. I remember the time she couldn't even get the words out, when I'd forced her to say them. She'd wanted to blame it on her outfit, her drinking, having led him on. But I hadn't bought that bullshit excuse. It had been sexual assault. And she'd needed to know that or she would never get past it.

Holden's whole body went rigid. "Fuck, Sloane. Damn, I'm sorry."

She shrugged, taking another spoonful of soup down. "I dealt with it. And I dealt with it because of my guardian angel sitting there next to you."

I blushed red. She hadn't called me that in a long time. She had, after everything had settled. After she'd made her police reports and started with the counseling, she'd gotten her life back on track. We'd been sitting in the dorms after midterms our second semester, midterms which she hadn't thought she had a chance in hell of passing and she had with flying colors. She'd turned to me with tears in her eyes, one of the few times I had ever seen Sloane cry, and told me I was her guardian angel. That I had been sent to earth, and in this place at this moment, because I had been meant to help her through this.

I'd told her I was honored to be. That I wouldn't want to be anywhere else.

Thinking of it even now, I teared up.

"She is the only person I told. And she kept my secret. She cleaned me up that night, and kept all my clothes under her bed for the police. She never left my side, missed half her classes for two weeks while she sat by me, helping me, making everything okay. She forced me to tell a counselor. She went with me when I told the cops. She sat out in the lobby during support meetings so I didn't have to go alone. She was my fucking rock." Sloane's voice cracked. "She still is."

"No, I'm not," I said, wiping my eyes. "You don't need a rock anymore, Slo. You're tough as nails."

"No. Sometimes I break, and you're always there. *Always*." She gazed at me with a soft smile. Then she focused her narrowed gaze on Holden. "So, yeah. She's a good girl. A *great* girl. The best there is. She's better than a fucking weekend *distraction*. She's better than someone to sow your wild oats with or whatever the fuck you were doing then settling down with Tish Syphilis Martindale." Sloane really geared up to go off here, so I stood to stop her.

"I'm going to show Holden out. We don't want to catch your sickness, anyway." I shimmied past Holden toward the door.

"What the fuck are you talking about, Sloane?" Holden asked, the muscle in his jaw straining.

"She heard you, you dickwad. That night of the wedding. When you told your mommy that Marley meant nothing to you. That all she was was a fucking distraction so you could get through the weekend without thinking about your brother. You said when the weekend ended, and you were back to your life, you would call up Tish and get together with her. Because she's more 'your type of girl'." Sloane used air quotes with her fingers for the last part.

Holden turned his eyes toward mine, his whole body pent-up tight and looking like a tiger ready to strike. I found myself moving farther back from him. "You heard that?"

I nodded. "Yeah, I did. And honestly, Holden, you didn't say anything I hadn't thought myself —"

"You heard that and didn't say anything to me?" His voice rose when he stood.

"I-I didn't know how," I said, backing and bumping into the breakfast bar behind me. Maybe I had known how, but maybe I'd also known deep down that if I'd said something, and he had confirmed all I'd heard to my face, it would have destroyed me.

"You didn't know how? You just *say* it. I was in your room that night, fucking you for hours."

"I know, Holden," I said, my voice quiet as he continued his march toward me.

"I had my dick balls-deep in your pussy, *my* fucking pussy, and you didn't know how to tell me?" His voice grew louder, tighter, angrier, bearing down fast. I had nowhere to go so I braced for impact. Then I got pissed.

This wasn't *my* fault! This was *his* fault!

"You were so fucking cold, so callous! You said it so goddamn easily, like 'Oh yeah, Ma, this girl doesn't mean shit to me and you're right that she's poor white trash and I could never have anything more than a fling with poor white trash. That's all they're good for,'" I shot back at him.

"I never said that." He shook his head, stopping his prowl.

"No, your mom said it. And you didn't disagree. So, I assumed that meant you agreed with her. And you told her Tish is your type! I'll be honest, Holden, I hadn't known you for long but I could tell within thirty seconds of meeting you that Tish is *not* your type."

"I told my mother that because I don't give a shit what she thinks," he said through gritted teeth, his fists clenched at his sides.

"Then why didn't you *tell* her you don't give a shit what she thinks, huh? Oh, I'm supposed to be the brave one who tells you what I heard, puts aside all my doubts and uncertainty and bares it all to you while you can't even tell your mom you like a girl from South Carolina!" I responded.

We were getting loud. We should move this out of the apartment and away from— Oh, Sloane had left the room. *Huh.*

He shook his head. "You have no idea what that weekend was like for me."

"No, Holden, I don't. I never lost my brother. And I know you miss Spencer something fierce—I will never be in your shoes. But I did what I could to be there for you and support you while you dealt with all the shit around you." I took a minuscule, tentative step toward him. "And maybe, you know, maybe you don't really think those things about me."

"I don't," he riposted.

"But you had said, many times over the course of that weekend, that whatever happened with us, you didn't think about it beyond the island. That it sucked that you could never fall in love with a girl like me."

He seemed shocked, as though he hadn't realized he had said that. But I remembered it. Those words echoed in my brain almost every two minutes, bouncing around and reminding me what a fool I had been all along.

"Marley— Fuck." He ran a hand through his hair. "We need—I want to talk about this. *Really* talk about this."

"Okay. I can give you my new number—"

"No. *Now.* I'm not letting this go unsettled. Come back to my place. I don't want to do this here."

I chewed my bottom lip and glanced toward Sloane's closed bedroom door. "Sloane is sick. I don't want to leave her if —"

"Just go!" Sloane shouted through her closed door. "I'm fine. And you two are a pair of idiots who need to work some shit out!"

I saw a hint of a smile on his lips. "Where do you live?" I stalled. I had to get myself together a bit here.

"Seaport, Financial District. We can take a cab. It's still raining." He nodded behind him toward the window.

"All right. I just— I need a minute." I walked past him into the spare room I was occupying.

I sat on the edge of the bed for a moment to catch my breath. I didn't know if what he said was true. Or if it was true on the island and now not true here, or perhaps a half-truth, a quarter-truth, a part-truth. I couldn't know. I had never been very good at math.

Holden had opened up to me on Martha's Vineyard, but I'd remained the same girl who knew in her heart she couldn't be meant for a man like him. That I wouldn't be able to make a life like his mine. So, whatever he had to say to clear the air seemed somewhat pointless. I mean, sure, I wouldn't hate him, or myself, for that weekend and those words he'd exchanged with his mother.

But I couldn't have him, either. That fact would never change.

I tugged on a different shirt and dragged on a new pair of shorts. I yanked on a pair of socks and my dry tennis shoes, then opened the door while rearranging my ponytail.

"I was still wet and I didn't want to get the seats—"
I started, but I didn't finish because Holden pressed his
mouth to mine.

It felt like it had on the weekend we'd shared—
zealous and forceful, him driving his tongue into my
mouth and pressing his lips hard on mine, tasting me,
devouring me, holding me so tightly, as though he
couldn't get close enough. I stumbled back into the wall
behind me and he came at me, not stopping.

Then I kissed him back just the same. If I could have
crawled inside him, I would have. I clung to his shirt
with one hand, spearing the other into his hair. I
pushed myself up on my tiptoes, moved my jaw to the
side to kiss him harder and deeper and he groaned into
my mouth in response. I'd missed that sound, missed
this man so fucking much it *hurt*. I felt an ache
throughout my body, one that would never be satiated
by anyone else.

I was destined to spend the rest of my life stuck in
my head and dreaming of the short time I'd had with
Holden Pierce and wishing it meant forever. One
weekend, on that godforsaken island, and now I found
myself cursed to spend the rest of my days living in the
memories of it.

I pulled back, my lips swollen and his breath coming
in pants. "Fuck, sweetheart, I missed you," he
confessed, resting his forehead on mine.

"I missed you, too," I whispered. I couldn't stop
myself.

"Come on. Let's go." He took my hand in his. It
fitted perfectly, just as it always had.

We didn't say anything else on the elevator ride, or
in the cab on the way to his place. The rain picked up
and I saw lightning in the distance across the river and

thunder rolled overhead. My thoughts were a jumble of words and actions that I didn't have the willpower to act on. Each passing traffic light, block by block, brought me closer to sealing my fate. To ending this for good.

The cab veered between cars at a clipped pace, and Holden kept hold of my hand but didn't touch me anywhere else. I figured he thought spot on what I did—that if we started touching each other, we wouldn't be able to stop. At least, I hoped so.

Twenty minutes later we stopped in front of a flashy high-rise, and a doorman in a cap came out and opened our cab door for us, holding an umbrella overhead.

Holden skirted out, reaching his hand out for me to follow him.

"Mr. Pierce, sir. How are you?" the doorman asked, keeping us sheltered from the storm. I slipped my hand into Holden's and set my feet on the curb.

"I'm good, George. You?" Holden asked, shutting the door to the cab after I'd climbed out then winding an arm around me and walking us into the building.

"Can't complain, sir," George replied. "Hello to you, too, Miss."

I gave the man a meek smile and let Holden lead me through the doors and across the lobby. This didn't look like Sloane's building, with its outdated furnishings and mid-century-modern feel.

Holden's building shone with glitz and glamor, its several-story atrium and fountain ahead of us. The floor gleamed black and sparkling and the busy lobby had white leather furniture and angular tables surrounded by a green garden area. The space imposed in an overwhelming way, but came across as welcoming at the same time.

"Mr. Pierce? Paul Hannigan called and he rescheduled the meeting about 535 Whittier." A woman in a smart suit came toward us, hustling in high heels that clacked on the slate floor.

"Good. Can you do me a favor and tell Paul to take my calls and emails for the rest of today? I'll get hold of him in the morning tomorrow," Holden said, his hand on my back as we reached the elevators at a swift pace.

"At once, Mr. Pierce," the woman replied, sneaking a glance at me.

"Thank you." The doors opened and Holden punched a code into a keypad, hitting the letter P.

"Penthouse?" I guessed, watching the button light up above all the others.

"Yes," he said, but he seemed a million miles away. Maybe because of the message about work, or having me here in his space, this close to where he called home. Maybe he regretted this idea and thought we should have met for coffee someday or exchanged some casual text messages, not gone full gusto with the kiss and the hand holding and the stifling sexual tension between us. I should offer to meet him at the Olive Garden in Times Square and we could split some breadsticks and salad, smack in the middle of cheap-looking fake-Tuscan décor.

"Holden," I started, but when he spun toward me, he seemed pained. Physically, like he hurt, aching and dejected. Maybe he'd picked up Sloane's superbug? "Are you all right?" I took a step into him and laid my hand on his face, then his forehead to check for a fever.

"Yeah, Marley. I'm all right," he croaked and heaved me into him. He hugged me, just hugged me, for a long time. The elevator doors opened, but he made no move to get out. He just kept me close to him, his arms wrapped all the way around me.

After a few long minutes, he pulled back, but held me tight with an arm around my shoulders. He walked me into his place, tossing his phone and wallet onto the table by the door, and went farther into the apartment.

It was *phenomenal*. An entire and impossibly high wall of windows made up the far side of the room, which enclosed a giant space with a kitchen at one end and a living area at the other. The rain pelted down against the panes, but I could still make out the tops of buildings, as far as the eye could see.

"*Wow,*" I breathed and he let me walk, mesmerized, to the windows. "It's stunning. You can see like the entire city."

"Not that much. But enough, yeah."

I moved along the wall, taking it all in and trying to find landmarks. Empire State Building, One World Trade Center, numerous skyscrapers that appeared as if they were kissing the clouds. *Intense, beautiful, mind-blowing.*

I gasped when a helicopter flew underneath us. "You see this every day?"

"Yeah." I could hear the smile in his voice.

"I wouldn't ever leave my apartment. The only thing I have a view of is the parking lot and the dumpster for the chicken shack next door. This is *amazing.*"

"God, I miss that," he murmured.

"Miss what?"

"Looking at everything through your eyes. The ocean, Edgartown, all of it. Just watching you be awed by another world."

We might as well get on with this. He'd given me the perfect opening for my impending I-am-not-the-girl-who-fits-here speech. "Holden, listen—" I took a few steps toward him.

"I fell in love with you, Marley," he said, his voice even and slow.

My steps faltered, then stopped.

"That weekend, didn't think it was possible. I've never been in love with anyone before, didn't even know what the fuck it felt like. But that morning when you left that house, rushing out of that goddamn bedroom like it was on fire, the thought of not seeing you again made me feel— I couldn't stand it."

He kept his distance from me, staying in the same place across the room. "I didn't know why. You had been so fucking responsive, so hot for me the night before—we went at it for hours. I didn't think of it as the end of something. I thought it was the beginning. But you didn't see it that way."

"I wanted it to be. The beginning," I confessed. "But I-I heard you. I knew how you felt about me. So, I thought we were over."

"I had this whole plan for us, in my head. Worked it all out for that day. I would convince you to stay just one more day, so we could spend your birthday on the island. Go shopping, get lobster rolls again, go to the beach. I planned to take you swimming in the pool at my family's house, take you on the boat—I haven't been on the water since Spencer died. But I wanted to go back out there, with you. Sail with you so I could watch you light up and experience something else new. I couldn't fucking wait. Then you left. You just *left*."

"I had to, Holden. I would never— I can't be the girl for you," I said this for both of us, not just him. I had to hear it, too, out loud. I had to keep myself away so I wouldn't fall further in love with the man who couldn't be mine. It didn't matter that he reciprocated those feelings. I should have been jumping for joy. But reality remained.

"Why?"

"Because I don't belong here." I gestured around me. "Your mom said it perfectly. I am poor white trash. I'm just a girl from Angler's Haven with a shitty childhood, a mountain of debt and a pretty face. She knew I was just a good time for you. She knew that it could never last outside of that weekend. And you agreed with her."

"No, I didn't. I told her that so she would leave me the fuck alone about it. I had already faced down too many demons that weekend. I didn't want to spend my last hours with you facing down more. I let her say what she wanted, but I didn't mean a fucking word of it. And I haven't spoken to her since I got back. Haven't seen Tish. I don't fucking want to."

"How do I know that's true? How do I know that this is true, and not what you said then?" I asked gently.

"Because I'm still in love with you."

My stomach, and my heart, dropped into my ten-dollar Payless shoes. I felt the floor shift underneath me, tipping from side to side while I tried to stay standing.

He couldn't be in love with me, could he?

I wasn't flawless, cultured, put-together. I didn't come from a family that took vacations to exotic locales and drove luxury cars. If they drove at all. I mean, they must have had chauffeurs, right? *See*? I didn't even *know*.

"Holden, it was just a weekend—" I started but he shook his head.

"It wasn't, Marley, not for me. I'm always going to be in love with you. And I tried to tell you that. I texted you. I called you. I paid your fucking rent for you —"

"You *what*?"

"I paid your rent. I got hold of your landlord and paid it up for six months so you didn't have to worry about it."

"He never told me."

"What?"

"He didn't tell me. Us. I mean, he didn't harp about the rent being late, but we paid him what we owed. Well, almost. Took every last cent I had. I had to roll pennies from the floor of my car to get the Subway fare from the airport to Sloane's place."

Holden clenched his jaw. "Fuck that motherfucker. I'm going to knock his teeth in."

"He only has like seven, anyway. Won't be too difficult."

I saw a whisper of a smile, then it disappeared. "I didn't know what else to do to get you to listen to me. I thought you were ignoring me."

"So you paid my rent?"

"I tried to impress you." He rubbed the back of his neck, uncharacteristically shy for a moment.

"I'm already impressed by you, Holden," I rasped. "But I-I don't know if I can do this."

"Do what?"

"Live this life with you. Be whoever you think I am, who you want me to be."

"I don't want you to be a goddamn thing but yourself. The girl you were on the island. The girl you are now. The one who loves her friends and her family with everything she is. The one who looked past all my fucking hang-ups and bullshit and brought me back to being myself."

"Holden, you didn't need me to—"

He shook his head once, cutting me off. "Marley, I didn't even fucking know how lost I was until I found you. I didn't even how far down I had fallen until you picked me up. And you didn't do anything but be *you* to make it happen."

I took a tentative step toward him. "I don't know how to start a life with you."

He gave me a slow grin. "I don't know, either. But can't we figure it out together? I want you to be here, Marley. Or if you want to stay in Columbia, that's okay. But I want—fuck, I'm in love with you. I don't want you anywhere but with me, for always. I want a relationship with you. A permanent one, long-term. I'm not the kind of man who thinks about much but his next deal and the next acquisition I have to make. Everything else I've ignored or thrown away. But *this*— I want this. For the rest of my life. *Our* life. You told me that you're not good at jumping off into the unknown, that you aren't brave. You *are* brave. And this isn't the unknown. This is a man who is telling you he'll take care of you and that he'll love you for as long as you walk this earth. I want forever with you, Marley Mae Jackson."

I had started crying before he finished. Every word rang so sincere and half-stilted and he struggled to get them out. I had never seen Holden like that. He had always been so quick with a remark or ready with an answer for everything. But now, he floundered and stammered and that made it real. That told me what he'd said that day, at Ava and Reed's wedding, wasn't his truth, just robotic and monotone words he had exchanged with a mother who didn't give a shit about her son's happiness, instead wanting to control and manipulate him.

He'd called me. He'd paid my fucking rent. He wanted me.

The spark blazed now, consuming me from the inside out. This was the man for me, without a doubt. Without any niggling reservations, without expectations or plotting our every step. *This is our truth.*

"I'll jump into the unknown with you, Holden. Because I love you, too," I said.

Any hesitation he had — *gone.* He flew at me and tugged me against him, kissing me deeply, cradling my face in his palms and stroking his tongue against mine. He poured all his emotion into this kiss, still crying but I didn't care.

I gave it right back to him, dancing my tongue against his, bruising my lips on his own.

"I missed you so much. Every fucking second." He dropped his mouth to my neck and held me against him. He cradled my face in his palms, kissing every inch of skin, brushing his lips against my forehead, my hairline, my eyelids.

He stroked my cheeks, moving his eyes over mine, searching. "Is this real? I've wanted you with me here for weeks. I was days away from driving down south to find you," he croaked.

"It's real. I promise. I thought about you all the time. Wanted this so much," I admitted.

He gave me a rare smile, one that reached all the way to his eyes. I got on my tiptoes and pressed my lips to his. "I'm here, Holden. I'm here forever."

He held me tight against him, his arms grounding me and keeping me standing, the strength I so badly needed flowing from his solid frame and into me, just as it had happened on the island when he held my hand. He gave me his all, without even knowing he could.

He leaned back, just enough to catch my gaze with his and give me another glorious grin.

"For once, I'm not going to plan anything out," I told him, beaming back. "I'm just going to —*fuck*, I'm going to have to plan this out. I have my lease, and Elle, back home. Sloane wants me to stay. She already said I could move in with her and I've been trying to find a job here." I chewed on my lip, my mind going off in all different directions.

He held me against him again. "You'll figure it out, sweetheart. I have faith in you."

"I don't want to be far from you. This last two weeks nearly did me in. I mean, I was fired and broke, but I've been jobless and poor half my life. Being without you made me miserable." I laid my hand on his face. "I don't want to be without you again, honey."

"Then stay here. Stay with me," he begged, his voice hoarse with emotion, with love. *For me.*

"I have to have a job. I don't want your money, Holden. I'm sort of pissed you paid my rent —I don't want you or anyone else to think that's what this is."

"I don't give a fuck what anyone else thinks."

I shook my head. "No, you don't understand. I heard your mother, I spent time with Cece and I met Tish —these people will think I'm a gold-digger only in this for your money. But I'm not. I don't want any of it. I need this to be fifty-fifty."

"Well, I'm not going to let you split the rent if you live here."

"How much is the rent?"

"Thirty-two thousand a month."

I stared at him. *"Dollars?"*

"Yes, dollars. It's my mortgage. Fifteen year fixed. Three point four percent interest. I'm two years in on my PMI."

"I have no idea what you just said."

"It's nice to be the smarter one once in a while. You can talk to me all about dirt to feel better if you want."

"So wait—*fuck.* I probably need a calculator for this, but thirty-two thousand dollars times fifteen years at three point four percent—"

"Is seven point four million dollars. Give or take."

I stared at him. "Holden, can't we move somewhere—I don't know, *cheaper?*"

He yanked me against him again. "We can do whatever you want. But you're not paying for it. Whatever you want, Marley, it's yours. I just want *you.* I love you. I really, truly love you," he said, kissing my neck. It started out soft and sweet then he started to suck gently behind my ear and I went limp in his arms with a breathy moan.

"Fuck, I missed that sound," he admitted, sucking my skin harder.

"I missed all of this, honey. All of what you gave me, every inch of you." God, his mouth. His body. His *everything.*

He kissed a trail from my neck to my shoulder, tearing my T-shirt to nip the skin at the bottom of my neck, then ripping the whole thing from my body as he got on his knees in front of me.

"I missed these tits, baby," he murmured, tearing one of the cups on my bra down and orbiting my hardening bud with his tongue.

My knees went weak and I put my hand on top of his shoulder to keep myself standing. "Holden," I whispered, stroking his hair.

"I missed your body," he said, his tongue flat and hard when he licked down my stomach to just above my shorts. "I missed your laugh, your smile, your kindness, the light in your eyes just for me—all of it." He tugged my shorts and panties down in one fell swoop. "But goddamn, I missed your pussy most of all." He dug his tongue inside my core and lapped at me.

"Holden, fuck," I cried, tossing my leg over his shoulder for him to open me up farther with his fingers and lick harder.

"This is my pussy, right? It belongs to me. For the rest of your life, Marley. No one else gets inside here, inside of *any* part of you, except me."

"No one, Holden. I'm yours. All of me is yours."

He went back to my mound, sucking and licking, biting down on my clit. When I couldn't stand any more, he picked me up, his arms under my ass, and tossed me onto the couch.

I bounced and he covered me with his body. "Love you, baby," he whispered and kissed me soft and sweet, all over my face.

But that didn't last long. Soon he was grounding his pelvis against me and pawing at his belt to try to get his pants undone.

"Holden, God, I'm aching for you." I grabbed my breasts and massaged them.

He didn't even get his pants all the way off before he surged inside me.

We both let out a long, deep breath. It felt—perfect, right, *just* where I was supposed to be. I ignored my doubts, my fears, the conditioned need in me to take care of myself, to protect what I had—as little as it might be—for fear that I wouldn't be able to have it again, that I would have to go without, the way I'd done my whole life. I lived in the moment with him like I'd wanted to all along.

And somewhere inside me, I knew the rest would take care of itself. That being with Holden meant never having to go without—not because of the billions in his bank account, but because we had each other. I didn't want his money, his wealth, the lifestyle he had grown up in. But I did want *him*. And the feeling I had with him that brought me solace, that let me believe I could rely on someone else to walk through life and lean on them, support them.

I felt loved. Unconditionally. For the first time in my life.

Holden started a slow, profound cadence with his cock, pulling almost all the way out of me then pulsing back inside, as deep as he would go. I moaned with every movement, holding onto him for fear he would vanish.

He stared at me while he made love to me, long and slow, both our bodies covered in a sheen of sweat and balancing on the brink, wanting to fall over together.

"I want you to come on my cock, Marley. I want to feel you come so I can fill you up," he murmured, his mouth against my ear.

"Oh, god, Holden, I'm so close," I groaned, clenching him inside me and causing his breath to stutter.

"Fuck, I love your pussy. I can't wait to wake you up with my cock, make you come with my hands and my mouth, worship every inch of you every day for the rest of our lives," he said, nipping the shell of my ear.

"I'll never stop wanting this. I'll always want you deep inside me, my body and my heart, forever."

"I want you to come, baby," he muttered. "I'm nearly exploding."

"Harder, honey," I whispered.

He complied and started a sharp and brutal rhythm, slapping against my skin, the sounds of our lovemaking echoing off the walls and windows.

The room grew darker, the storm just overhead, and I came to the loud clap of thunder and a streak of lightning blazing the room.

"Fuck, Marley, Fuck!" Holden was coming as I was, pumping in and out until he emptied, totally spent, several minutes later, his cum deep inside and leaking out of my pussy.

"God, I love to see that." He peered up from between my legs. "I love you, baby."

"I love you, too."

He got a towel to clean us both up, grinning like a maniac as he did. Then he gave me a tour of the apartment.

I had been blown away by one room, with its towering windows that spanned two stories, and the enormous chandelier hanging from the center of the second story. But the rest of the place brought me to my knees in ridiculous, awe-inspiring fashion.

It had three bedrooms, four bathrooms, three freaking balconies. The bathrooms had gold fixtures. *Real gold*. The master suite was the size of my place in Columbia. Not exaggerating—the bedroom's dimensions equaled those of a two-bedroom, one bathroom apartment. And he had the biggest bed I had ever seen.

"I just—I don't know how I'm going to do this." I sat hard on the edge of the bed.

"Don't know how you're going to do what?" Holden sat beside me and took my hand in his. "I told you, sweetheart, you're braver than you think you are. And together we can handle anything life throws at us."

"I don't mean that." I rested a hand on the side of his face. "I love you. Being with you is the easy part. But how the hell am I supposed to clean this place? It's going to take a week and as soon as I finish I'm going to have to start all over again!" I threw my arms up.

He looked at me strangely a moment then burst out laughing.

"It's not funny, Holden. I don't even know how to clean gold faucets. Is there, like, some kind of special version of Lysol? I mean, I don't see a speck of dirt anywhere." I glanced under the dresser on the flawless oak floor and saw nothing.

"Sweetheart, you're not cleaning this apartment. I have someone to do that."

"Oh," I said. "I guess, yeah, you would. But I mean, I don't have a job right now, so I could do it for a while. Save you money."

"I realize this is going to take a while for you to get used to, but, Marley, you're not doing jack shit around here. You're not mopping floors or making beds. That isn't your life anymore."

"I like making my bed. I mean, of all the shitty chores there are in the world, that one I don't really mind." I shrugged.

"Okay, fine. You can make the bed."

"But maybe not change the sheets." I twisted around on the massive mattress. "I mean, do you have special blankets made or something? This thing is gargantuan."

"No. It's a California king. It's pretty standard."

"I have a twin."

He stared at me. "What?"

"Yeah. It's my bed from when I was a kid. It still works. Never replaced it."

He cracked up so hard, his eyes started to water.

"It's not funny, rich boy," I mumbled, swatting him on the arm.

"Oh, baby. It's *so* funny. I cannot *wait* to spoil you." He fell back on the bed and took me with him.

He turned us on our sides, facing each other, and laid a hand on my hip. I wore his shirt and he had on his pants, since what I'd arrived in had been destroyed downstairs. "You look so good here," he said, voice low, leaning in and bestowing a gentle kiss on me.

"This place is amazing without me in it. I'm just decoration." I gestured around the lavish room.

"You're more than decoration, Marley Mae. You're one of a kind."

"No. There's tons of poor girls from the south just like me."

He shook his head. "No. There's no one like *my* Marley."

"Holden." I gripped his hair in my fingers. "I love you. I want this for us, being together, being in love. But you have to know that if you have nothing, if you lose all of this and it's just you and me, I will still love you. Just as I do now."

"Sweetheart, if I had any doubt about that, you wouldn't be here." He kissed me again. "But I'm not losing shit. So don't worry about that. Don't worry about *anything* anymore. The days of digging for pennies to pay for a cab or begging your landlord to wait another day for rent are over."

"I still need to take care of my parents. Ross can't do it alone," I told him. "I'll use my own money —"

He shook his head. "No. I'll do it. I'll get them groceries delivered, buy a house for them, get a fucking maid — whatever they want. Whatever it takes so you don't worry about it ever again."

"They're not evil people."

"I didn't think they were, baby. If they were, you wouldn't be you."

"Elle is going to flip when she sees this place." I grinned, sitting and staring up at the sweeping wood-beamed ceiling.

"Yeah, well, if it's okay with you, I'm not sharing you with anyone for a while. No more Instagram posts with Mitch or nights out clubbing with Sloane."

"We didn't go out much. I pined," I admitted to him with a small smile.

He smiled back at me and his face shifted to serious. "I have something for you."

I watched him walk across the room, loving how the ridges in his back moved up and down as he went, how he seemed so at ease here, just like he did eating lobster rolls in a dinky old restaurant or lying on a twenty-dollar blanket on a beach crowded with people. He had confidence that most men try desperately for, and he had it without even thinking about it.

But underneath that confidence and swagger, there existed a man in love, a man who missed his brother, a man who struggled to be who others wanted him to be while still being himself, who threw himself into his work to avoid all the expectations of the people he didn't want to let down, living and dead. But with me, he knew he could be whoever he wanted to be, without judgment, without me holding out my hand asking for something, without wanting to know how many zeroes he had in his bank account. I just wanted Holden's happiness, however that came, wherever he found it. And I would give him all I was to get him there.

He walked back to me, a box in his hands. I tilted upward and kissed him. "I love you, Holden. I'll tell you every day. I'll be here for you no matter what. You're the man for me, honey. You said on the island you didn't even know who you were anymore. But I do. You're loving and fun and strong and ambitious. You're so many wonderful qualities that I can't even begin to enumerate them all. You said you had already faced down too many demons on the island, and you couldn't handle one more. But I'm here now. And anything you need to face, we face together."

"Fuck, Marley." He tugged me against him. "What did I do to deserve a girl like you?"

"You said you gave to charity. Maybe that's it," I joked. "And you taught me how to swim. You gave me at least a dozen orgasms. You offered to take me on your plane, to take me sailing. You're a good man, Holden. Even if you don't believe it, I do."

He held out a square velvet case. "This is your birthday present. I got it that day I had to get the garter in town. Couldn't resist." He had a boyish smirk on his face.

I ran my fingers along the indented writing along the top. *Ippolita.* I tugged the box open and all the breath left my lungs in a whoosh.

Inside sat a bangled charm bracelet, its shine almost blinding me when it hit the light. There were two vertical lines of diamonds on one end, and on the other hung a charm in a jagged, triangular shape. I held it between my fingers. Inscribed were the words *Martha's Vineyard* with a large jewel encrusted in the center.

The bracelet felt heavy in my hand, the weight of the gold and its significance hefty as its mass.

"Holden," I said, my voice just audible.

"Do you like it?" he asked, hesitant and vulnerable.

"It's— I love it. It's incredible." I swallowed back tears. "This is—you got this just for me?"

"Yeah, it's just for you. You think you have to share it with someone?"

"I've never had anything with a diamond in it."

He stared at me a long moment and I wiped away a tear with the back of my hand. "Will you put it on me?" I asked.

He nodded, his eyes still boring into mine. He took the bracelet and unclasped it. Then he wound it around my wrist and closed it with a soft *click*.

"Wow." I stared at it, moving it back and forth on my arm.

"It looks good on you."

"It's that island tan." I swiped at another errant tear.

"No, sweetheart. It's just you. Tell me something."

"Anything."

"Why didn't you want anyone to know about your birthday?"

I took a deep breath. "My mom didn't do anything for my birthdays as a kid. Maybe she always intended to, and maybe she did try to save a little to get me a gift or throw me a party, but my stepdad would always take all our money and lose it. Or she would decide something else was more important, like cigarettes or a new pair of shoes for her. Anything they had put aside was gone before you could even blink. Year after year, I would sit on my bed at the end of my birthday day and I'd have nothing to show for it." I confessed. "It shouldn't matter, I know that. You know I don't care about material things. But it sucked."

He tucked a loose strand of hair behind my ear.

"Elle didn't grow up with much, either, and we had these homemade cakes her mom baked every year. Sometimes they were lopsided or half the frosting had been licked off by one of her sisters, but we still had it. There'd be a handful of us who played games, and she opened little trinkets from friends and family. I never had that. It made my birthdays feel empty. It made *me* feel empty."

"I'm sorry."

I shook my head. "Don't be. This" — I held up my arm — "this makes up for twenty-six years of shitty birthdays."

He grinned. "Yeah, well, if you give me twenty-six more, I promise each year will be even better."

I threw my arms around his neck and hugged him. "Thank you. I love it so much. Thank you." More tears fell, but I didn't care. I held onto him like a lifeline and he held me right back.

Twenty-six years of birthdays to look forward to with the man of my dreams? That was going right into my planner.

Epilogue

After the Blaze of Glory — I couldn't wait to teach Holden all about Jon Bon Jovi — aka our makeup sex and life-altering declarations — there was still a lot to be sorted out.

I sat on his beautiful Italian leather sofa, peering out at his magnificent view over the city. The sun had come out after the storm passed, and the metaphor set against the current backdrop of my life did not get overlooked. I dialed Sloane's number to tell her I was staying at Holden's — most likely for the rest of my life.

"I'm glad I was wrong. Then right." She sneezed into the phone.

"I feel bad leaving you there when you're so sick." I chewed my bottom lip. Maybe I needed to go back and bring her some Nyquil and crappy magazines.

"Don't. How the hell do you think Holden Pierce knew my building was for sale, anyway?"

"Wait, you —"

"Yeah, babe. I called his office. Gave his secretary a tip, made up some story about how he and I were old friends and I looked up potential for prospects for him. Which was not totally a lie. I have known the guy a long time and I was looking out for him. Sure, more like helping along his love life than his business interests, but whatevs. It did the job."

"Sloane, I-I don't even know what to say."

"There's nothing to say. It took me like ten seconds to get you to go out and buy me chicken noodle soup — which is terrible by the way — because I knew he was in the building. I'm a freaking genius. I should start a match-making company or sell my story to TMZ. I fully expect the two of you to name your first-born after me."

I laughed. "That's a promise, Slo. I swear."

"He loves you?"

"He does," I confirmed, watching Holden pace with his cell phone in the kitchen, glancing over at me every once in a while, bringing me something to drink, sitting down and rubbing my feet. God, the man gave a damn good foot massage.

"Are you happy?" she asked.

"I am."

"Are you going to let someone else take care of you for a while and not try to do everything by your goddamn self for a change?"

"No. Well, maybe a little. He has a maid!"

"Live it up, girl. If anyone deserves the good life, it's you."

"Love you, Slo."

"Love you, too, MJ."

I hung up the phone and dropped it in my lap. My beautiful, loving friends. The best in the world.

Holden finished his call and walked over, sitting down next to me with a smile. It hadn't gone away once yet.

"Hey," he said, curving my eyes to his with a finger under my chin. "Why are you crying?"

"Because I have the good life now."

"Yeah, baby, you do."

I told him how Sloane had orchestrated our running into each other today.

"Wow, didn't think Sloane was that crazy. Or a fan of mine," he commented.

"She's a fan of mine. And I think she gets that we're a two-for-one deal now."

"Yeah, baby, we are."

Then we had sex on the couch again. It was a sexy couch — what could I say?

After that, I felt like I needed to get back to reality. Which for me meant planning. I had ingrained that in myself for a lifetime and I couldn't help it. So, I started my favorite Get Shit Organized task and made a list with a steno pad, keeping several pens close by in case one ran out of ink.

"Okay, first things first. Where do we live?" I asked Holden that night, with discarded Chinese food boxes all around us and *Slippery When Wet* on in the background. I wrote HOME at the top of the paper.

"Here." Holden sat back and folded his arms. He had decided not to budge on that one.

"Not someplace, less, um, well, *less*?" I asked.

"No. This is my place. It's yours, too."

I looked around. "It is really pretty."

He lifted an eyebrow at me.

"I mean masculine and tough." I deepened my voice and got a laugh out of him.

"I got this apartment when I made my first half billion on my own. I'm proud of it. I want you to be, too."

His first half billion. *Swallowing that down and moving on.* "I love it." I squeezed his hand. "I do. Maybe someday I'll get used to it. And there's lots of rooms to have sex in." I wiggled my eyebrows at him. He agreed by tipping the corners of his mouth up in return.

"That's settled." I tapped my pen on the paper. "Now, a job." Next word written down was JOB.

"I've gone to a fair share of charity events. You want to work at another food pantry? I'm sure there's someone I can get in touch with," he offered.

"Maybe. But I don't know, there's some really cool urban farming organizations around. I sent my résumé to a couple," I admitted.

"Whatever you want, baby." He stroked my skin with his thumb.

"I want to try to do this on my own," I told him. "I appreciate your offer but—"

"But Marley Mae Jackson can do anything herself. I know, baby."

I gave him an appreciative smile for understanding.

"What really sucks is that I don't know if Ben imploded my career so bad I won't be able to get in somewhere. I mean if they call for a reference will Richland Hope tell them I'm some kind of insipid socialite who doesn't know what she's doing? I did a great job there. My performance reviews were perfect. I got raises every year. I won employee of the month four times!" I started to get amped up.

"Marley, I have no doubt you did a great job there. They fucked up. It was wrongful termination," Holden said. "And I'm going to take care of it."

I had no idea what Holden meant when he said he would take care of it, until I got a letter and a severance package two weeks later in the mail.

Ms. Jackson,
We here at Richland Hope believe your employment was terminated under false pretenses. Due to this error, our CEO Ben York has been let go and enclosed is a lump sum commensurate with your years of dedicated service and lost wages. We apologize for any inconvenience or distress this has caused.
Please consider returning to our organization. We need more employees of your caliber.
Sincerely,
Wyatt Franklin, Chairman of the Board of Directors

"Um, Holden!" I called out once I had read the letter, my voice cracking. I found him in his study, one of the many rooms we had 'christened' since I'd gotten there two weeks ago. I'd worn a short skirt and he'd spanked me with the blunt end of a letter opener. It had been hot and we still had eight rooms left to go.

Holden sat, using his computer, his cell phone and his desk phone all at once. One thing I'd learned about Holden — the fierceness with which he loved, he also poured into his work. The man was a machine. He slept five hours a night, then woke up and checked Japanese markets, read real estate blogs and got through all his work for his dad's firm. He never stopped, except to pay attention to me. Sloane had been right — total workaholic. But he poured that passion into us, as well, and I *always* came first.

The second I walked in, he clicked off one phone and told the person on his cell he would call them back. "Hey, baby, what's up?"

I held up the letter and the check for two thousand five hundred dollars made out to me. "What is this? I mean, I know what it is, but how?"

He took the papers from me and read them over. "Pretty pathetic severance but the letter is good."

"You did this." I didn't phrase it as a question. I knew he had.

"I didn't. My lawyer did. Sent them a pretty standard wrongful termination letter. I see that was enough."

"How did they—I mean, why did you... I don't..." I swallowed. "*Holden.*"

"Sweetheart, I told you I would take care of you. This is me doing that."

"I'm not— Shit." I wiped away suddenly falling tears.

"Baby. You got fucked. I'm just righting a wrong. Don't feel bad about it."

"But you did this *for me*," I said, sniffling.

"Yeah, and I'll always do this *for you*. Always." He kissed my forehead.

Well, we had sex in his office *again*. I mean, how could we not? I was falling more in love with the man I'd had only glimpses of on the island and fallen for anyway. Getting the whole package? All the time, day and night, week after week? *Even better.*

The next week we went down to Columbia so I could get my stuff. I was running out of clothes—even though Holden's daily maid did all my laundry—and it seemed the second I took something off, it was clean and back in my closet like magic. But I had more clothes and furniture at my apartment and loose ends to tie up.

Of course, Holden came with me. He said he wanted to see where I lived, but I knew now what that meant — he wanted to take care of me. I got it now. *Well, I'm in the process of getting it.* We both knew it would take time for me to accept all he had to give and not try to do everything on my own.

First thing he did upon our arrival? He gave the landlord a stern talking to — which I'm sure made Mr. Vindap pee his pants — and got the money back he'd paid in rent, our security deposit and another five hundred dollars somehow.

Elle was on her way out of town, as well — to New York. To move in with Slater.

Martha's Vineyard was like the Spanish fly of love lives, it seemed. A person went there, fell in love and came home with a hangover. Then lived happily ever after. I wasn't sure that was how actual Spanish fly worked. I'd never had it.

Elle and I split the deposit, said goodbye to our crappy furniture, which we donated to the Salvation Army, cursed the burned-out light bulbs and death-trap shower stall and cried for a while.

We were both emotional. We had been living together for over eight years. I would miss our late-night horror movie sessions, where we would get scared out of our wits then leave the lights on all night and sleep in each other's rooms. Or when we'd headed up the street to the dive bar that had dollar cans of Pabst and played porn on the TVs for Porn and Pabst night. It had brought out some sketchy dudes, for sure, but we'd always had each other there to talk the other out of going home with a creep. Or when we would sit on the little hill behind the outdoor amphitheater when cool acts came to town, unable to afford a ticket but sharing a six-pack between us while we listened to music.

Slater lived in Brooklyn, so we were a mere Subway ride away from each other, but we both knew it wouldn't be the same.

"I love you, Marley. I'm so happy you found someone to love you as much as I do, who has a dick," Elle said when we hugged one last time beside our cars.

"Me too. I mean, I'm happy he has a dick, for sure, but I'm happy for you and Slater."

She beamed. "He has so much dick it's unreal." She showed me again with her hands how big he was.

Holden cleared his throat behind us and raised an eyebrow at me. Elle and I just laughed.

She took a step closer to me and lowered her voice. "Are you freaking out?"

She knew me so well, my oldest friend. "I'm trying really hard not to."

"Are you out on that limb? Does it feel like it's going to splinter?" she asked, glancing at Holden who gave us a private moment, standing a few yards away.

"I'm out there — and I don't think it's going to break. It's definitely platinum plated," I told her.

"I am always here. I am always in your corner. And I believe that you deserve a big life, Marley Mae. I believe that you can live on the edge sometimes and still be happy."

"I hope so. I'm on the edge." I peeked behind me at Holden, who shot me a sexy grin. "But it's such a fucking great view that I'm not even freaking out."

She hugged me tight to her. "I'll call you in a few days. We'll get brunch or whatever it is ladies of leisure do." She kissed my cheek, gave Holden a hug and threatened him not to break my heart or she would break his face, then took off in her beat-up little Honda that sputtered a cloud of black dust when it went.

"Gonna miss her." I wiped the last tear away and watched Elle go.

"She won't be far, sweetheart," Holden said, draping an arm across my shoulders.

"I know. But it'll be different."

"Different is okay, Marley. Different with me — it's good. It's not going to ruin you."

"I know that, honey. And that's why I love you. Not just because you take care of me, but because you know I need to hear that you will."

Holden insisted our next stop was Angler's Haven. He said he wanted to see where I'd grown up and sample the local delicacy, fried sea bass aka burnt hair. He agreed it tasted as gross as I'd described it.

Afterward, we went to the house I'd grown up in. I was a little sheepish, considering I had seen Holden's place and he'd taken me by the building that housed the penthouse he had been raised in and it was just as formidable and immaculate as his place, maybe more so. Holden *knew* I'd come from nothing, but seeing it in all its overgrown and abused glory was another thing.

"I planted those roses." I pointed to them when we headed up the beleaguered walkway to the front door.

"They're pretty."

"I cut them back every year, but they go crazy there, growing like mad. Can't keep them down, I suppose."

"Just like you," he whispered and kissed my temple.

God, I loved this man.

My mom threw the door open as soon as we hit the front stoop, smiling. "So, here's the rich boy you told us all about!"

I hadn't told my mom he was rich. I'd told my mom he was a boy, sure. But she'd worked her Facebook magic and made some clever deductions. When she'd figured out he had money, she'd texted me, *Bill and I have a business idea for weight loss shakes – think your new boyfriend could help us set up the ground floor?*

I hadn't told Holden about the text. I'd just told my mom Holden was far too busy for things like that. But now that we were here, I had a feeling she would hit him up on her own.

We sat at the dinky kitchen table, the one I had missed many meals at, swinging my feet from the worn, wooden chairs and hoping food would materialize to fill my empty stomach. Where I'd done the homework my mom had never helped me with, where I'd sat and listened to my parents argue because my stepdad had yet again lost all they had, when I'd watched my childhood pass by me in a blur of want and worry.

Straightaway, Bill launched into his plans for his future, hitting Holden up for cash for the track.

"I'm not a betting man," Holden replied.

"Well, I gots dis tip that is a doozy. It's a sure thing. Guar-an-teed," Bill bragged, giving Holden a slimy grin.

Holden leaned forward, looking Bill straight in the eye. "I've heard about your years of sure things and all the money you pissed away when you should've been taking care of your kids and your wife. I can promise you one thing—you will never get a fucking dime out of me, or Marley, again."

Bill sat back, aghast. My mom gasped. "But we have this idea for diet shakes—"

Holden took my wringing, balled-up hands in his under the table. "Marley has taken care of you long enough. And I know her. She will want to keep doing that. Getting you food and helping you with bills. I can't stop her, and I told her I would put food on the table and buy you a house if you wanted it."

Bill licked his lips at that prospect.

"But once that's done, we're done. I won't have her working herself to the bone to help people who never did the same for her. She should never have gone hungry. She should never have had to worry for you. And she sure as shit won't be doing it anymore."

I stared over at Holden, my eyes brimming with unshed tears. I hadn't expected this tirade, but, I would admit, it made me all gooey inside. He'd taken care of me again and said all the things I had wanted to say since I was a little girl. All the years of swallowing the mistreatment, afraid to make things worse by rocking the boat.

"We raised her right. Took care a'her when no one else wanted her," Bill sneered at me, like I was a mangy street dog they'd taken in out of the rain.

"She's your fucking daughter. You should've busted your ass to make her happy. That's your job. You're her parents," Holden shot back.

"She ain't my kid." Bill sat back and folded his arms across his chest. I'd heard that one before. Plenty of times. "I'd never give birth to somethin' that scrawny and useless."

My stepdad was pissed about the money, I could tell. And when he didn't get what he wanted, he got mean. He had anticipated my boyfriend being their meal ticket. That had evaporated fast and he'd lashed out.

But Holden hadn't seen it before. And didn't take it very well. He stood and sucker-punched Bill hard in the jaw.

Bill's chair slammed backward into the floor when he tipped down and started bleeding from his mouth. "You sonofabitch!" Bill screamed and scrambled to his feet but didn't make a move to retaliate. He wasn't that stupid.

Holden stood and locked our fingers together. "We're done here. Food. House. That's it," he said to my mom, who sat there just staring at us. She nodded in slow understanding.

He nodded, just once, and hauled me out of the door. He slammed the car door to my small hatchback, rubbing his knuckles and grimacing.

"You hurt your hand?" I asked, quietly, as we sat in the driveway for a moment.

"No," he said, his voice tight. "I'm sorry, Marley. I just— Fuck, I lost it."

"I know, honey."

"You deserved better than that life."

"I know that, too."

"I'm going to give it to you, Marley. I'm going to give you the world."

I leaned over and cradled his face in my hands. "I know that, too, Holden." I kissed him softly. "You could give me nothing and I'd already have the world. Because I have you."

He kissed me deep and long and, when Bill came raging out of the house, threatening to sue, I took off. And didn't look back.

The last stop on my terrible trip down Memory Lane was to see Ross. We caught him at the garage, working, as usual, but I wanted Holden to meet him before we left.

"So, this is the guy who's taking my baby sister up north, huh?" Ross said, with a half-smirk and hand held out to shake.

Holden nodded and shook his hand. "Holden Pierce."

"Yeah, I know. Ma already called and said you laid Bill out flat. Appreciated. I've been wanting to do the same since for about fifteen years now."

Holden gave a slow grin. "Yeah, well, it was my pleasure."

"I'll bet." Ross chuckled. He gave me a hug. "You all packed?" He nodded toward the car.

"Yeah. I am. No idea who I'm going to find to fix this piece of junk when it goes wonky again."

"I'm sure your man will find someone. And do you need a car in New York? It's all cabs and Subway, right?"

"It is. But I'd miss her. We've put a lot of time and effort into this baby." I patted the trunk gingerly.

Ross snorted. "We put a lot of second-hand shit into that car to make it limp along, Marley. Don't get too sentimental. It's a piece of garbage."

Holden laughed and I hit him on the stomach. "Hey, man, back off. You'll hurt her feelings."

Holden examined Ross for a brief moment. "Marley said you want to start your own garage."

"Working on it. There's a lot of business around here. I work seven days and we still got cars here for weeks we can't even get to." Ross nodded at the line of vehicles parked in the lot beside us.

"How much do you need to start something like that?" Holden asked.

"I got it, man. I don't need a handout," Ross replied, proud as ever.

"Not a handout. An investment. That's what I do. I make investments," Holden said.

Ross rubbed his jaw and looked Holden over. "You serious?"

Holden nodded once.

"Need to think on it," Ross said.

"Do that. Then get back to me." Holden handed him a business card. "And don't worry about your mom and Bill anymore. I got that covered, too."

Ross looked from Holden to me and shook his head. "You gonna be good to her?" he asked and I got misty-eyed.

"Always." Holden extended his palm.

Ross shook his hand then gave me a hug. "She doesn't need much. A couple Bon Jovi CDs and a beat-up Hyundai will make this girl happy for life."

"Don't tell him that. I want him to shower me in diamonds and furs."

Ross and Holden both cracked up. "Yeah, not you, little sis." Ross tugged my ponytail and gave us a nod. "I'll talk to you soon," he said to both of us and went back to the garage.

"He's a good guy." Holden wrapped an arm around me.

"He is. Solid. Smart. The best brother a girl could ask for. He threatened all the bullies who came around and he put all the Band-Aids on all my boo-boos when I needed him to. I'm going to miss him." I teared up again, for like the hundredth time since we had hit the city limits.

"He can come see us anytime, sweetheart. And whenever you want to visit, I'll be right there with you," he said, kissing me, his lips soft on mine.

"You're a good guy, too, Holden," I whispered.

He rewarded me with one of his stellar smiles. And I think I fell a little more in love with him, though I hadn't thought it possible.

We drove my car back to New York. A couple of times, Holden wanted to leave it by the side of the road, especially when the air went out and we had to pour water in the radiator to keep it from overheating during a traffic jam.

"She's been around longer than you have, Holden Pierce. We have history," I told him.

The car made it to New York in one piece with us in it although it looked so pathetic parked next to Holden's Bentley and Mercedes.

"I think it needs a tune-up," I told him as we hauled bags up to his apartment.

"I think it needs a junkyard," Holden muttered, but I ignored his comment.

Once we got all my bags and boxes in our room, I whirled around. "Wow. So, this is it."

"This is it," he repeated.

"You still love me? Even with all my junk here?"

"You know I do."

"You still going to give me twenty-six years of birthdays?"

"At least," he replied, holding me close.

"You going to take care of me?"

"Always, Marley Mae. Always."

"I'm going to take care of you, too, Holden. And not because I have to. But because I want to. Forever."

* * * *

Later that summer, Holden told me we were taking off for the weekend just before Labor Day. I had landed a job at an organic farming initiative that worked with low-income schools and neighborhoods to build sustainable urban vegetable and fruit gardens in vacant lots. It mixed the two things I loved the most — the environment and feeding the hungry. I had been there about six weeks when I asked for a day off, which they had no problem with. It was just a great place to work, and I had already logged a week's worth of overtime in a month and a half.

Holden told me to pack light, and by light he meant as few pieces of clothing as possible, including the infamous orange G-string bikini.

Friday morning, a car picked us up and took us to the airport.

Holden held my hand, both our bags clasped in his other one, and we walked across the tarmac to a small jet.

"Is this your plane?" I breathed, staring at the shiny white Gulfstream in front of us.

"Yep. Like it?"

"If it doesn't crash, I like it."

He chuckled. "I think you'll like it."

The pilot introduced himself, as did the stewardess, who poured us champagne the second the plane taxied the runway, and soon we were in the air.

"How long is the flight?" I asked Holden, trying to get him to reveal our secret destination.

"Not long." He gave nothing away.

"Tease."

True to his word, we touched down about thirty minutes later on Martha's Vineyard.

I looked over at him with an eyebrow raised. "Returning us to the scene of the crime?" I asked.

"Something like that."

After we taxied and parked, we climbed down the stairs and into a waiting black sedan, just like the ones we'd had when we'd been there just two months ago.

"I'm having déjà vu." I told him, watching the scenery of the small town go past in a blur of clean lines and bright colors out of the window.

"Not a bad thing, is it?" he asked.

I snuggled beside him, resting my head on his shoulder. "Not at all. It's wonderful. This is where we met. I'll always love it here."

His chest sank when he let out a long line of air. "I was really hoping you would say that," he replied, kissing the top of my head.

The car slowed and steered into a small drive beside a gray, clapboard house. It rose narrow and tall, with pale-yellow shutters and a periwinkle blue door in the center of a long, spindled porch. A white picket fence lined the front yard at the street and gorgeous purple and blue hydrangeas dotted the landscape beyond the gate.

"This is so pretty. Is it your family's?" I asked, glancing over at him, hope in my voice.

"Yes," he replied with a single nod.

"It's so beautiful." I ran my fingertips along the top of the fencing, reaching out to smell the flowering shrubs. Holden followed me to the front walk, taking it all in while I headed up to the porch.

A lockbox hung on the door handle and I glanced at Holden when he went to enter the code. "You don't have a key?" I asked.

"Not yet."

He'd said this was his family's place — why wouldn't he have a key? And this didn't seem like the kind of summer home his mother would like. Too simple, delicate and subdued. I loved it, but Kitty Pierce didn't strike me as the kind of woman who would.

The porch swing drifted slightly in the breeze and a small package sat on top of it.

"Holden, there's a box over there." I pointed.

"We'll get it in a minute." He tugged the door open and held it for me.

I stepped in, taking in the plain walls and tan wood floors. The furniture was all understated and clean and no pictures hung on the walls or were grouped on the tables. It had no character or charm — like an empty hull.

"It's pretty." I wondered why his family hadn't bothered to put their personality into it.

"Yeah?" he asked, his hands set in the pockets of his shorts, watching me.

"Yeah, don't you think so?"

He shrugged. "It could be."

"For sure! I mean, it has great potential." I peeked around the corner hallway, leading toward the back of the house. "Is it on the ocean?" I asked.

He nodded at me. I walked down the hall into a wide, bright kitchen with a butcher block island in the center. The back of the house had an enclosed porch with screened-in windows and a door that led to a small, grassed lawn squared off by more picket fencing, and a gate that opened to the sand leading down to the beach.

"Wow," I said, stepping out and walking right through the yard and onto the sand. I glanced behind me to see Holden following wordlessly, his hands still in his pockets. "The beach is right here."

There were people out and about along the water, families and couples, rainbows of umbrellas lining the shore as far as I could see in either direction. A few young kids ran by, shouting hello and waving when I did.

Holden came up and wrapped his arms around me from behind, pressing his lips into the back of my head. "You like it."

"I love it, Holden. It's beautiful here. How lucky you are to have a place like this."

"This is for you, Marley," he whispered.

I twirled in his arms and stared at him. "What do you mean, it's for me? It's your family's house, right? Their home here on the island?"

He shook his head. "No, Marley. It's yours. You're my family, now. I bought it for you."

I swallowed, tears filling my eyes. "You bought it for me?"

"I knew you wouldn't want one of the mansions on the other side of the island and that you wouldn't be happy staying in the gold villa my parents have. I wanted you to have something that was all yours, something we both wanted — near the town, on the beach, big enough for us and our kids — someday."

"Holden." Tears fell down my face as I wound my arms around his neck. "It's perfect. Just — perfect."

"Not yet. There's one more thing." He took my hand and led me back into the house. We went to the front porch and he took up the box that sat there. I perched myself on the end of the swing as he tore the top open, reading the papers inside then glancing over at me.

He took a seat beside me, setting the box in my lap.

I gave him a wonky smile, tears still leaking out of the corners of my eyes. Inside rested a few papers with pictures of a boat, along with a key connected to a floatable key fob. "*A boat?*"

"I haven't wanted to get on the water. Not since— Spencer. But I want to now. With you."

"Holden." I hugged him close, the box still between us. "You didn't have to buy me a house. Or a boat."

"I know that. I wanted to."

"Why?"

"Because I want the life I've always fucking fought against, Marley. My parents insisted I did what they did, work in the city, come to the island for weekends and holidays—and I told you that wasn't me. Not who I wanted to become. But with you—it's all I want. Not the way they are—no fucking way. But the way *we* are. To give you a place that's all ours, let you hang pictures, put out roses in mason jars and make it totally ours. To go out into the water and swim, now that you know how, and sail to Nantucket and anywhere you want to see. Anywhere in the world you want to go, Marley. I'll take you there. And where I wanted to take you first is right here. On our island."

Holden slunk down to the floor of the porch in front of me, on one knee. "Marley Mae Jackson," he started, retrieving a small velvet box from his pocket. "Not one more day without you. Not one more wasted fucking day. I love you. And I want you with me, wherever you want to be, always."

He cracked open the top and a large square diamond sat nestled in the center, catching the light coming through the tall maple tree near the porch.

"*Holden*," I gasped.

"Marry me."

"Yes," I said without hesitating and he rewarded me with the most amazing smile I'd ever seen in my life.

He took the ring and slipped it onto my finger, fitting it snugly against my knuckle. "You like it?"

"Yes," I breathed, staring at it. "I like it, Holden. I like this house and the boat and — without all of it, I would love you more than ever."

Later that night, after we'd christened the master bedroom upstairs, and the master bath, and the kitchen island, he took me out on the boat.

It was a long, stark-white craft with a big blue sail. It didn't have a name yet, but I told Holden if we were thinking of our future children, we'd better name it the *Sloane*.

"Or the *Jackson*," he reminded me.

He seemed nervous at first, reminding me he hadn't been on a boat since he'd lost his brother.

"I'm here, honey." I kept his hand enclosed in mine. "I'm always here."

We didn't stay out for long and he insisted I wear a life jacket the entire time. Of course, I did. Just for him. I would do anything for him.

All that weekend, he didn't take one phone call. He never looked stressed or hunched his shoulders. We spent every waking minute together and all our sleeping minutes, too. And Holden was the man I had fallen in love with, and the one he wanted to be. Generous, sweet, fun.

We sat on the porch swing of our new house Sunday afternoon, gently swaying back and forth, delaying heading back to the city. "I'll never break your heart, Marley. You can plan on that," he told me, cuddling me against him.

"I know that, iPhone boy." I snuggled up closer to him. "I want to get married here. On the island. Next summer."

"Done," he replied.

"I want something small, no life-size cut-outs of us. And no paparazzi anywhere."

"Agreed."

"I want to put a picture of you and Spencer on our mantel," I continued, my voice soft.

He nodded. "Okay, sweetheart."

"I want you happy. Always. When we had our weekend here, when we met, all I wanted was to give you the lightness you feel now, the grace and joy you feel without all the other shit you let cloud your mind," I confessed.

"I am happy, Marley," he murmured.

"I'll be there for you, Holden. I'll never say goodbye. You were born to be my baby. It's my life and who says you can't go home?"

"Those are Bon Jovi songs, aren't they?"

I laughed and wound my arms around him, squeezing him tight. "The most perfect man in the world, and he's all mine. My island distraction."

Want to see more like this?
Here's a taster for you to enjoy!

Beautiful Sinners:
Secrets, Lies and Vegas
Pamela L. Todd

Excerpt

Excitement fizzed in my stomach as I followed the girls, who talked a million miles a minute and barely paused to take a breath. We walked into the restaurant...or was it a circus tent? Soft, floaty material of all colors was our ceiling and the wall panels displayed vintage art from the big tops of days gone by. In fact, the only clue that we hadn't stepped into a 1940s circus was the window that overlooked the world-famous fountain display. It took my breath away even in daylight, but now, lit up against the backdrop of darkness, I could barely tear my eyes away.

Hayley introduced us to the hostess, who led us to our table, the most central in the restaurant. Eve scanned the room, her hunter instincts on full alert as she surveyed her prey. Beth looped arms with hers, giggling in her ear.

The moment our waiter appeared, Hayley ordered a bottle of champagne.

"Well, I think we should make a toast," Hayley announced once our glasses had been filled.

"Here, here," Eve said, raising her glass. "To Marley! For without her, I would never have met that cute investment banker from Chicago."

Hayley rolled her eyes. "Yes, Eve, that was exactly what I was thinking."

Beth giggled, flipping her long, shiny black hair over one shoulder. "Yeah, because it should be about Ken from Kentucky."

I snorted a laugh. "You do remember that his name wasn't actually Ken? And the fact that he only put up with the nickname was because you left your bra pinned to the wall in Coyote Ugly and he could see your nipples through your dress?"

Beth waggled her eyebrows. "Well, I do have very nice nipples."

"You should send that to Hallmark," Hayley said. "Okay, in all seriousness guys, I really do want to make a toast to Marley."

Beth and Eve raised their glasses, eyes on Hayley as they waited for her toast.

"Marley, you know we love you," Hayley said with a smile, "and I think it goes without saying that this trip has been ridiculously overdue. So here's to our last night, and going as hard as we can."

"To Marley!" Beth and Eve chorused, chinking their glasses at mine.

I forced a smile and took a gulp of champagne, which tasted sour on my tongue. That toast, whilst heartfelt, felt like a needle in my heart. It was just another reminder of how different I was from my friends.

Eve tossed back the remainder of her drink. As she placed the empty glass on the table, her eyes darted between us all when she noticed us staring. "What are you all looking at? You said go hard."

"I said hard, not sloppy," Hayley said, shaking her head, the small smile pulling at her lips, ruining any scolding she may have intended. She tugged on the end of Eve's shoulder-length blonde hair. "You might want to pin this up before bed, because no one will be holding it back for you."

Eve leaned closer to Hayley, pursing her glossy red lips. "Honey, I plan on burning all the alcohol out of my system with vigorous exercise."

Beth laughed. "Let's make a toast to that!"

We ordered our food when the waiter returned, Beth and Eve still sizing up their potential prey. I circled the rim of my glass with my fingertip and felt a set of eyes on me. Hayley studied me with her curious blue eyes, a tiny crease between her eyebrows.

Out of everyone, it was Hayley I was closest to, the first out of this group of girls I'd met. They pulled me into their orbit in a blur of cocktails and club music. Beneath the man-eating exterior of these women were big hearts and kinder spirits. I adored them all, but Hayley was the one I felt the deepest bond with. But like any close relationship, it had its perks and its downsides. Like right now, when I knew she could see more than the others.

"Last night blues?" she asked, her tone light.

I gave a swift nod. "Something like that."

Hayley patted my knee under the table. "We'd better make it a memorable one then, hadn't we?"

"It's already been pretty memorable, Hayley," I said, giving her a genuine smile.

And it had.

Surprisingly.

None of us had been to Vegas before and I had been hesitant to come. *Sin City...* Who wanted to go there? A city where people flocked to make stupid decisions and change their lives…for better or worse.

Maybe that isn't such a bad idea…

I wasn't altogether sure what I'd expected of this place. When the plane had begun its descent toward the ground and I'd seen the bright lights of this unusual world, a flicker of excitement had rumbled low in my body. I'd all seen the movies, the TV shows, but really, nothing could have prepared me for the intensity of Vegas. I'd had my preconceived ideas, the mental image that was a far cry from the glossy, fluorescent reality. I'd thought I'd known what to expect, but it wasn't until we'd driven down the Strip with the lights reflecting off the windows that I'd discovered there wasn't actually anything — real or imagined — that could have prepared me for Vegas herself.

It felt like I was a Lilliputian in a glittery and exotic setting — only the buildings were Gulliver, and these were *my* travels. Truth was, I had looked down my nose at the thought of a trip to Las Vegas. I wasn't a snob. It was just the white-trash stories that went hand in hand with the city which made it a less than desirable vacation spot. But when I'd got here, I couldn't have been more wrong.

Wealth and luxury screamed from most places and it was larger than life. A playground for those looking for an escape from reality, even for a short while.

Maybe this was exactly where I needed to be.

After a delicious meal that was served on a plate with pictures of monkeys, the girls tried to decide where to go for the night's activities. Well, Hayley tried to narrow down the options — Eve and Beth were still admiring the specimens on display. I, on the other hand, ogled the dessert tray.

God, I hate diets.

Beth subtly pointed out a target to Eve. "Look at that one, over there."

"Oooh…." Eve crooned.

"Oh! That one!"

"Oh my God, are you serious? What are you, blind?"

"Over there then."

"Mmm-hmm."

"Wait a minute… I've got it… By the bar. See?"

"Dibs."

"You can't call dibs!"

"I just did!"

"But I saw him first!"

"Then you should have called it."

"Fine. Whatever. I don't care."

"You so do."

Beth and Eve's shameful game of man window shopping was a welcome distraction. It was an impressive feat that they found so many desirable men in the restaurant, considering there were only nineteen tables. When I'd first met them, I'd thought the guys they favored were lucky to have such beautiful girls fawning over them. Now I felt sorry for the poor bastards. It was like watching a lioness flirt with an innocent springbok. There was no doubt that these girls were predators—and they were hungry.

They thought of this vacation as a buffet table, and the helpless male habitants and visitors of Vegas were the only meat on the menu. I'd lost count of how many business cards and cocktail napkins with carefully written phone numbers they'd acquired this weekend. With tonight being our last night, they would be bringing their A game…and no one was safe.

Hayley giggled, breaking my reverie, and leaned over the table to whisper, "A guy at the bar is staring at you."

My eyebrows shot up "So?"

She rolled her eyes. "So go talk to him!"

"Yeah. Right," I said, folding my arms across my chest.

Hayley frowned. "Why not?"

"I can think of a few reasons." Maybe it was because Hayley had made me aware, but I felt a pair of eyes on me. The little hairs on the back of neck stood on end and it was all I could do not to turn around.

Hayley gave a slight shake of her head, as though admitting I was a lost cause. "So where are we going?" she asked, the question aimed for no one specific.

"I really want to go back to Coyote Ugly," Beth pleaded, clasping her hands together under her chin and pouting.

Eve arched a perfect eyebrow at our friend. "And lose another bra to the wall? Good thing we're only here for the weekend. Imagine the loss if we were here for longer."

I rolled my eyes. "Please. Like Beth needs an excuse to buy new underwear."

"We are so not going back to Coyote Ugly. Come on, you guys. We need to make this a stellar night." Hayley's eyes flickered to me. "For Marley's sake."

I frowned. "Why for Marley's sake?"

Beth shot me a pointed look. "Like we could get you on another vacation. It was hard enough getting you to come this time!"

I dropped my eyes, unable to look at their accusing faces. Though they were messing around, I doubted they would ever know how much their words stung. How quickly they forgot the easiness of their own lives.

Hayley cleared her throat. "Guys, focus. Where are we headed next? We've already been sitting in here for more than two hours. And I nominate Marley to be in charge of tonight's festivities."

"Why don't we just stay in the hotel tonight?" I suggested. We were staying in one of the best hotels on the Strip, yet we hadn't even experienced its nightclub yet.

Hayley nodded her agreement. "Vault? Yeah, I heard it's meant to be one of the best. We're staying here anyway. May as well keep close to home."

Beth looked disappointed at being outvoted, but when a group of well-dressed and devastatingly good-looking men walked past our table voicing their own plans to visit the same club, she soon perked up.

Beth wriggled in her chair. "You guys done?"

Sign up for our newsletter and find out about all our romance book releases, eBook sales and promotions, sneak peeks and FREE romance books!

About the Author

ML Uberti is a Metro Detroit native who has a degree in English and Film from Wayne State University. She was the copy-editor for three nationally published books by Bottom Dog Press and has been writing since the fourth grade, receiving high praise for her totally implausible but entertaining story about a young girl who turns into a praying mantis. She is currently married to a musician, teacher and Netflix junkie, is a stay-at-home-mom to three mischievous children and a (slightly) overweight beagle named Matilda.

ML Uberti loves to hear from readers. You can find her contact information, website details and author profile page at https://www.totallybound.com